FOUR CORNERS WAR

Four Corners War (Pacheco & Chino Mystery #3)
Ted Clifton
ISBN 978-1-77342-089-9

Produced by IndieBookLauncher.com
www.IndieBookLauncher.com
Editing: Nassau Hedron, Stanley Nelson, Lisa Nelson
Cover Design: Saul Bottcher
Interior Design and Typesetting: Saul Bottcher

The body text of this book is set in Adobe Caslon.

Also Available
Ebook edition, ISBN 978-1-77342-088-2

PROLOGUE

Tyee began talking as soon as Ray entered the computer room. "The research on this San Juan County stuff is pretty amazing. If what I'm finding is correct, the sheriff has managed to accumulate enough military hardware to start a sizable war."

Ray was frowning. "Well, crap. Pretty sure that's not going to make the governor happy."

"Looks like it's worse than just the governor being unhappy. I could track these military vehicles because they are required to have special permits due to their weight. And it appears they've left the state and entered Colorado. I have no idea where this equipment went once it crossed the state line. But I've checked, and it definitely didn't leave Colorado."

Ray shook his head. Not only had the wacko San Juan County Sheriff accumulated old military hardware for his white supremacist take-over of something, he had taken what amounted to State of New Mexico property and moved it into Colorado. *How did these people get elected?* "How much equipment do you think we're talking about?"

"Over the last eighteen months, I can track twelve armored vehicles; some described as having mounted weapons, one tank, and two armored troop carriers. Of course, what I can't tell you is what's inside them."

"Did you say, 'tank'?"

"Yep, just what a sheriff's department needs in case they're invaded by the Chamber of Commerce, or maybe the Lions Club."

"The governor's going to shit. Why would they be moving those vehicles into Colorado?"

"It's pure speculation, but my first guess is that they have some kind of joint operation with like-minded morons in Colorado, and they're combining forces for some sort of action."

"Action? What the hell kind of action?" Ray knew perfectly well that Tyee didn't have an answer. He was just yelling to blow off a little steam. They both knew he needed to call the governor and give him an update on the San Juan County military movements—Ray could hear the governor yelling already.

"What the fuck are you telling me, Ray? The San Juan asshole sheriff is gathering an army in Colorado with New Mexico fucking equipment? Is the guy a complete moron? Is every sheriff in this state a goddamned idiot?"

Ray hadn't said much. The governor was asking some of the same rhetorical questions Ray had hurled at Tyee.

"Ray, you know I could send in the National Guard, but I can't let them cross into Colorado. That bastard of a governor in Colorado hates my ass and would gladly keep all of the stupid fuckin' equipment if he found out. Do you think this guy is going to take some kind of action with these weapons?"

"No. I don't. That would be too strange. I know these people, or at least people like them. We had people just like this back in Las Cruces. They just want to dress up in their uniforms and play war. I'd think the only people actually at risk are the militia members—there's always some chance they could be shot by one of their fellow loonies."

"Yeah, that sounds about right to me. But hell, I can't let him take New Mexico assets into Colorado and not do something about it. Ray, I know this is beyond the scope of what we talked about on this, but could you and some of your people just go up to Farmington and snoop around? Find out what the hell's going on?"

"Sure, governor." This was Ray's business after all, and the governor didn't like people who told him no, so he would go, but he sure wasn't happy about it. "It's a long drive to Farmington. Any chance the state patrol or somebody would have a plane we could use?"

"Shit, Ray, I've got a plane. And I hate to fly. Consider it yours, along with two pilots. You now have an official air force to attack the Farmington sheriff." Ray sure hoped the governor was just being his usual oddball self—he didn't want to go to war, with or without an air force.

1

Fly Away

1989. George Herbert Walker Bush becomes 41st president of the United States of America. First World Wide Web server and browser are developed. Tens of thousands of Chinese students protest in Beijing's Tiananmen Square, facing off against tanks. Thousands are killed. The Berlin Wall comes down, marking the end of Communist control of East Germany and the USSR. Average cost of a new home is $120,000, average income $27,450, and average price of a new car $15,300. Best Picture is Rain Man, and the song of the year is "Don't Worry Be Happy."

Farmington, New Mexico

"Tyee, I can't force you to get on the plane. But it's a long drive to Farmington, and if you don't want to fly, you'll have to drive—alone." Ray tried to persuade Tyee, who was pouting like a two-year-old—a very big two-year-old—about ready to have a tantrum. He kicked at the ground and gave Ray a dirty look. "Okay, I understand. You're not comfortable in a small plane. But this," Ray pointed at the aircraft behind them, "is really a big plane. It's got two engines and two professional pilots. They know what they're doing."

"Bullshit, Ray. This is the crazy governor's plane and two guys who may or may not know what they're doing.

You can fire me if you like, but I'm driving." Tyee's stubborn expression dared Ray to demand he get on the plane.

Sue walked up to see Ray and Tyee glaring at one another. "What are you two arguing about?"

"Tyee's afraid to fly."

Tyee's face got a little darker. He crossed his arms and gave Ray a decidedly cold stare.

"Well, if Tyee isn't flying, neither am I."

"What? Have you both lost your minds?" Ray stomped away toward nothing in particular, mumbling. Nothing was going as planned. Sue was supposed to come along for the ride to offer moral support and take a break from her routine. Big Jack was babysitting Happy with help from his new girlfriend, Beverly. Happy liked staying at Big Jack's bait shop for reasons only a dog could understand. Now, what was supposed to be an easy plane ride of an hour or so was turning into a civil war. Ray continued to stomp around in the dirt, watching as Sue and Tyee engaged in some kind of conversation.

"We go." Tyee made the statement in his infamous minimalist Indian-speak. He climbed aboard the plane.

"What did you say to him?"

"None of your business, Ray. Let's get on the plane before he changes his mind."

They boarded to see Tyee slumped in his seat, frowning out the window.

"If everyone will get buckled up, we'll be taking off in just a minute or two," the pilot told them before he sealed the door. It was reassuring to Ray that he wore a professional-looking uniform and had the classic look of a pilot from the movies, complete with a broad smile. Of course, like Tyee said, that didn't mean he knew how to fly a plane.

Soon they were in the air. Everyone relaxed a little. Tyee was still not speaking, but he did smile at Sue. Ray just sighed.

Ray Pacheco had retired from being sheriff of Dona Ana County, New Mexico, not that long ago. He had then moved to a remote cabin on Elephant Butte Lake near Truth or Consequences, New Mexico, or "T or C," as the locals called it. He soon found himself bored with retirement and took up fishing, which was how he met his two partners and friends, Big Jack and Tyee Chino.

Big Jack owned Jack's Bait, Boats, and Beer. Ray first went to the otherworldly bait shop to seek advice about how to take up fishing. Big Jack considered fleecing Ray by selling him fishing gear he might not need. But, succumbing to his better nature, he instead suggested that Ray seek out Tyee Chino, the best fishing guide on the lake.

Those first encounters laid the groundwork for friendship and eventually a partnership in the private investigation business—Pacheco and Chino. Big Jack preferred to remain low profile, and was a silent partner.

After what seemed like a short trip, the pilot announced that they were about ten minutes from Farmington and everyone should buckle up.

The approach into Farmington's airport has put the fear of flying into many a seasoned traveler. The airstrip sits on top of a small mesa in the middle of the town. While the location is convenient once you land, the visual coming in for a landing is more than a little disturbing, with the approach making it seem as if the plane is headed directly into the side of the mesa. Common sense tells you that the pilot is not going to crash directly into the side of a cliff; however, your eyes will tell you that your common sense is lying. Especially on a windy day, with the plane tossing about from side to side and up and down. And most days were windy in Farmington. Tyee glanced from the window to Ray with a look that suggested his friend had condemned him to death. But then, just when disaster seemed imminent, the plane easily cleared the mesa wall and settled onto the runway. Sue applauded, Tyee actually smiled, and Ray let his breath out.

Ray had been to many places where the locals described the landscape as rugged. But this had to be the very definition of rugged. The natural terrain was jagged, with no level ground. Its rocky faces showed a variety of colors of stone, but little vegetation. There were hills everywhere. Everything seemed exposed. It was an odd place to put a town. After they deplaned, the wind immediately caught their attention, cold and gusty, making Farmington seem doubly inhospitable.

"The governor says we're at your disposal for the next several days, Mr. Pacheco," the pilot said. "We're less than an hour away from our base in Santa Fe. So, if you agree, we'll head back there. When you need us again, just give us a call and we'll leave immediately." With that, he gave Ray a card with names and numbers.

"Sounds great, captain. Not sure about our schedule at this point, but I'd guess we'll want to head back to T or C in a day or two. I'll give you a call as soon as we know." They shook hands and Ray moved quickly toward the small terminal.

"Sheriff Pacheco, hello. I'm Chief Deputy Thad Trujillo—welcome to Farmington."

"Thanks, appreciate you meeting us."

"No problem. The governor and the AG made it clear we're to assist you in any way we can. Even without the big brass giving me orders, I'm very pleased to meet the famous sheriff from southern New Mexico."

"Well now Deputy Trujillo, I think you might be messing with me." Ray smiled at the chief deputy and Trujillo grinned in a mischievous way.

"Your associates went to the restrooms. The luggage has been placed in a patrol car outside. That car is yours to use as you see fit. Sorry we didn't have an unmarked car available, but I imagine you're used to riding in a patrol car."

"Yeah, I've done that some. Any word from Sheriff Jackson?"

"Nothing direct. One of his ex-followers came into the office yesterday to tell us he thought the sheriff had gone off the deep end." Trujillo looked down and shook his head. "The guy belonged to Americans for Liberty—the group the sheriff's been active with—and he said the sheriff told them they'd begin seceding from the country as of October 1st. The guy said he enjoyed all the rah-rah stuff and the military crap, but he didn't want to leave his country. Seems like the sheriff may have taken his truck. He wanted to report it stolen."

"What do you know about the Americans for Liberty?"

"It's a long-term, anti-government militia group. Been around for maybe ten or fifteen years. Never thought they would cause any real harm—just a bunch of beer bellies pretending to be tougher and meaner than they really are. The sheriff got involved about five years ago, though, and he seems to take it pretty seriously. Lot of the softer guys dropped out after he started making them exercise and do real training." He chuckled.

"Does Sheriff Jackson have a family?"

"He's married, although they've been separated for a couple of years. Wife's name is Barbara—she lives in an apartment downtown. Don't believe they ever got a divorce, but lots of bitterness between them. His wife's active in local politics and the sheriff wanted her to stop, but she said no and moved out."

"I'd like to talk to her. Could you get me an address and phone number?"

"Sure."

"Sheriff have any friends who might know what's going on?"

"Our sheriff was a loner. The only person I know that he was close to was his mother, who died some years ago. Mostly what he cared about was work and stuff to do with the militia."

"Did you think he was a good sheriff?"

"That's kind of a loaded question. He was—or is—my boss. He's a difficult man to get to know, not very friendly. But in terms of running the department, I'd say he did a good job. A lot of people didn't like him much. I think that was mostly because he just wasn't friendly. Some people thought he was a real asshole—generally lawbreakers or people who wanted a special favor and didn't get it. He didn't play politics and more or less treated everyone about the same, even if a little cold. Occasionally, he'd drink a bit too much, which could create problems. But that mostly had to do with his estranged wife."

"Deputy, do you know where he is right now?"

"Not for sure, sheriff. My guess is that he's in Colorado at the militia's base camp. I think it's close to Ignacio, but definitely in backwoods territory. The guy who came in to file the stolen vehicle charge said the headquarters was in a very remote part of La Plata County. That's a sparsely populated area with limited access. The guy also said they've more weapons and ammunition up there than you can imagine. He said it would be a bloodbath if anyone tried to get them out of that camp."

"How about the military surplus equipment? I understand that he took some of that gear with him into Colorado?"

"Yeah, I've definitely gotten an earful from the governor about that. Most of the equipment is missing from the armory, where it was stored. I guess the sheriff and his people took it. Most of that old junk was useless. It's old army crap that I think they just wanted to unload on law enforcement. But it was all in bad shape and would cost a fortune to maintain—even assuming you had a use for an armored troop carrier. The sheriff loved that military crap, though. Almost every weekend he would have his militia people out there, washing and oiling. But we never used any of it in the sheriff's department. It just took up space. I told the governor it was a waste of money and he should just let Colorado have it—turns out that wasn't the thing to say. The governor went nuts, telling me the goddamn governor of Colorado was not getting any of our shit. Then he hung up."

"Our governor and the governor of Colorado seemed to have their own little war going on."

"Well, what's our plan, Ray?" Tyee had forgiven Ray for the plane ride, given that he had survived.

"We'll get checked into the hotel and then go back to the sheriff's office and get the contact information for the sheriff's ex-wife. Might go talk to her and see if she knows anything about the sheriff's plans. Want to talk to Deputy Trujillo some more, but my first impression is that he has everything under control. If that's the case then I think the issue of the sheriff stealing equipment and then holing up in some remote part of Colorado with a small army is a problem for some federal agency, not anything to do with us. Once we're comfortable that Deputy Trujillo has everything handled in Farmington, we can report to the governor and go home."

No one objected to that.

2

Warmer Climates

Many Years Ago

"Ladies and gentlemen, it's with pleasure that I introduce my great friend and one of the best representatives this country has ever had, Congressman Jeremiah Johnson." There was thunderous applause at the event held to honor the congressman. No one expected otherwise, after all it was his retirement dinner; and many were glad to see him go.

Johnson took the lectern. "Thank you, Senator Graham. Good to see you back in Colorado for a change. Tommy and I have known each other for many years and have generally had good things to say about each other, although I do have some stories I've been saving in case we ever became opponents. But I guess I'll just keep saving those little gems."

Graham smiled, but directed a noticeably suspicious eye toward his not-so-great friend.

"When I announced my intention not to run for re-election," Johnson went on, "I know some of you were surprised, maybe even a little upset. But I also know many of you were happier than pigs in shit. Well, I'm going to make that crowd even happier. My wife, Jane, and I are moving to Las Cruces, New Mexico. I've enjoyed my time representing the great state of Colorado, but my old bones request that I move to a warmer climate. By the way, 'old bones' was not a reference to my long-suffering wife."

Jane looked pained, but kept smiling. Loving the old bastard took real fortitude and a great deal of patience.

Johnson's speech didn't go much longer, which was good, but he wasn't very kind. He had a way of pissing people off. It was one of his most consistent qualities. He had been elected and re-elected because he also had a way of getting things done. But his skills were more those of a bully than a diplomat. Not many people would be sorry to see him leave, especially Senator Graham.

"You know," his wife told him after, "it's not your job to make the senator angry."

"I know, Jane. I should learn to be more diplomatic. But if I did that, I wouldn't be me, now would I?"

"No." Jane snuggled a little closer for a quick hug and a little peck on the cheek.

"I don't deserve you, Jane."

"No, you don't." She smiled at her husband. "It was nice of the senator to come to your going-away party."

"Well, I'm sure it was because of the going-away part. He's nothing but an old crook dressed up in fancy clothes and hiding behind a law degree. If I could make his life more miserable, I would." His eyes narrowed. He had sighted Graham nearby.

Jane knew the look and tensed for what was about to come.

"Senator, mind if I have a few private words?"

"You know, Jeremiah," Graham sighed, "there's no reason for us to be enemies. Why don't we part as friends?"

"Tommy, you are the biggest bullshitter I've ever met. Plus, you're a crook. Why the fuck would I want you for a friend?"

Graham scowled. "Listen, ya dumb son of a bitch. I've had it with your foul mouth and holier-than-thou attitude. Fuck you!" The senator turned to leave, an ugly expression on his face.

"I know what you and your lowlife brother are trying to do in Pueblo," Johnson fired back. "I won't stand for it. I have documentation on who owns that land, and what'll happen to its value if that road project you're pushing happens. That road to nowhere is a boondoggle, designed for no reason except to line your pockets. Either drop the project, or I'll expose you."

The senator stopped, turning slowly. His face was red. He was starting to perspire. "You do anything like that, and I'll have you killed." He spat the words in Johnson's face.

"I would rethink that, ya two-bit thug. Your little threat is on tape." Johnson pulled a small recorder out of his pocket. "Now, unless you want to go back to Pueblo and work in your idiot brother's construction business, you better do what I told you." Jeremiah Johnson's first instinct had been to punch the fat senator in his fat face. But he saw Jane glaring in that familiar stop-whatever-you're-doing way, so he walked off.

"You know my dear," he said to her, "I think it's time we move to another state."

The next few months were full of activity. They sold their house in Colorado Springs and rented one in Albuquerque. They decided to park in Albuquerque for a while and get a feel for things, then decide whether they wanted to buy a house there or in Las Cruces.

But the congressman couldn't sit still. He got involved in Democratic Party activities in Albuquerque, and soon was being talked about as a potential state leader for the party. Jeremiah was happiest when discussing politics—it was his life. He hadn't been active in New Mexico politics for some time, but it was amazing how similar the issues were to those in Colorado. Being an ex-congressman gave him status and respect that pushed him up the ranks in the party pretty quickly, and his witty, bombastic ways opened a lot of doors.

His family had been long-time residents of New Mexico and were once considered one of the "noble" families in the state's political hierarchy. The problem with that, though, was that all members of his famous family were Republicans. Jeremiah became the black sheep when he declared himself a Democrat; he might as well have declared himself the devil. Even after the passing of many years, there were still certain family members who wouldn't talk to him.

After Jane and he lived several years in Albuquerque, occupying the same rental house they had first moved into, they were still not sure whether to stay or move to Las Cruces. But they had firmly established themselves as active political beings in all things New Mexican.

The years moved along. The Johnsons were happy, and

very active for people in their mid-sixties. Senator Tommy Graham had just run for governor of Colorado and won. Jeremiah had debated with himself about offering some of his nasty tidbits to the senator's opponent, but had decided he didn't need the grief. He and Jane were satisfied with their life as it was—why stir up old pain and anger?

Then tragedy struck. Driving home from the grocery store, Jane was rammed broadside in a busy intersection by a speeding police car. The cruiser was pursuing a car thief and wasn't using its siren. She died instantly.

Jeremiah withdrew from everything and became a recluse. He had his phone disconnected and would rarely answer the door. There were days when he couldn't get out of bed. The man of action, full of piss and vinegar, had been defeated. He dreamed of being dead.

There was loud knocking on the front door. "Hey anybody home? Mr. Johnson this is the police—we need to make sure you're okay. Hello? If you can hear me, I need you to come to the door or we're going to break it in." They banged on the door some more. The doorbell hadn't worked in months.

Jeremiah lay on the couch, listening to them. He hated the police. He knew it wasn't rational, but that didn't change how he felt. They had killed his wife and now they were going to break into his house. Something snapped. He blinked very quickly several times and his mind began racing. *What the fuck!*

He threw open the door.

"You better stop pounding on my door ya moron. Do you know who the fuck I am, you little piece of shit? I'll tell you who I am—I'm an ex-congressman, I am friends with the mayor, I am friends with the police chief, I know the asshole governor. And I am pissed. You need to get off of my property and file your goddamn report saying that the old fart who lives at this address is alive and well. Now fuck off!"

Slam!

The police left. Their report said the man living at the house was up and apparently not in any physical danger. They added they suspected he might be crazy.

Jeremiah began attending political meetings again. It was hard. He moved out of the house he and Jane had shared; the memory of her was too strong there. He moved into a small apartment in downtown Albuquerque. Sometimes he would go to his new home and cry. He had never done anything like that before. After a while, he cried less.

The incumbent governor of New Mexico, Richard Hawthorne, was a Republican, and he was running for re-election unopposed by anyone in his party. He was a colorless man who talked a lot about money—mostly his—and about arts and culture. He was expected to win in a landslide.

The Democrats were having a difficult time finding a viable candidate who was willing to run—and most assuredly lose. In a why-the-hell-not moment, the party chair approached Jeremiah and asked if he would consider running.

"Lookin' for someone to get stomped on by that elitist

asshole of a governor."

"I understand, Jeremiah," the party chairman sighed. "More than likely, he's going to be re-elected. It'll be his final term, though, which means the next election will be wide open. All of our eager beavers want to wait and run then. We need someone who can run a good campaign and talk about Democratic values."

"And be willing to lose."

The chairman nodded. "Yeah, I guess that's the deal. Will you do it?"

"Hell yes, I'll do it." Jeremiah Johnson smiled. "And I'll beat that pompous ass!"

Johnson had been a politician his entire life and knew every trick in the book. But there was something else. He wanted to do the right thing. Not that he had ever not wanted to do what was best for the people, but there was just a new intensity to his drive to help the ones who were being stepped on by the assholes of the world, like the present governor.

He ran a populist campaign from the heart. He denounced the incumbent governor in words not often heard in public. The crowds grew. He was an overnight sensation. He held nothing back, saying what he wanted to say, and people loved it. The incumbent called him foul-mouthed, crazy, a communist, another Hitler. People loved that, too.

They only had one head-to-head debate, and Johnson was in his element. His opponent, who had spent years saying almost nothing of substance; now found it impossible to shift gears, was not. By the end of the debate it almost seemed even he had decided to vote for Jeremiah

Johnson.

Jeremiah was elected in a landslide. Within months of taking office, he implemented most of his campaign promises. He became the most popular and colorful governor New Mexico had ever had. He lived a simple life and spent every day trying to make Jane proud.

3

Arrival

Farmington, New Mexico

Chief Deputy Trujillo had made reservations for the Pacheco party at the Casa Blanca Inn, a short distance from the airport and a few blocks from the sheriff's offices. Check-in was easy. And they were pleasantly surprised by the Southwestern charm of the building and the uniqueness of a hotel outside the usual national chains. The overall effect was cozy and romantic.

"Ray," Sue gushed, "this place is beautiful. Guess I wasn't expecting such Santa Fe charm in Farmington."

"Plus, it's about half the price of those Santa Fe joints."

"You're always so romantic."

Ray paused a minute to see if Sue was upset or just kidding. From her look, he couldn't be sure. He was still getting used to a lot of new things in his life, with marriage being one of the areas demanding most of his attention. He couldn't have loved Sue any more than he did, but there were many times he wasn't sure what she was thinking. At those times he felt like he didn't know her. He had a very reliable gut instinct about crooks, but much less about his wife.

Tyee's scowl suggested he wasn't pleased with much of anything. "Man, this place just screams 'romance.' Maybe you two should stay, and I should go down to the Holiday Inn."

"Okay, look—both of you. Let's just get on with the task at hand and enjoy a nice place to stay at the expense of the governor, then head home. Okay?"

The biggest problem with that plan of action was there didn't appear to actually be a specific task at hand. Sheriff Jackson's actions were beyond anything Ray, or even the governor, could likely deal with. If anyone was going to do something, it would have to be the FBI or ATF. It was also apparent Chief Deputy Trujillo had everything under control. The obvious course was for the governor or his attorney general to appoint Trujillo acting sheriff, set a special election for a while down the road, stand back, and let the man do his job. End of assignment.

Sue smiled at Ray in a way that told him clearly she wasn't angry, and he should go do whatever he had to do. "I think I'll hang around the hotel and have a leisurely lunch while you two go about your duties. See you later." She gave Ray a peck on the cheek along with a wink, then set off for their room.

"Listen, Ray," Tyee said, "I know I'm being a pain in the butt. Guess it was the plane ride; not real sure. But there's something else. I know this is going to sound silly, but ever since we landed, I've had a feeling of foreboding. I know you're going to mock me for getting mystical. But I really feel a powerful sense of danger."

Ray let out a deep breath. "Tyee, I trust your instincts. It's not silly. I feel on edge, too, for some reason. I think we need to be careful. The whole thing with Sheriff Jackson is strange. But right now, I think the most important thing to do is to get as much information as we can on Trujillo so we can give the governor a heads-up on whether he can take over the department until there's an election."

It was a short drive to the sheriff's downtown office. Ray and Tyee were both quiet, absorbed in their own thoughts.

"Get everything squared away at the Inn?" Deputy Trujillo seemed overly concerned with Ray and Tyee's comfort, or maybe just nervous at being responsible for people sent by the governor. Either way, it felt a little overdone to Ray.

"Yeah, the place is great. Really appreciate all your help. Wonder if we could get that phone number and address for the sheriff's wife." Ray was ready to do something, and not just stand around chatting.

"Sure, got that right here." Trujillo handed the information to Ray. "You also can use that office just behind you while you're here. No one's using it now."

"That's great. Thanks, Deputy. Well, we'll let you get back to work; no need to entertain us. Maybe sometime tomorrow we can get together and go over some of the issues that might come up if Jackson doesn't come back."

"Great. I'll look forward to that. As I'm sure you know, small towns have a pretty efficient communication system—gossip. So your visit isn't a secret. I received a call this morning from one of our leading citizens, Mr. Lewis Grimes. He owns Grimes Oil Company and wanted to know if you had time, could you drop by and see him? He did mention that he's a major contributor to the governor."

Ray wasn't sure how to respond. He sure as hell didn't want to spend time talking with some pompous business-man just because he had political clout with the governor. "Let me get back to you on that. Our plan is to gather some information regarding Sheriff Jackson's actions and to make sure everything is under control in the depart-ment, and then head home. Not so sure how much time there'll be for glad-handing."

"With you there, sheriff," Trujillo nodded sympatheti-cally. "But Mr. Grimes is as about as important as anybody gets around here. Not only is he our leading businessman, worth millions, he's also head honcho on almost every-thing political. His latest wife—think she's the third or fourth—is a very attractive twenty-something blonde bombshell. Rumor is she's threatening to file for divorce, and she's made it clear the reason was Mr. Grimes's sup-posed affair with—" his eyes widened "—Barbara Jackson, the sheriff's wife. My guess is he wants to talk to you about more than politics."

Ray got Grimes's contact information and assured the chief deputy that he would contact him and see what he wanted.

The edgy feeling Tyee talked about was starting to take shape. Almost all small towns had secrets, and sex and money were the common themes. This was the ugly side of law enforcement, when you had to get involved with upstanding citizens because of their personal weaknesses. Ray hated it.

Tyee was not pleased with the turn of events, either. "Sex and politics—not our strong suit." His goal had been to gather some facts, pass them along to the governor, and head home, not talk to politically connected rich businessmen.

"Yeah, not a good surprise. But let's just see how this plays out." They had called Barbara Jackson from the sheriff's department and didn't get an answer. Now they headed for her apartment to see if they could learn anything. It wasn't very scientific-sounding, but a lot of law enforcement amounted to poking around and seeing what happens. Stirring the pot. Shaking the trees. Ray was from the old school where you had to be out in the field doing something if you expected to make progress.

Barbara Jackson's apartment building was a few blocks from the sheriff's department. They pulled into a parking spot right in front. Tyee walked up and rang the bell on her unit. There was no answer. He got the sense no one was inside. They went to the unit next door and rang the bell.

The door opened a very small crack.

"Hello," Ray said. "My name is Ray Pacheco, and this is my associate, Tyee Chino. We're assisting the local sheriff on some matters. We were wondering if you knew where Barbara Jackson might be today."

"Are you here because I called?" The lady responding looked to be in her eighties or maybe nineties—and very nervous.

"Not sure what you mean, ma'am. Did you call someone?"

"Yes. I just called the sheriff's department and told them they should check on my neighbor."

"Well, we're from the sheriff's department, but we

didn't know you had called. We wanted to talk to Mrs. Jackson about her husband."

"I think her husband may have killed her." The elderly lady made her bold statement and slammed the door. They could hear her set several safety locks. Apparently, the conversation with the neighbor was over.

A patrol car pulled up and parked next to Ray and Tyee's car.

"Hello, Sheriff. Deputy Trujillo said you might still be here. I'm Deputy Clark. We got a call from the neighbor of Barbara Jackson. She wanted us to check on her welfare."

"Good to meet you, deputy. We've just talked to the neighbor lady. She seems to think something might be wrong with Mrs. Jackson. She also indicated she thought it involved her husband. We didn't question her because after her comment that Barbara's husband may have killed her, she slammed the door and locked it."

"Yeah," Clark nodded, "that sounds like Shirley. She's ninety-two. And about every week, she'll report some kind of crime, from alien invasion to mass murder. But before I left out for here, I called the mayor's office where Barbara does volunteer work, and they said they hadn't seen her in some time. So, there may be reason for concern." The deputy went up to the door and rang the bell. As expected, there was no response.

"Might not get away with this in a big city, but I believe I will just force this lock and see what's going on. Might want to hide your eyes if you or Mr. Chino are sensitive to such actions."

Ray and Tyee gave Deputy Clark slight smirks, but did

not hide their eyes. Using an appropriate small tool, he had the lock picked in a matter of seconds and opened the door. They were confronted by the equally unpleasant and familiar odor of a dead body.

4

Encampment

Ignacio, Colorado—Days Before

"Colonel Jackson, where do I put these boxes?"

Sheriff Jake Jackson, sometimes called "Colonel" by the men of the Americans for Liberty, allowed his shoulders to sag. He rubbed his face with a weathered hand and silently counted to ten. "Son," he said at last, "I believe I told you just about thirty minutes ago to place all the boxes behind the main house until we can get one of the tents set up."

"Oh, right. I wasn't sure you actually meant all of them. But I'll get them over there, right now."

Jackson sighed.

When he was a little boy, all Jake Jackson ever wanted was to be a soldier. He would play with his toy army men for hours. They were his best friends. His mom told him his father was a soldier and had died in Vietnam. He didn't remember his dad, but his mother said he was big and handsome and that Jake looked just like him. By this time, his mother was always introducing him to "uncles" who visited her late at night. Jake dreamed that someday he would be the big soldier, and he would kill all those uncles. They were all ugly and smelled bad.

The little boy Jake never smiled. When anyone talked to him, he kept his eyes on the ground. When forced to speak, he would say little more than "yes, sir" or "yes, ma'am."

When he was a young man, he tried to join the Army. They told him he had several serious medical issues and hadn't tested well. They advised him to seek counseling. Jake knew they thought he was crazy, just like all his teachers.

He became a big man with broad shoulders, but he still felt small and weak. A friend of his mother's got him a job at the sheriff's department for the summer after he had graduated from high school. It was mostly running errands, but he got to wear a uniform. That gave him a new goal. He wanted to be a deputy.

Jake struggled with the tests. But he was big and strong, and he had a calm manner that suggested to others he was under control. Eventually, he passed the requirement exams and became a deputy in Farmington, New Mexico—his hometown.

Farmington was in the Four Corners region, so named because it is where New Mexico, Colorado, Utah, and Arizona meet. The area had been inhabited for over two thousand years by a diversity of Native tribes, Spaniards, Mexicans, and European settlers. It remained a harsh, rugged land that still held many secrets about its past.

Jake achieved success in the sheriff's department, with only a few incidents involving excessive force to blemish his record. He was known as a loner and very seldom socialized. He ran for the office of sheriff, and won. Some believed he won because no one else wanted the job. His mother had directed his campaign, and the prevailing opinion was that she got him elected. She knew a lot of people in town.

During his first year as sheriff, his mother died. Jake was alone. Most people commented that he had aged a decade in that one year. He said nothing about it.

To his militia in the backwoods of Colorado, he said, "I want to thank each of you for your commitment to the AFL. You have made an important decision to fight for your freedom and to establish a base of security in the midst of this troubled country. I hope in only a few years we will be free and living the life we all expected in our own country." That brought only a spattering of applause. The Colonel was respected and feared, but he wasn't a dynamic speaker. However, the intensity was evident in his eyes. No one challenged the Colonel. "We have established 'Americans for Liberty' so we can escape the tyranny being forced on us by the U.S. government. We have worked for many years to reach this point. Now we are going to take action. As of this morning there are about a hundred of us ready to build a better tomorrow. In the next few weeks, I expect that number to grow into the thousands. Once we reach a certain mass of people, there's no way the government will send in the ATF, or the FBI, or the fuckin' Army. They will be forced to leave us alone." That hit the right chords and got shouts of approval.

Most members of the AFL were ex-military, and many were in law enforcement. The country had changed, and they didn't like it. They were angry and frustrated over a lack of control. They would meet to talk about how things had to change. Many years ago, before many current members joined, they began a fundraising drive to buy land in Colorado. They managed to get enough money to buy a hundred and sixty acres in La Plata County near Ignacio. The land butted up against the San Juan National Forest near Navajo Lake on the north and adjoined Bureau of Land Management land to the south. There were some high-dollar cabins worth many millions in the area, but they were mostly in the west, toward Durango.

It was remote land, and very rugged, mountainous terrain with steep ravines and almost no flat surface. This was going to be AFL's new country: "Freedom".

Over the years they built primitive structures and moved a tremendous amount of weapons, ammunition, and other gear into the zone. The Colonel announced the target date to set in motion all of their plans was October 1st. It had arrived. Many members became nervous and dropped out, but newer, meaner, and crazier ones had just joined. They were intensely loyal to Colonel Jackson.

"Freedom—our new country—is within our grasp. We will claim thousands of acres of this land as our new home. We will secede from the screwed-up United States, and we will become our own country. Freedom is within our reach. We will not fail."

Many cheered wildly. A few looked a bit nervous.

"Freedom or die!"

5

Murder by Skillet

"Looks like she was hit on the head with that skillet over in the corner," the assistant coroner told Trujillo. "My guess is she died sometime within the last three days, and as late as yesterday morning. But that's only a guess at this point. Once we do an autopsy, I'll be able to pinpoint that better. No question in my mind, though—she died almost immediately after being struck."

"Any chance there are prints on the skillet?"

"Sure, could be. The surface of a cast-iron skillet is not the best to get prints. But we'll try."

Trujillo began directing his men as to how he wanted the crime scene searched and secured. He went outside to find his visitors.

"Ray, sorry you had to be involved in this. I know the governor didn't send you to assist in a murder investigation."

"Don't worry about it, deputy. Let us know any way we can help." Ray knew the unspoken message was to stay out of the way.

"Once we get everything secured and some preliminary autopsy results, we can meet and discuss how this might affect what you're doing here. It's pretty obvious the most likely suspect is going to be her husband, our absent sheriff. But let me get more details, and then we can talk later."

"Of course." Ray thought Trujillo seemed on edge—and hell, maybe he should be. Murder couldn't be a normal thing in Farmington, unless it occurred in a dark bar between folks nobody much cared about. But murder of the sheriff's estranged wife, who worked for the mayor and supposedly had an affair with the richest man in town—now, that would make any law enforcement officer nervous. No matter what you did or didn't do, someone important was going to be unhappy.

"Tyee, I think Deputy Trujillo would like for us to leave town."

"Okay with me. Don't see how we can be much help in a local murder that might involve important people. My Apache sense says we should get the hell out of Dodge."

"I agree. Way too many loose ends around here. We'd just be in the way. I'm going to call the governor and give him an update but suggest to him that we go back to T or C until we have a better idea how to proceed."

"What the fuck, Ray? Things get a bit nasty, and you want to go home?"

Ray's conversations with the governor always posed a challenge to his self-restraint. He was aware, after many such exchanges, that Johnson exercised no self-control over what he said. It just came out. He would yell and cuss at the slightest provocation, and only after a little cooling down did he start to think. While it was a very annoying quality in a private conversation, the pattern had served the governor well during his years in politics. It was how he bullied his way to some very important positions. And he was not going to change his ways at this point in his life.

"Look, governor," Ray replied cautiously, "if there was something useful we could do, then we'd stay. But for now, the acting sheriff has it under control. Our main goal coming to Farmington was to make sure the sheriff's office was being properly run. And it is! So, if we hang around, Trujillo will decide the only reason we would do that is to spy on him. He'll clam up, and there'll be no more cooperation. Plus, governor, he's your best bet to run the sheriff's office. We piss him off, and he might quit. As far as we have been able to see, that would mean you'd have to send in someone from the State Police to manage the department. That'd mean more problems, more headaches, and more chances for more screw-ups."

The governor went quiet on the line for a moment. "Shit, Ray. You're right. I just don't like it. Feels like we're leaving a lot in the hands of a guy I don't know and I'm not sure I trust. I don't like it."

Ray understood the governor's concern. "We can go back to T or C and start doing research on Trujillo. Plus, I'll stay in touch with him about the murder investigation. And I'll contact the FBI to discuss our wandering Sheriff Jackson and see what they think should be done. I think there are still areas we need to explore. But it's just not necessary to be in Farmington."

"Okay, okay. I agree. One thing before you leave. I'd like you to visit with Lewis Grimes. Now, Ray—you need to be very careful with that old crook. He's dangerous in a lot of ways. He's been a contributor to my campaigns, and a royal pain in the ass because of it. I'd like your impression of this man."

Ray frowned. First Trujillo, now the governor wanted him to meet Grimes. He didn't like it. Still, he acquiesced. "I can do that, governor, if he's agreeable to meeting with me. This murder may affect that. The most likely suspect is her husband, but Grimes will be on the list. Trujillo advised me that it was common knowledge he'd had an affair with her. He might decide he doesn't want to talk to anyone without a lawyer."

"Nah, I doubt that. That old bastard hates lawyers about as much as he hates cops. If he'll see you, I'd like you to do that. But he worries me, Ray. I don't want to cloudy up the picture too much more, but I've been told by the Director of Revenue there's good evidence he's been underreporting the fuel taxes he owes to the state. We think it's a scheme he developed on the Navajo reservation, in cahoots with the tribe's officials, to report more gasoline sales there while those gallons are actually being sold in the state. He's collecting the tax but not paying it. This is a monster deal, Ray, and one I could end up in the goddamned middle of. We're talkin' millions."

Ray was by no means a math wizard. But he had a good idea that what the governor talked about could amount to an amazing sum of money. He had dealt with a smaller instance like it in Las Cruces. A station owner falsified his sales records to understate them so he could siphon off money to pay gambling debts. That guy owned just one little station, but in a matter of months he had accumulated over two hundred thousand dollars in unreported fuel taxes. Grimes's businesses were hundreds of times bigger. The money involved would be a huge sum anywhere, and almost unbelievable in Farmington, New Mexico. Now Ray's interest was piqued.

He nodded as if Johnson could see him. "As soon as we're done, I'll call and see if we can get an appointment to talk to Grimes. Before Barbara Jackson's body was discovered, he'd wanted Trujillo to ask if I'd drop by and see him. So, unless her murder changes things, I believe he is expecting me to call."

"Great. Listen, Ray—Grimes is a different kind of crook, with all his lawyers and political connections. But you should remember that, at his core, he's nothing more than a thug. And he'll do anything to protect what he's got. Be very careful."

Ray called Sue from the sheriff's department. "The governor called his pilots for us, and they should be here in about two hours. Are you ready to get back to T or C?"

"Sure, I guess. You know, we just got here. Something wrong?"

"Yeah, some things have happened. And I think it's best if we leave while it gets sorted out. I still need to run by and visit with the local tycoon, either to please the governor or piss the local guy off, I'm not sure which. Anyway, Tyee and I are headed over to this guy's mansion. My guess is it'll be a short meeting. So, hopefully we're back to the hotel in about an hour, and then we can go out to the airport."

When they approached Grimes's neighborhood, a couple of things stood out. One was the ominous, substantial fence all around a vast area with three large houses. Another was the armed guards stationed at strategic spots.

"Looks like Mr. Grimes is expecting some kind of trouble," Tyee noted gravely. "Maybe we should have called first."

"I'm sure it would have been the polite thing to do," Ray agreed. "But, under the circumstances, I thought it might be more useful just to drop in. Of course, I was not expecting an armed encampment."

"A couple of those guards look like Navajo warriors," Tyee observed. "From the stories I heard growing up, not the guys you'd want to mess with. Apaches and Navajos have a long history of fighting each other. The only time there was any sort of truce was when we joined together to fight the white man. I might just wait in the car."

"I thought Apaches were the toughest of all Indians."

"Takes all kinds, Ray. I'm working on being the smartest Apache."

"Your timing is perfect."

"Okay," Tyee sighed. "One more rodeo. But this walking-into-danger thing is getting tiresome."

"One more rodeo?"

"Old Apache saying."

"Yeah," Ray sighed. "Should've called first."

They parked in front, keenly aware of the many eyes watching them. Once inside the fence, they could see the three houses were connected by breezeways, creating a sense of one huge structure. The compound was massive, covering probably more than 30,000 square feet. The entrance to the main house would have been more suitable for a castle in England than a mansion in Farmington. Its massive front doors looked like they weighed a ton each; impressive, but not friendly or inviting.

Ray was looking around for some way to signal someone that they were there—a doorbell or some kind of knocker—when the door swung open.

"Well, son-of-a-bitch! You've just got to be the famous sheriff who cleans up the governor's shit piles." Then his eyes went straight to Tyee. "And you must be his famous Indian sidekick."

He held up one hand, with a gesture like a cop telling traffic to stop, obviously imitating the stereotyped aboriginal characters in old western movies. Still looking at Tyee, he put on a serious face and spoke gravely, though what he said was nonsense.

"How! Ugh!"

Tyee didn't react, and Grimes quickly reverted to playing host.

"How exciting to have you guys just drop in. This calls for a drink."

With the flamboyance of royalty, he turned back into the house and called for someone named Mable. Before any explanations could be sought, a friendly-faced, middle-aged woman appeared and took immediate instruction to bring drinks out to the pool. Grimes waved to Ray and Tyee, indicating they should follow him through the house and outside into a broad space under towering oaks. The scale and audacity lent the house, pool, and yard an unreal, mystical quality.

The surrealism of the situation was capped off by the much younger, very attractive Mrs. Grimes, who was enjoying the warm New Mexico sunshine, lying beside the pool wearing nothing but a perfect tan. Completely naked and unconcerned.

"Shit, Vickie," Grimes snapped. "Can't you see we have guests? Put somethin' on."

With the deliberate movements of a graceful feline, Vickie rose up on one elbow to peer at Tyee and Ray without the slightest hint of embarrassment. She slowly rose from her chaise lounge to find her robe. If anything, she seemed reluctant to put it on.

"Sorry about that, guys. Vickie's my wife. She's not exactly shy." Grimes's expression bore a strange combination of irritation and pride.

Tyee and Ray struggled to recover and stop gaping. Being in proximity of the beautiful Mrs. Grimes seemed to remain a distraction, even now that she was somewhat clothed.

Mable arrived pushing a cart loaded with drink options. Both Tyee and Ray chose diet cola. Grimes took a bourbon and water and Vickie a tall gin and tonic, which she almost consumed before she made it back to her chaise.

Grimes opened the discussion. "That's some awful news about Barbara being found dead. It's hard to believe that moron of a husband of hers would murder her. But you should know, that guy's not all there. I'm not going to say he's crazy but, my god—that man's crazy. And now he's off with his make-believe militia, threatening to break away from the United States. Now, is that not crazy?"

Ray cleared his throat. "It's a tragedy. But we have nothing to do with that investigation. I'm sure Acting Sheriff Trujillo will get to the bottom of that matter very soon."

Grimes smirked. "Yeah. Sure. He will, without fail, pick someone to accuse and make sure the evidence proves it."

Ray raised an eyebrow. "Are you suggesting Trujillo is not honest?"

Grimes shook his head. "What I'm suggesting is that Governor Johnson better send some more people out here to watch over the local yokels as this thing progresses. The governor has enemies here, and so do I. My message to Johnson needs to be very clear—either he helps control these people and his tax bastards, or some bad shit is going to happen."

Ray stiffened. "Are you asking me to threaten the governor for you?"

"Shit, call it whatever you like. He'd better take some kind of action to put a stop to this right now. Got that, cowboy?"

Tyee answered, "If you're going to be a rude old bastard, you should at least say, 'cowboy and Indian.'"

His retort seemed to surprise Grimes. He glowered at the giant Indian. "I'm tired of you guys. Get the fuck out of my house." With that, he stormed off.

Mrs. Grimes rose slightly. "He really is a rude old bastard." She offered a weak smile. "Would you mind showing yourselves out?"

Once away from the guarded compound, they headed straight for the hotel to find Sue waiting out front with their luggage. Ray pulled up and quickly began tossing their bags into the patrol car.

"I sense things did not go well," she observed.

"I think we need to go home for a few days and figure out what's happened. But, for sure, I can say there's going to be one angry governor in Santa Fe."

6

Lewis Grimes: Navy Pilot, Lover, and Businessman

1964. The war in Vietnam continued to draw attention from anti-war protestors, political pundits, and the president. The beginning of campus unrest created doubt about the war for many. Lyndon Johnson, who had assumed the presidency after the assassination of John F. Kennedy the previous November, was elected in a landslide victory. The Civil Rights Act of 1964 was signed into law, signaling a change in the political environment and a reshuffling of party loyalties. The Beatles became the most popular band in America. Music fans also discovered The Rolling Stones, The Animals, The Supremes and Bob Dylan. The brash Cassius Clay won the heavyweight boxing title from Sonny Liston.

"What the hell is wrong with you, lieutenant?"

"Nothing, sir."

"One more move like that, Grimes, and I will personally see to it that you do not fly for the Navy ever again. Understand?"

"Yes, sir."

Lieutenant (j.g.) Lewis Grimes stepped smartly away from the angry deck officer to meet up with a deckhand, who muttered to him, "I guess you know—you're nuts. Nobody in their right mind drives that F4 into the deck of this carrier the way you did. You knew you had the admiral's chickenshit nephew in your back seat. They're probably gonna kick your butt outta here." Although such a relationship was certainly unusual for a naval officer, the deck hand, who handled planes after they landed, was the closest thing Grimes had to a friend aboard the carrier. And even he had trouble with him, because Grimes made it difficult to care what happened to him.

"Well, fuck the admiral and his nephew. You're supposed to pound them into the deck, right?"

"Yeah—but not at that speed or that angle. You're lucky that didn't turn out to be one big fuckin' fireball. My god, lieutenant—do you *want* to kill yourself?"

"Okay, so you think they're gonna kick me out? That admiral needs people like me to drive these machines into harm's way, and people willing or able to do that aren't standin' in no fuckin' line for the job. I'm the best goddamned Phantom pilot on this carrier, and he knows it. I'm older than any of these guys, and I'm still flying these fuckin' machines. Why? Because I'm good. Maybe a pain in the butt, but I get the job done. Period."

Grimes was right. He probably was the best goddamned pilot flying the F4 Phantom off of the USS Kitty Hawk's deck into high-risk operations over Vietnam and Laos, and yes, at forty-five he was the oldest pilot on the carrier. Even though he kept getting busted in rank he knew more than anyone about the task at hand. But the admiral's sister had more power over the admiral than even wartime considerations, and to humiliate her weak-willed son was a step too far. The admiral had the wiseass lieutenant (who no one, not even the deckhand, really liked) mustered out.

Even during a made-up war, it was an unusual thing to do to your best pilot. But family harmony held greater sway than national security.

Still, Grimes was shocked that such a stupid thing could happen at all, let alone to him. He vowed to never again underestimate the power of rank and money, especially after learning that the admiral's sister was married to one of the richest men in the country. Her moron son was in the Navy only because the admiral promised not to put him in harm's way. The plan was that after two years he would have built a fine enough résumé to run for the House of Representatives out of New York. Being shown up by a hotshot pilot as a whiney coward was not what the family wanted, and someone beneath them, namely Grimes, had to pay with his career.

After months of paperwork maneuvers, Grimes was flown unceremoniously back to the states and discharged into civilian life in Miami, Florida. And, oddly, he had also been given a handsome payment by the father of the admiral's idiot nephew, on the condition that he accepted his discharge and kept silent about it. So, for his cooperation in getting the hell out of the picture, he had more than enough to begin a new life. He had no interest in politics—he was hardly aware of the damage he had done to the nephew's chances to run for office, and cared even less. He did what he did just because he couldn't stand the pompous ass.

Still, the Navy had given him structure and purpose. Now he was at loose ends. He had no idea what his next move would be. But the amount in his bank account, unimaginable for a lieutenant unceremoniously booted from the Navy, would be a big help.

He settled into a sleazy part of Key West and enthusiastically began a sordid life of drinking, womanizing, and smuggling. Some of these came naturally to a man of his talents, and some he learned on the fly. The whole area was busy with smuggling cigars, rum, marijuana, women, coffee, and other temptations from Cuba. The operations were mostly run by Cuban-Americans out of Miami, in business with relatives still on Castro's island. The Miami Cubans hated Castro and, to a lesser extent, Cuba. But business and family took precedence over politics.

Grimes's little operation running cigars and rum was mainly ignored by the Cubans. They did not want trouble with a white guy some thought to be insane. Law enforcement, meanwhile, kept a tacit understanding with the Cubans: so long as they didn't interfere with the tourism business and didn't kill anyone who wasn't Cuban, the police would look the other way. The Key West cops had no desire to go to war, and for good reason. They most likely would have lost. Besides, the Cuban Miami connections were all active in local politics and could make things very uncomfortable, if desired.

Grimes didn't fit into the picture, but that tended to his benefit. The cops were never sure what to do about him. And the Cubans seemed reluctant to cut off his adventures into their part of the world.

Being Lewis Grimes, however, he found a way to unsettle that nice, stable arrangement. He began an affair with the married daughter of the head man in the Cuban connection.

"You know, Vickie," he remarked drunkenly one day, "I think you're about the best-looking woman I have ever seen."

The woman to whom he made that observation narrowed her eyes at him. "Lewis, you are nothing but a drunk and a con man. Although, I do think you're very sexy. But you're also a moron. I've told you dozens of times to stop calling me Vickie. My name is Angela—Angela Orlando. Got it?"

Grimes being Grimes, he only shook his head. "I really like the name, Vickie. Angela is okay. But I prefer Vickie."

"Lewis," she hissed, "you do know my father is Nathan Cruz, and if there is something called the Cuban Mafia, he's the head of it. One word from me, and you're dead. Do you understand this?"

"Angela, I think you make an excellent point. I'd forgotten about Dad and his tendency for violence."

"Make a joke if you want," she huffed, "but you are risking your life down here doing whatever the hell you think you're doing. I think they've ignored you because they think you're nuts, which means it would be bad luck to kill you. When they find out that you are just a wiseass drunk who enjoys playing silly games, you'll soon be dead."

The next day, Lewis Grimes's old dilapidated Jeep was blown to tiny bits by people who knew their way around explosives. He decided it was time to seek a new life somewhere else.

With the Jeep turned into shrapnel and no insurance to settle, he packed all his belongings into a suitcase and walked downtown to the Greyhound bus depot. On his way, he stopped by the bank and transferred all of his money—the very large sum from his navy discharge and now his ample savings from smuggling—into an account he had arranged at Chase Manhattan Bank. While his destination wasn't New York City, he felt secure with his money being housed in the nation's largest bank.

At the bus station, he settled on going to St. Louis for absolutely no reason other than it was far from Key West. The bus ride was beyond miserable. It took forever, and his traveling companions were generally most unpleasant. After one night in a clean but annoyingly noisy motel, he took a taxi to the airport and purchased a ticket to Denver with cash.

He had no intention of actually staying in Denver— going there was just a ruse to confuse anyone who might be interested in following him. He didn't know if that might be the Cubans or the federal authorities, but either way he wanted to disappear. In Denver he bought a rather tired-looking 1955 Ford and headed toward Albuquerque.

Grimes had been born and raised in Manchester, New Hampshire, and he thought of himself as an east coast person. His parents were reasonably well-off, but he knew their snobbery far outstripped their actual wealth. After he left for college, he had almost nothing to do with them. Then when he surprisingly joined the navy, under threat of being drafted, he completely avoided his parents and intended to keep it that way. Going to New Mexico felt like he was headed to a foreign country, and that suited him just fine.

He settled into an old motel on Albuquerque's Central Avenue. He would go out occasionally for food but generally kept to himself. After about two weeks, he started exploring the city a bit more, venturing into the downtown area and finding a Merrill Lynch office. Thinking it might be a way to explore some local business opportunities, he opened an investment account with a hundred thousand dollars from his Chase account. It was enough to get a little attention from the staff, but not so much as to set off any alarms. He met with the manager and was introduced to an account executive name Larry, who assured him they could help him with any of his needs.

For the next month Grimes went into the Merrill Lynch office almost every day to make trades. Most of these he directed himself, although Larry would always make time for him and offer suggestions. He had a nice run of luck, and soon Larry was asking *him* for advice.

Grimes mentioned to the manager and to Larry, that he was considering making a substantial investment in an operating business in New Mexico. He wasn't sure it was actually true, but he knew he needed something to do and thought that finding a small business might be a way of hiding in plain sight. During the second month of his routine, visiting the Merrill Lynch office daily, Larry asked if he would join him in his office.

Larry shut the door in a conspiratorial manner. "Lewis, I want to talk to you about something—but it doesn't exactly follow Merrill's policies, so I don't want to do this if you might be offended in any way."

Grimes chuckled. "If this has anything to do with my

roving eye when Miss Clarkson walks by, then all I can do is plead that I'm a red-blooded American man and can't help myself."

This got a grin from Larry and seemed to relax him. "No, no—nothing to do with watching Miss Clarkson. That's actually the main reason she works here. This has to do with a business opportunity outside of Merrill Lynch."

"Look, I asked you about local opportunities. If you know about something that might be a good fit for me, I'd be very grateful, and of course, I completely understand that it would have to be private, not in any way associated with Merrill Lynch."

Larry proceeded. "My wife's older brother ended up owning a couple of gas stations in Farmington. Do you know where that is?"

"I assume New Mexico?"

"Yep. Farmington is in the northwest corner of the state; the area is called Four Corners because four different states meet at a single point. Well, not a whole lot is going on in Farmington, but my brother-in-law said he's looking to sell, and I remembered that you asked about some kind of business. I wasn't sure whether that would be something you were interested in, but I thought I'd bring it up to you."

"You said he 'ended up' owning these stations—what d'you mean by that?"

"Well, he owned a trucking company operating out of Albuquerque and he was hauling gasoline from the refineries to independent stations. Not real sure my wife's brother is much of a business man—he was just mostly a truck driver. Anyway, some guy who owned the stations ended up owing him a bunch of money and offered him the stations to settle the debt. No question that, in hindsight, he should have sued the guy and tried to get the cash, but he thought he could run the stations and make some money." Larry shook his head. "Didn't turn out that way. About a year ago he closed both stations and now he wants to unload them for whatever he can get. Thought it might be something you could at least look at."

"Sure. Not sure that fits me, but I'll look at it."

For the next several months Grimes visited Farmington numerous times, exploring the gasoline business. He introduced himself to other station owners and soon discovered none of them were happy in the business. It seemed the only person making any money was the Phillips 66 distributor. Due to the remote location of Farmington—but the proximity to a refinery, which lay about a hundred and fifty miles south—Phillips had something of a monopoly. The local Phillips distributor, Bill McCullum, was universally despised by everyone who knew him, but amongst the gas station owners, the degree and intensity of that hatred was unmatched. Grimes met McCullum and could immediately understand why he was hated—he was the most hateful person Grimes had ever spoken to.

Grimes asked him if he would ever consider selling. McCullum said "hell no," and that if he ever did, he sure the hell wouldn't sell it to "no damn Yankee."

Still, Grimes was intrigued with Farmington. Its somewhat isolated setting and the possibilities he saw interested him. He rented a house there and spent the next two months meeting the dignitaries of its community. He also introduced himself to the leaders of the Navajo Nation.

A short time later on a cold, rainy, winter night Bill McCullum's car ran off the road, down a steep embankment, and exploded in a deadly fireball. How it happened was not known. Speculation by the sheriff's department was that a wild animal had run into his path and, in his effort to avoid a collision, had lost control. Any evidence otherwise was washed away by the rain.

Everyone expressed sorrow, but few felt any real loss. Even his widow, the downtrodden Ann McCullum, seemed more concerned with what would happen to the business and their money than any questions about the untimely and slightly suspicious demise of her husband.

Grimes sent flowers for the funeral and introduced himself to the grieving widow three days after. He told her he had been in secret negotiations with her husband to purchase the business, and even if McCullum's sudden death did unfortunately lower its value, he was still interested in pursuing the matter—if she was. There were many complications, including approval from the Phillips 66 company in Oklahoma, but after two months of negotiations and piles of legal paperwork, Grimes bought the distributing company and renamed it Grimes Oil Company.

Within a few years, Grimes had purchased most of the gas stations in the area and had established a heavy presence on the Navajo reservation. He discovered his knack for business and fell in love with profit-making. He had come to town with a sizable fortune and in short order had amassed a business empire. Most people openly admired his business skills. Grimes just smiled.

7

Back Home in T or C

The flight to T or C was uneventful, and even Tyee was pleased to get on the plane since it meant going home. They had only been in Farmington a short time, but they had shared a sense of stress and worry. Something uncomfortable was going on in Farmington, and they wanted to be away. The comfort of home sounded much better.

Until—

"I have had it! Fuck this! I am quitting—right now!" Big Jack glared at Ray like he was the problem causing him to shout and stomp about the dock at his bait shop. "Look, Ray," he paused to admit, "I know this is not your fault. But somehow, I decided I could be a normal person—and you were part of why I thought that. So, maybe it is *your* fault."

Ray had, upon his return home, found Big Jack's urgent message that he had to see him at once. Big Jack and Ray were partners in the PI business, but more importantly they had become good friends. Big Jack's message conveyed urgency. So, early the next morning, Ray headed over to Jack's Bait, Boats, and Beer on Elephant Butte Lake.

"Tell me what's going on, and maybe I can help."

"First off, did you know that the mayor of T or C is

not paid? Zero, nada, not one damn dime. Can you believe that?"

"Well, I guess I hadn't thought about it, but it doesn't surprise me. These small-town mayor jobs are mostly ceremonial, anyway."

"Ceremonial? Ray, you do not know what you're talking about. I'm getting twenty or thirty calls a day. Calls about trash pick-up, about jobs for somebody's nephew, about the librarian being snooty, about the absurd cost of electricity—these people are driving me nuts!"

For no sane reason, Ray started to laugh. He could not help it. After a moment of shock, Big Jack joined in. Happy, Ray's dog, began to bark and circle the two men, who by now were bent over in something resembling pain.

"Oh, my god, Ray," Big Jack gasped at last. "I'm so sorry. I must sound absolutely crazy."

Ray collected himself. "I never really thought too much about the actual job while you were running for it. I guess I totally underestimated the hassles involved. As far as quitting—if that's what you want, you know you have my full support."

Big Jack sighed. "I know. It just feels like I'd be doing something bad, though. Especially after all those people helped me get elected. How can I just walk away because the job is annoying? It would make me feel like a small, petty person if I turned my back on the people who put in time and effort to help me. What am I going to do?"

"Hire an assistant!"

Big Jack blinked. "What?"

"Go to the city council and ask for money to hire an

assistant. Tell them you need an assistant mayor to handle the day-to-day stuff so you can stay focused on the big picture. Tell them you're working on a long-term strategic plan to bring new prosperity to T or C, but can't do that *and* take care of every little petty matter that pops up."

Big Jack grinned. "My goodness, Ray. You have a very creative, if devious, way of thinking."

"Thank you. I think?"

"Not sure Big Jack can hang in there as mayor. He was telling me about all of the calls he gets from people who want something from him and how he doesn't want to deal with any of it." Ray and Sue were enjoying catching up on their drive into T or C for lunch at Sue's old workplace, the Lone Post Café. Ray was convinced the red chili sauce served in this part of the world was addictive, and that every once in a while, one had to have a chili fix. The Lone Post was his supplier of choice.

"In another bit of news," she replied, "Nancy Clark has decided to go back to school and get a law degree. She's going to be enrolling at NMU in Albuquerque for the next semester. She hasn't told Tyee, and she asked me how I think he'll react. Any ideas?"

"Hmm. Pretty sure he's not going to be happy about it. He seems to be in a great place right now, and Nancy's a big part of that, which makes this bad news for him. What prompted this?"

"It'll probably sound silly to you, but I think a big part of it's because of Tyee."

"What, she doesn't want to be with him anymore?"

"Of course not, Ray. She's madly in love with him. But she's afraid that she's getting too dependent on Tyee, and she doesn't want to just hang out with him. She thinks some time apart might be best to bring them together."

"OK, you really think that sounds like it makes sense?"

"Yes."

"Maybe this is me being a sexist old fart, but I don't understand the logic of being apart so you can be together—seems like some kind of female double-talk." Ray was frowning—this wasn't his area of expertise, and he really didn't want to keep talking about it.

"Fine. I'll tell her you think she's just a stupid woman and should just do what her man says!" Sue let a little anger show in her voice, though she knew it was a mistake.

"Sue, you should tell Nancy that I don't have a clue how Tyee will react and that she should do exactly what she thinks is best for her."

They reached the main drag in T or C, and Ray made a U-turn that was more aggressive than necessary, pulling into a parking spot in front of the Café and jolting his old, ugly, but very reliable Jeep—along with its occupants. Happy ended up on the floor. The conversation was over, and no one was pleased.

They took some time to order and visited with people they knew, but the mood was still chilly. Ray took a breath and tried to set things back on course.

"Look Sue, I'm sorry. I know you're just trying to help. But I don't understand Nancy—or Tyee, for that matter. You seem to think these things have to be managed, and

I know you've told me before that I just don't understand how relationships happen, but from my point of view they should just get married and live happily ever after. Am I wrong?"

"I'm sorry too, Ray. And you're not wrong, but the problem is that Tyee's told Nancy that he doesn't want to get married again. She knows he loves her, but he's afraid he'll have another failed marriage, so he's being really cautious. She's ready to jump into a commitment and he's not. She thinks if she just hangs around waiting on him, then nothing permanent will ever happen, so she figures she needs to get on with her life. And it's possible that once she's not around for Tyee all the time, that he'll realize what she means to him and he'll come after her."

"Well hell, why didn't you say it that way before—that makes all kinds of sense."

All's well that ends well, Sue thought. She smiled and began to actually enjoy her lunch.

Everyone went back to their routines. Ray went fishing a couple of times. Tyee did research on the Farmington matter and helped the FBI on unrelated projects. Big Jack hired an assistant, Johnny Baca, and immediately delegated to him all aspects of the mayor's job except rights to criticize and otherwise annoy his new assistant. A sense of an orderly and calm existence began to prevail.

Until—

"Goddammit Ray," the governor thundered over the phone, "I thought I told you to handle the Farmington situation, and now the whole damn thing has blown up. Farmington! Middle of nowhere Farmington! Nothing ever happens there, and suddenly people are being murdered. Fuck, what am I supposed to do now? Ray, are you paying attention? That's not a rhetorical question—I genuinely want to know what in the fuck I'm supposed to do."

"Governor, sorry but I don't know what you're talking about. What happened in Farmington?"

"That idiot you left in charge of the sheriff's department, some guy named Trujillo or something, has arrested some other guy named Kee for the murder of that woman. Kee's a Navajo. I don't know the details, but he's an old goddamn Indian who can barely walk, and your man Trujillo arrested him with no proof at all."

"Look governor, I'll have to call Trujillo and find out what's going on, but he's not stupid. He's not about to arrest someone without a reason."

"Bullshit. I just got off the phone with the president—yes, the fuckin' president of the Navajo nation. He told me that my official in Farmington had illegally arrested a Navajo Nation citizen and he wanted the man returned *immediately*. I'll tell you, Ray, I didn't like this guy's attitude. And how the hell did that moron become my official? Anyway, I asked Mr. President if he was threatening me with some kind of goddamn Indian war. I told him that if he was, well, my ancestors had been through that once already, and I was sure as hell not going to take any of his Indian bullshit. He hung up! This bastard Begay actually *hung up on me*. What the hell's going on in this world—has everyone gone crazy?"

Ray was reluctant to respond to the governor, whom he had always suspected was a little off-center. Anyway, he was sure that wasn't the point the governor wished to make. "Governor, all I can do is call, and see what's happening and get back to you."

"Ray, that's not good enough. I also got a call from Grimes. He's angry and he said your Indian threatened him—what's that about?"

That did it for Ray. "Grimes is a bully," he seethed, "who only wants to shout at people and make them do exactly what he says." *Sound familiar?* Ray thought, but didn't say. "He wants you to interfere with a local murder investigation and reign in some tax people who are annoying him, and he wanted me to give you that message. He was rude, and when Tyee made a wiseass remark he got angry and left. No one threatened him."

"Okay, okay. I know Grimes is an asshole. He's also in big trouble. It's not just the state, but huge sums he owes the feds, too. And it involves the Navajo leaders, especially the president, Begay. Ray, I know I get angry and start to shout and sometimes don't make a lot of sense. I'm sorry. But I do need your help. There's been another murder in Farmington. It's one of the city leaders, a councilman named Thomas Martin. Jeez, Ray, it sounds like that place is coming apart. I can send in the state police, but I'm concerned it could make matters worse. I know you're pissed at me right now, but what I need is for you and Tyee to go back to Farmington and untangle this mess. Will you?"

"Tell your pilots to come and get us." Ray hung up. He had a bad feeling. Again.

8

Murder, Murder Everywhere

A message from Acting Sheriff Trujillo was waiting for Ray when he arrived at the Farmington airport's fixed-base operator's office. It said a squad car was outside for Ray and Tyee, and the keys were in the airport office.

Tyee raised an eyebrow. "Guess someone warned him we were coming?"

"Yeah. Could've been the governor or someone he told to call." Ray's mind wasn't entirely on that matter. "I think this could easily turn into us against everyone. We should assume at this point we don't have any allies. My feeling about Trujillo being a good cop still stands, but we need to be cautious while we proceed."

"Indian Sidekick starting to wonder about White Man Leader."

"Very funny."

At the sheriff's office they asked to see Trujillo and were told he was out and not expected back that afternoon. Ray left a message indicating he needed to talk, and that they would be staying at the Holiday Inn.

"Not exactly a warm welcome," Tyee observed.

"No. This is not a good sign. Could be just a little push-back after being yelled at by the governor. Or could be Trujillo's not who I thought he was. What do you think about trying to contact the Navajo president to see if he wants to talk to us?"

Tyee fidgeted. "First reaction is I have no desire to enter the Navajo reservation. Most white people think the idea of Indian sovereignty is some kind of joke. It's not. We enter their reservation and they decide to throw us in jail, the governor can't do anything about it. An official of the federal government can eventually get to see us, but we'd be stuck for weeks until they work it out. More than likely," he admitted, "that won't happen. They wouldn't want the publicity or ill will with the feds. Still, it could."

"That's not very comforting. But my gut says they won't want to start that kind of trouble either way. I'm thinking the worst that happens is they ask us to leave—unless there's something about you being Apache that will cause them to act differently."

Tyee shook his head. "Apaches and Navajos have good relations. That's not the risk. The risk is you and the governor. If the president's involved in some kind of crime like stealing from the state or federal government, then that's what will make them do something stupid. Actually, they'd probably just arrest you and would let me go—you know, on account of our cultural bond."

"The Indians win again. Oh, wait a minute, I remember now—you guys lost."

"White Man becoming very annoying, again."

"Sorry. I think it sounds like we might want to touch base with our FBI friends regarding a few things before we venture onto foreign soil. Let's go check in and make some calls."

"Couldn't get hold of Agent Crawford, but did talk to Agent Sanchez in Albuquerque. He wasn't very reassuring. Like you, he said if there's trouble on the reservation, we'd be shit out of luck for a few days. Personally, he thought they wouldn't harm us, but they could hold us for a while without much reason at all. He did give me a name and number of the agent in Farmington who has the most contact with the Navajos."

Tyee smirked. "So it's like, 'You create a mess on the rez, call that guy. Not me.'"

"Yeah, I think that's what he was saying. Also, he seemed to think somehow it was funny that we were concerned about being captured by the Indians. Or maybe I misread his reaction."

"FBI folks not known for their sense of humor. Maybe it's something they're workin' on to improve their image a little."

"Trying to be more like us?"

"Yeah, that's it."

"Glad they're trying to improve themselves."

"I talked to a low-level guy at Indian Affairs," Tyee said. "He told me there were all kinds of rumors about President Begay being dirty. He said we should be extra careful how we approach this, because there's a lot of tension on the reservation right now. He's hearing from some of his contacts that they think something might explode any day."

"Hmm. We'll need to talk to Begay at some point. But maybe we wait until we have a better idea what's going on.

Right now, I think we should go visit with Trujillo. He left me a message saying he was sorry he missed us. He's back in his office and wants us to come back by so we can talk."

"Ray, Tyee," Trujillo greeted them, "I've got one big mess. Two mysterious deaths of prominent people, and the most likely suspects are the richest man in town and the missing sheriff."

Ray frowned. "I don't understand. I heard from Governor Johnson that you arrested an old Navajo named Kee in the Barbara Jackson murder."

Trujillo widened his eyes and exhaled. "Not sure I can say anything good about my conversation with the governor. All he did was yell at me. I tried to give him an update, but he kept interrupting and somehow it got all confused. I tried to straighten him out, but he just yelled some more and hung up."

"Believe me, I understand. The governor did not learn listening skills in grade school. So, why did you arrest Kee?"

"This may not be the nicest way to put it, but Kee is a known drunk. He mostly lives on the street, and he's had numerous run-ins with our department. He's claimed for years to be Sheriff Jackson's father. You can imagine that did not sit well with the sheriff. Jackson hated him. One time Kee was arrested, and he was beaten up in jail. There was an investigation, and a cellmate was charged, but one has to wonder what really happened. It's all an ugly, tragic story for both of them. Whether he was Jackson's father, I have no idea. But his mother was known to have been 'friendly' with Kee, who, back in the day, was somethin' of a wild man.

"Then," Trujillo sighed, "he walks in here a couple of days ago and confesses to killing Barbara Jackson. Said he hit her over the head with a cast-iron skillet. Well, that's not a detail that's been released to the public. We had to take him seriously. I put him in jail, and as I was *trying* to tell the governor, we had to wait for him to dry out so maybe we could get a better idea if he really did it. My guess is he didn't—he's almost eighty, and in poor health. I'm not real sure he could lift that skillet, much less use it as a weapon."

"Why would he confess?"

"No idea. I don't think anyone would claim he's of sound mind. So, it could be as simple as he's crazy and just confessed for no good reason. I don't know. My problem is that if this news gets out, then everyone wants a lynching—not literally, of course. But they do want this guy to be guilty."

"Guess that would solve some people's problems. What about the councilman who was killed? What happened there?"

"That happened after Kee was locked up. So, even if he could be a suspect in the Barbara Jackson murder, there's no way he killed Thomas Martin. And we're still not sure whether Martin's death was murder. The governor jumped to conclusions and never let me give him all the information we have. Martin was found dead at his house from what *could* have been a self-inflicted gunshot. There was no note found. We did find a gun, and while we don't have ballistics results yet, we're fairly sure it's the one he was shot with. We're still gathering evidence and talking to people. But, as I tried to tell the governor, we can't rule out murder, yet. It's still an open question on what really happened."

"What do you think?"

"I should tell you that I believe Barbara Jackson's murder and the death of Thomas Martin are connected. It's just too big a coincidence; there's no question in my mind. The connection could be that Martin killed Jackson, or was involved in some way, and committed suicide because of his involvement. Or it could be two different killers, or that both are murders committed by the same person. But I think they are connected. And the person who I think is in the middle of this mess is Grimes."

"Guess that doesn't surprise me too much. But how is he connected with Martin?"

"Martin was Grimes's man. Grimes got him elected with huge contributions to his campaigns. Everyone knew Martin did what Grimes told him. He didn't even try to hide it—he was actually very proud that he was seen as the representative of Lewis Grimes in city politics."

"Was there any connection between Martin and Barbara Jackson?" Good question from Tyee.

"Only a rumor that after a rather stormy and visible affair with Grimes, she turned to Martin for consolation. Martin's wife left him about two years ago. She accused him of all sorts of things, including affairs. Their divorce was settled quietly with the help of what our gossips say was a large cash settlement, courtesy of Lewis Grimes.

Martin's wife took the money and the kids and went back home to Indiana. After that, Martin became Grimes's buddy on many a late-night adventure involving almost every attractive woman in Farmington, and quite a few from Albuquerque. After Barbara's last argument with Grimes, it was rumored that she'd moved in with Martin."

"Not exactly your Chamber of Commerce picture of Farmington."

"No, it's not. There are many good people in this town, mostly Christians who find Grimes and his pals undesirable. But Grimes is a very powerful man. It's believed he's secretly purchased a controlling interest in the biggest bank in town. He has an unusually cozy relationship with the Navajo nation, and he owns the largest employer in the county, Grimes Oil Company. He's not someone anyone wants to go to battle against because most people are afraid of him. So, his rather juvenile sexual habits are ignored."

Ray thought a moment before he responded, "Let me be clear why we're here. The last thing in the world I'll do is spy on you or question your decisions. If I think you're making a mistake, I'll address it with you first. But we're working for the governor. He may be bombastic, or maybe insane, but he's in charge. My feeling is that he only wants to solve problems, and you and Farmington have become a problem. What we'll do, if you let us, is observe and assist, but not interfere. That also means we'll handle communications with the governor. In that regard we definitely can be a benefit. He yells at us, too, but after some time working with him, I can usually wait him out and calm him down enough that he'll listen. He has some problems with Grimes that aren't involved with anything you're trying to resolve. And as you know, he could come in here with a bulldozer and damage a lot of people's lives. I think that would be a mistake. I've told the governor you're the best man to handle the problems in Farmington, and the best man to run this department, if it comes to that. I still believe that. Let us help you, and maybe we can avoid hurting more people than we have to."

Trujillo chuckled. "My first reaction with the governor was to tell him to go to hell, and just move on down the road. But Farmington's my home, and I can't just walk away. I welcome your help. I just ask that if you know something I should know, that you tell me."

"Agreed. And consider yourself officially Acting Sheriff." Ray told Trujillo everything he knew about Grimes's alleged tax crimes and how they could have an impact on the president of the Navajo Nation. Doing that risked the wrath of the governor, but Ray was once again trusting his gut that Trujillo was who he seemed to be. Besides, he needed allies, even one he wasn't yet a hundred percent sure about.

9

Mayor and President

Ray and Tyee had been waiting almost twenty minutes in the reception area of the mayor's office in Farmington. When Ray called, Mayor Frank Chavez had agreed to meet with them and had told them to just come on over. Now, keeping them waiting felt like one of the power games some people played that drove Ray nuts.

"To hell with it. Let's get out of here. This gamesmanship bullshit drives me nuts." Ray was losing patience with everyone and everything. Just then the door opened and a rotund fellow with a strange comb-over waddled out of his office like he was the judge in a county hog contest.

"Oh, so sorry. I was on the phone with President Begay and he just talks and talks. Don't that just drive you crazy—someone who just goes on and on? Well, you must be Sheriff Pacheco, and Mr. Chino, so glad to meet you. I visited with Acting Sheriff Trujillo and he said wonderful things about you both. Did you know that Sheriff Trujillo and I both attended Jefferson High School right here in Farmington? Isn't that something? And now, I'm mayor and he's sheriff. I sure wouldn't have guessed that when we were in school. We were nowhere near the best students in the school, but look at us now. You just never know how things are goin' turn out—who would've guessed it? Well, look at me just blabbing on like nobody's business. It's great you had time to stop by. Both of you. It's so impressive. I mean you're almost famous. Right here in my office. Isn't that something? Please come on in so we can talk in private. Isn't this great?"

All Ray's instincts were screaming at him to run like hell from this amazingly obnoxious man. He glanced at Tyee, who seemed in a kind of trance, staring at the little round mayor. Ray nudged him to break the spell. They followed Chavez into his office.

"Isn't this something? Please, have a seat. Would you like some coffee or tea? Or maybe something stronger? After all," Chavez winked, "it's getting late in the afternoon."

"No, we're fine, Mr. Mayor."

"Great, great. Well, if you don't mind I think I might have a little cocktail. Just a tad early for me, but this is so exciting to have you as guests, I think I'll make it a special occasion." The mayor pulled a whiskey bottle from his desk drawer and poured a considerable amount into a red plastic cup. "Well, cheers." After a couple of deep gulps, he appeared to be calmer, more ready to talk.

Ray began. "I'm sure Acting Sheriff Trujillo mentioned to you that we're here as representatives of the governor. He wanted us to make sure we paid you a courtesy visit since we're going to be in your town."

"Well, isn't that something? I didn't even know the governor knew my name. How about that? Man, that calls for a drink."

Ray and Tyee began to surmise that almost anything

called for a drink as far as the mayor was concerned. The question crossed Ray's mind once more: *how do these people get elected?* "The governor," he continued, "appreciates the good job you're doing. Also, while we're here, I thought I might ask you about Councilman Martin. Did you know him well?"

Chavez seemed to deflate, if only for their benefit. "My god, we were like brothers. I still can't believe he'd kill himself. My god, what a tragedy. I still can't believe this has happened right here in Farmington." To soothe his pain, the mayor prescribed himself another good slug.

"Was there any indication he might be suicidal?"

"Thomas, suicidal?" Chavez frowned dubiously. "Well, of course not. He'd gone through a tough divorce, but that was *years* ago. He was, by most accounts, having a blast—drinking and palling around with Lewis Grimes. Thomas wouldn't have committed suicide. I've already told Trujillo that—no way he killed himself. I don't know what happened, but he didn't commit suicide." Now the mayor was feeling no pain and appeared for a moment to be headed toward discussion of more details. But he stopped and looked a little strangely at them. "Gosh, this is great having you people visit me today and bringing greetings from the governor—just great. But I just remembered, I need to be across town for a meeting on a zoning matter. Hate to give you the bum's rush, but I really have to get going." He got up, a little wobbly, and showed Ray and Tyee to the door.

Ray blinked outside. "That was one strange man. I think he got pretty soused in record time. Then he realized who he was talking to. I don't know what to think about him. What about you?"

Tyee nodded, still puzzled. "Strange person. But no question—he suddenly realized he was talking too much. And I imagine that's not a very common realization for him."

"Where's the Navajo Nation headquarters?"

"I think it's located in Window Rock, Arizona. But there's a lot of stuff in Shiprock, here in New Mexico. I think Window Rock's a couple hundred miles from here, and Shiprock maybe thirty miles—but that's only a guess."

"Well, shit," Ray grumbled. "I had no idea their headquarters was that far. I guess we need to call and set something up. Maybe see if we could meet in Shiprock."

"Yeah. Need to get our act together before we go popping in on the reservation."

"Is Shiprock on the reservation?"

"Yep. I think I remember from school that the reservation is almost 30,000 square miles spread over New Mexico, Arizona, and Utah. That's bigger than most states back East. But it's sparsely populated. And much of the land is basically uninhabitable. That's probably one reason the government gave it to the Navajos. The nation," he explained, "is autonomous to a degree. It exists in the middle of the United States, but based on treaty it can govern itself. Still, the federal government holds a kind of veto power, just in case they do something really stupid," he added with irony. "But both sides take the autonomy of the nation very seriously."

Ray and Tyee headed back to the sheriff's department to make some calls.

"Looks like the president will be very pleased to meet us in Shiprock in about an hour," Ray said after hanging up. "Didn't talk to him, but his assistant seemed very nice. He said the president would be honored to meet a representative of the governor's office."

Tyee didn't look impressed. "Maybe it's a trap?"

"I did mention I was bringing a giant Apache bodyguard, but that didn't seem to faze the assistant. Maybe they already know about you."

"You know, I'm a much better wiseass than you. That just doesn't sound right coming from a respected lawman."

"I sense jealousy."

"If we're going, it's time to giddyup."

The terrain was very stark outside Farmington. It somehow gave Ray the same feeling he imagined he would have if he were leaving port on a schooner and venturing into the ocean—a hundred years ago. The desert floor was barren and seemed lifeless. In the distance there were large rock formations, and prominent among them was the likely inspiration for the town's name: Shiprock. A massive chunk of rock rose up from the desert floor in the shape of a sailing ship. It was hard to gauge at a distance, but must have reached several thousand feet into the air. Ray felt as if he had left the familiar world behind.

"Kind of spooky."

"Yeah. That's one big rock out in the middle of nowhere. But don't get scared Tyee, I'm here to protect you."

"White man wiseass remarks increasingly tiresome."

There were only a few buildings in Shiprock, the largest clearly marked as the Navajo Nation's offices. Ray pulled up in front and paused.

"We've been joking, but I do take this very seriously. These are real crimes, possibly including murder, that may have been committed by some very powerful people. We need to be very alert and cautious."

"Yep, I agree. We're now in a different country."

"Sheriff Pacheco and Mr. Chino, it's a great honor to meet you both. I've heard from many people about how you've handled some very messy deals for the governor. I must tell you, I'm not a fan of Governor Johnson. Not sure if it's his style or if it's the substance of his policies, but we don't agree on much. With that said, though, I welcome you to the Navajo Nation."

It was obvious by his greeting, warm and cold at the same time, that Begay was a politician first and foremost. It also was immediately clear they weren't going to learn anything from him unless he thought it benefited him.

"Thank you, Mr. President. We do appreciate you seeing us on such short notice, and we won't take much of your time. We do work for the governor, but we recognize he can sometimes be a challenge. We originally made a visit to Farmington to get a handle on what was happening in the sheriff's department after Sheriff Jackson's sudden departure. Of course, that was soon complicated by the discovery of Barbara Jackson's body and then Councilman

Martin's demise."

Begay shook his head. "Hard to believe such things are going on in Farmington, but I'm sure Sheriff Trujillo will get to the bottom of it soon."

"Yes, sir. We agree. We're not trying to interfere, just help. The governor asked us to drop by and assure you that we're monitoring the situation. He said you were upset with the arrest of Mr. Kee."

"Well, yes. I called the governor while I was a little hot. Since then I've been told that Kee, for whatever reason, confessed to killing Barbara Jackson. I'm sure he didn't actually kill her, but in the circumstances I can't exactly blame Sheriff Trujillo for holding him. We're in the process of hiring an attorney to assist Mr. Kee."

"That sounds like the right approach. We don't have any special information about these killings. As I said, we were asked to look into the sheriff's department and make sure the citizens of the county had a functioning department. And I believe they do."

Begay smiled. "Is there anything else I can help you with? Or did you just drop by because the governor thought I might literally go on the warpath?"

"I'm sure it will please the governor to know the situation is now in the hands of the sheriff's department and war has been averted. However," Ray cleared his throat, "there was another matter we thought might be good to bring to your attention. I'm sure you're aware that there's some concern regarding a considerable amount of fuel being reported as sold on the reservation by Grimes Oil Company. The governor and his people believe that amount seems rather substantial considering the population on the reservation. Do you have any information that might help us to understand that?"

Ray and Tyee felt a significant drop in the room temperature, from friendly to icy. President Begay might have been mostly politician, but his expression changed, becoming a lot closer to warrior. Ray tensed.

"Had no idea you were here to investigate tax matters. You should contact our financial division. I'm sure they can assist you." Begay began to rise, as if to indicate their meeting was over.

Ray kept his seat. "The governor just wanted to make sure you had a heads-up from him regarding this investigation into Mr. Grimes's business dealings. He didn't want you to be blindsided."

Begay wasn't having it. "You and your governor are full of shit. You can tell him that he'll play hell getting anything from us. We are a sovereign nation, and we'll not play along with a witch hunt. If New Mexico wants to go after Grimes for his business activities in New Mexico, go right ahead. But what happens on this reservation is none of the state's business." With that, President Begay started to leave the room.

"I'm sorry, President Begay, if that came out sounding like a threat. I had no intention to suggest anything. I was only conveying information. If I could, there's one other area regarding Mr. Kee that maybe you could help us clear up."

"I don't wish to be rude, sheriff, but you have worn out your welcome. Good day."

Outside, Tyee smirked. "Well, Sheriff Smooth-Talker, I think we've pissed off everyone we've talked to today. Should we continue on, or go home?"

"Doesn't feel like we've made any real progress, does it?"

"We have two bodies, numerous suspects, one dubious confession, a missing sheriff, and we're surrounded by hostile people. Actually feels kind of normal."

"I know. Pretty typical. What really confuses things for me are the tax issues and how they relate to all this and Kee's confession. Why was Begay so upset that Kee was being held by the sheriff? I can't imagine him taking a great deal of personal interest in a less-than-upstanding citizen in that situation."

"One of my very wise uncles used to say, when you cannot understand someone's current behavior, look at their history."

"Doesn't sound very Indian."

"Well, he was an English professor at New Mexico State and only spoke Indian to entertain his grandchildren."

"Sorry."

"Apology accepted, Big Chief."

Ray and Tyee plodded along for a few more days, making little, if any, progress. It became clear that being in Farmington was again a waste of time. Until something happened, they were just waiting, and they could do that at home. Ray called the governor's pilots.

10

Home Sweet Home

"You know, Ray," Big Jack looked at him, "it seems to me you go away a while, create a big mess, then come back home and hide. That about right?"

"You do have a great way of summarizing things."

"My goodness, Ray. You have been around that old crazy governor so much you've turned into a bullshitter yourself. Why don't you just tell me to go to hell and get it over with?"

Conversations with Big Jack had started to become more confrontational after he was elected mayor. The easy-going "grab a beer and go take a nap on the dock" Big Jack had been replaced by the "why the hell am I talking to this guy" Big Jack.

"Go to hell."

"Hey, I like it! An honest response from the famous retired sheriff of Dona Ana County."

"Are you trying to piss me off?"

"Good question. I've lost my charm, haven't I?"

"Maybe a little." Ray gave Big Jack a smile, and they chuckled. Ray knew Big Jack was still struggling with being the mayor and having "responsibilities."

"Tell me what's happening in Farmington," Big Jack offered. "Sounds like there's some kind of crime wave going on."

That felt like safer ground. Ray related what he knew and speculation about what it might mean. "There's little question that somehow Grimes is involved in the deaths. Maybe he didn't do either, but I bet he has a good idea who did. Those tax charges are big, though. And even if he believes he's too rich and important for anybody to charge him with a crime, I think that's what the governor intends to have his people do. How that fits with the Navajo Nation and its president, I don't know, but that's also an explosive situation. Barbara Jackson's death was murder for sure, based on the evidence. Martin's could be suicide or murder; still don't know. Have an old Navajo who confessed to killing Jackson, but it seems unlikely he did it. Still, he had inside information and it gave him some credibility. How he came to know that information is still a question and so is what made him confess if he didn't kill her. And of course, all of this seems to possibly have some connection with Sheriff Jackson taking off with military equipment and hiding out somewhere in Colorado with a militia."

"That's a lot of bad stuff in a short time for a small town."

"No question. And my gut says it's all connected. These just don't seem like isolated events. Plus, the old Navajo, a guy name Kee, has claimed in the past to be Sheriff Jackson's father."

"What? Come on Ray, you're making this shit up."

"Nope, this is beyond anything I could make up. A heck of a mess, and I'm guessing there's no way it's going to end well."

"I think I'd be worried about another murder."

Ray stood in his kitchen hugging his wife.

"If you squeeze me any harder, I might scream."

"Oh, Sue. I'm sorry. It's just so good to be home and to hold you."

She gave him one of her great smiles but noticed trouble in his eyes. "What's really wrong, Ray?"

Ray's whole being felt like it sagged. His arms even felt heavy. He looked at Sue. She deserved an answer. "I'm feeling like I can't handle things the way I used too. I know, the physical part's been going on for years. But this case has made me worried about my mind. Nothing in particular, just a sense that I'm not picking up on subtle things that always used to be so easy for me. Plus, I'm just flat-out tired."

"There's nothing wrong with being tired. Young people get tired. I bet Tyee's tired. I'm tired. You focus too much on your age. You've been so busy and in stressful situations—Ray, you *should* be tired. And just because you can't figure out every aspect of this case right off doesn't mean you're losing your edge. I think you need to go fishing a few days and think about what happened in Farmington and how it can all fit together. Agreed?"

"Yeah. At least on the fishing part. I also need more time with my lovely wife and my devoted dog." At the mention of "dog," Happy came up wagging his tail to rub up against Ray's leg. It felt good to be home. Some of his sadness was already gone.

Over the next few days, Ray and Tyee spent considerable time fishing on Elephant Butte Lake. Fishing is something that can be done alone or with a companion, and if you have someone with you, you can talk or not talk. Ray and Tyee found a comfort in being alone together as they fished, each keeping company with his own thoughts.

"Seems to me," Tyee broke the silence, "the deaths of Barbara Jackson and Martin are both murders. A town like Farmington's not going to suddenly have multiple murderers. So I think it's one." He had given the matter much thought.

"Makes sense. Why do you think this murderer killed them?"

"Lust or greed have to be involved. Maybe it's someone who was mad at Barbara for her affairs, and at Martin for being with her. Or somehow this has to do with all the money Grimes stole from fuel taxes. Maybe they were all involved and had a falling-out," Tyee made his cases with no hesitation.

Ray was not so sure. "Hmm. Both those scenarios would seem to point to Grimes. Do you think he killed them?"

"Why not? We know he has a violent temper, and I believe he's a ruthless bastard who'd do anything for money and power." Tyee thought he could see Grimes clearly.

"Even so, we've got no evidence that it's Grimes. Plus, if the Martin death is murder, then whoever staged it did a good job. The assistant coroner told some of the deputies that other than a bruise on Martin's jaw, and a limited amount of powder burn on his hand, all indications are that it's suicide. Of course we don't have a coroner's report yet, which is a problem, but unless the assistant coroner is an idiot, or hiding something for some reason, the fake scene was handled fairly well. More like a lawman than a businessman. Not sure Grimes would know how to stage a suicide that convincingly. And there's still no official ruling that it's murder. Maybe Martin really did kill himself. Maybe this is about lust and he impulsively killed Barbara over love gone wrong, then suffered remorse and shot himself." Ray still had questions, but the obvious answer might still be the correct answer.

"Well, that would sure make it nice and neat. The killer committed suicide—case closed." Tyee was ready to be done.

"Yep, almost too tidy." Ray knew that tidy could happen, but in the real world it mostly didn't.

They resumed fishing and thinking, and the boat drifted slowly toward the shore. Both men settled into the serenity of the setting. It was a good amount of time before either of them spoke.

"I got some bad news and I need some advice," Tyee said at last.

"I can't believe this. The famous Apache sage needs my counsel."

"You know; you don't make things easy."

"Sorry." Ray actually did feel sorry after he saw how serious Tyee was. He knew what he was going to ask him. He shuddered to himself. He hated talking about personal stuff.

Tyee began, "Nancy's going back to school. Says she wants to get a law degree and that she can't just waste away here anymore." He shrugged. "I had no idea she thought she was wasting away. I thought we had a great thing going. I guess I was wrong. Anyway, she's going back to Albuquerque. I don't want her to. But I'm not sure what to do. Has Sue talked to you about this? Is there something I'm not getting?"

"I'm the last person to ask about relationships. Not sure why, but it seems to be an area where I have no expertise at all. Sue's told me several times that, without her pushing, I would have never asked her to marry me—and all along, I thought I was the assertive one. What I do know is that you and Nancy seem like a great couple. I believe you love her and she loves you, so you need to figure out how to not let the two of you drift apart."

"Yeah, maybe. I know I care about her, but marriage? It wasn't that long ago that I was the reclusive lake drunk. It scares me to think about another failed marriage. She planned on leaving for Albuquerque this morning. Said she'd already enrolled. So that's it—goodbye."

"I think you should talk to Sue. She'll give you better advice than I can."

"Come on Ray—what should I do?"

"You have to do what you think is right."

"What kind of bullshit advice is that?"

"Okay, my advice is that you go find her in Albuquerque, ask her to marry you, and whatever happens, good or bad, it's just life. Live with it. Time to giddyup!"

Tyee was always amazed at non-Indians who, for some reason, got it into their heads that everything was different for an Indian. When he had first ventured off the reservation and began meeting white people in their own world, it wasn't uncommon to have a someone ask him how an Indian thought. These were usually people who had gotten to know Tyee a little, but still thought he was somehow different from a "normal" person—whatever that meant to them. The image of the stoic Indian who grunted responses was a silly stereotype. At one time, when he had been a fishing guide, Tyee had actually acted out the cliché as a way of getting clients. He thought he had gone a little over the top, but the tourists who came to him hadn't even recognized that it was an act. Even within Tyee's small circle of friends on the reservation there were shy Indians and vocal outspoken ones. Bad and good, mean and kind. Just like people everywhere, they came in a variety of shapes, sizes, and personalities.

Tyee was very large, by anyone's standards. He was also a very kind, gentle man who was a little shy in most of his dealings with people outside his own family. Because he was big and standoffish, many people assumed that he was cold and unfeeling, when he was nearly the opposite. His emotions were often strong, his feelings lay very close to the surface—and he was sensitive to the feelings of the people around him.

When Tyee first met Marsha, who would later become his wife, at the University of New Mexico, he fell in love, deeply and without hesitation. She was gorgeous, blonde, fun-loving, and smart, and seemed to care for him despite coming from a very rich, very white, very prejudiced family. He was completely out of his element. He was honest to a fault, while Marsha was all about laughs and fun, with a bit of defiance thrown in to irritate her family. And she almost never told the full truth about anything—deceiving was like breathing for her.

What may have started as merely a lark for Marsha eventually led to them being married. It happened fast and without anyone's approval—both families had forbidden them from marrying, predictably leading them to rush straight into matrimony. They moved to Denver, where Tyee took a promising job with a software development company. From the beginning, though, their marriage wasn't quite right. Marsha never really settled in. She would go back to Albuquerque to visit her family and be gone for weeks, having little or no communication with Tyee. Meanwhile, he would try to ignore her behavior and concentrate on his new job. His love for his wife was blinding him to the obvious: they were headed for the rocks.

One weekend, after she had been gone for days, Marsha had called and said she wanted a divorce. As hurtfully as she could, she told Tyee she had fallen in love with someone else, someone more like her. She abruptly ended the call, and Tyee went into a tailspin. Against all logic, he still loved her, and still couldn't see her obvious flaws—which meant he blamed himself. His promising world collapsed.

After months of depression and despair, he was fired from his job. He headed back to New Mexico and settled into an odd existence, with no home, living in a tent on Elephant Butte Lake. He eventually started taking a few jobs as a fishing guide, which gave him money for booze, which he used to drown out the pain.

Even after all this time, after he had given up alcohol and made a new beginning working with Ray, Tyee still blamed himself for his failed marriage and for his lost years of self-pity and drunkenness. He was terrified the past would repeat itself, and it made him afraid of any new commitment.

11

Field Maneuvers

"Just got off the phone with Agent Crawford," Ray said. "Looks like the FBI and ATF have been pressured by the governor of Colorado to take some action against the Americans for Liberty camp out in southern Colorado. Crawford said some teenagers were out hiking and accidentally stumbled onto the camp. They said they were threatened and basically scared to death, but unhurt. Anyway, that's all Graham will take, so either the feds do something or he's sending in the National Guard."

Tyee raised his eyebrows. "Can't let a bunch of make-believe military types take over part of your state and do nothing, even if it's a remote part."

"Yeah. Their governor may be as nutty as ours, but you've still gotta do something. Speaking of our governor, Crawford talked to him, and he of course agreed they needed to break up this gathering of nuts *and* give him back his equipment. However, *our* always-wacky governor insisted we go along with them."

Tyee peered at him. "Are you sure we're being paid enough for this kind of work?"

"Probably not. I don't want to go 'observe' this nonsense any more than you do, but the governor wants someone who'll give him direct info on what's happening to go along with the feds, because they'll only tell him what they want him to know. So, I think we're kind of stuck."

"I wonder if my old job as a drunk Indian fishing guide is still open?"

"Excellent emergency fallback position."

Ray shared the plan as far as he knew. They would meet up with a team of feds in Albuquerque. Then they would go from Albuquerque by helicopter to the camp in Ignacio, Colorado. There was already a small group of ATF officers near the campsite, covertly keeping an eye on things while they waited for the rest of the team. The operation was scheduled for early in the morning two days later, but Crawford wanted Ray and Tyee to be in place for the planning session in the afternoon, so they would need to head out the next morning.

"By helicopter? Helicopter!" Tyee was not happy.

"Can't be in this man's army without riding in helicopters."

"I don't want to be in this man's army." Tyee frowned. "Really, Ray—why're we doing this?"

Ray threw up his hands. "I don't know. We got ourselves into the middle of a mess, and it just doesn't feel right to walk away. I'm really sorry I dragged you into this whole deal. I just don't know how to say 'no' to the governor. He makes everything seem like a personal affront if you don't do what he wants. So here we are, getting ready to go on a military-style mission, riding helicopters and carrying automatic weapons. This is my fault. You don't have to do this. Matter of fact, maybe it's best if you don't go."

Tyee didn't like that idea, either. "Oh, great. Just when

the fun starts, I have to stay home."

"Okay. If you insist, you can go." Ray peered at him seriously.

"Wait a minute. Did you say, 'automatic weapons'?"

"Small ones." Ray tried to hide a grin.

"How 'bout if I just carry water or something?"

"Water boy? So you want to be the water boy for the military?"

"Guess they don't have water boys in the army."

"Probably not. Maybe the Navy."

"How about radio guy?"

"Yep, probably have those. I'll ask Sanchez or Crawford if you can be a radio guy or a water guy, or maybe a map guy. I bet they have a map guy."

"Forget it. I'll go as an observer—*neutral* observer. I like that."

"Neutral observer, it is. In a helicopter."

"Jeez, I forgot about the helicopter. I think I need a raise."

Ray laughed. "Yeah, I think we both do."

12

The Sheriff's Return

Some Days Earlier

Sheriff Jake Jackson knew his wife was having an affair with Councilman Thomas Martin. At least, he thought he did. Hell, everybody else seemed to know it. What really teed him off was that this affair came right after she had one with Grimes. And my god, Grimes had to be seventy years old. How could she do such a thing?

Still, he didn't hate her. He knew he was a hard man to be around, much less married too. Jake Jackson sensed, instinctively, that he was going crazy. Not being one to dwell on introspection, he was nevertheless keenly aware that he had never felt mentally secure. Instead, he always felt he was on the outside of reality, looking in. And lately he could tell he was moving further from sanity. That did not alarm him. It only made him more conscious that he had only a little time left to settle things.

He had left with his primary militia contingent for Ignacio to establish a camp and was excited to be on what he called "maneuvers," even if half of the men seemed to him nuttier than he was. Once they arrived and started setting up camp, he made his decision. He had to go back to Farmington and contact Barbara.

He had to because one of the most troublesome loose

ends in his life was his father, Chris Kee. As angry as he was with Barbara, she was the only one he could ask to look after him. Jake knew the most likely outcome of this misadventure with the militia group would be armed conflict with the feds. He didn't expect to survive.

He had protected his dad over the years, while Kee fell deeper and deeper into alcoholism. It was his responsibility; he couldn't ignore it. He owed it to his mother, too. So he needed his slutty wife to help just this one last time.

After a couple of days in camp, he told his followers he had to leave for an emergency meeting with the governor of Colorado and would be back soon. He headed to Farmington.

He didn't have a plan. He knew Barbara would probably be agreeable with some of what he wanted, as long as he stayed cool and didn't yell at her. He wasn't sure he could do that. He knew if he lost his temper, she would yell back and everything would go to shit. Their split happened after a yelling match about her spending too much time at work.

After she left, his world started to collapse. He did love her and thought she was the most stable thing in his mixed-up world. He lost focus. Everything and everybody turned into threats. Madness found Sheriff Jake Jackson in Farmington, New Mexico.

By the time he arrived in Farmington, he felt calm and thought he would be able to talk to Barbara without getting angry. First, however, he had to find his dad. He knew his most likely hangouts—three hole-in-the-wall downtown bars. He had gone to them many times to get his dad, either to take him home or put him in a cell to sleep it off. When Jake was a child, he hadn't known Kee was his dad. He instead believed his mother's stories about his father being a war hero. Kee just hung around the house a lot, and except for a few times, when he drank too much, he was usually nice to Jake. Jake didn't hate him or like him. He was just one more "friend" who came to see his mother.

When Jake was in high school his mother took a bad fall. She was drunk and had fallen down the stairs. He rushed to the hospital, where he was told she might not live. He had never been as scared as he was that day. His mother was his world, and without her he would be lost. She didn't die—in fact, after a few days she was her old self again—but while she lay in the hospital, she told him Chris Kee was his real father, and that if anything should happen to her, he should go to Kee for help.

Jake could not believe it. He screamed at her, ran out of the hospital, and wouldn't talk to her for more than a week. He had even stayed with a classmate to avoid her after she returned home. He tried to pretend she had never told him about Kee. But as time moved on, he began to accept this turn of events. What did it matter to him, anyway, who his father was?

Later, after his mother died, Jake began to watch out for Kee. They never talked much, but Jake was always there to get him out of trouble.

At the second place he checked, Angel's Bar and Grill, he found Kee passed out in a storeroom in back.

"Listen, sheriff," Angel muttered to him, "I know you

watch after this guy. But I can't have him comin' around here anymore. He bothers my customers, always begging for drinks, and when they say 'no', he gets mad. I'm going to be at your office tomorrow, and I'll file a complaint against him. I don't give a shit what you think."

Jake hardly reacted. "Don't get excited. I'll make sure he stays away."

"Well. Okay. Look, I don't want to cause trouble, but I've got a business to run. You understand, don't you, sheriff?"

"Sure. I understand." They hauled his dad out to the truck, and Jake drove to Barbara's apartment. He thought about how everybody he knew had a fucked-up life. And he was tired of all of the grief. It was time for it to be over. He left Kee in the truck and went up to the apartment door to ring the bell.

"What the hell do you want?" Barbara greeted him. "Hasn't this been the worst goddamn day in my life, and now you show up? Just leave, Jake. I don't want to talk to you about anything. Just go!"

"Goddammit," he seethed. There went his calm. "Why are you always such a bitch? I just need to talk to you for a minute. Then I'll leave."

"Shit. Okay, come in, before my neighbor calls the cops."

He tried to become calm again. "Look—the first thing I want to say is I'm sorry. I'm sorry about our marriage going to shit, and I'm sorry I'm such an asshole. I really thought we could make it work. But it didn't." He cleared his throat. "I've got some things I'm going to have to do, and I think there's some chance I won't be back."

She arched a skeptical eyebrow. "Are you talking about your crazy army shit?"

Jake felt anger return, but fought it. Maybe this whole idea was a mistake? He just couldn't have a conversation with her anymore. "Maybe I should just go."

She sighed. "Shit, Jake. Just tell me what you want." She turned to walk back into the tiny kitchen, turning her attention to something cooking on the stove.

He took a deep breath. "There's some chance I won't be returning to Farmington, and I was wondering if you'd look out for my dad if I'm not around."

Barbara gave a dismissive laugh. "Your dad. You know what I think? I think your mother made all that shit up just to mess with you. She was as nutty as they come. I don't think she had any idea who your dad was."

The rage pounced on Jake, blinding him. He sprang toward her, grabbed the skillet and swung it. He heard the sound, loud and sickening. She dropped to the floor, dead. Jake stood, stunned. *What just happened?* He stared at her body. He turned to see Kee standing at the open door. The old man seemed to be screaming. But there was no sound.

He pushed Kee out to the truck and into the cab. His mind was racing. He went back inside again and looked at Barbara. *My god, what have I done?*

He had to get back to the camp. He knew that. *I've screwed up everything for everybody.* All he could do for his dad was give him money. He drove his dad to an old hotel to get a room, stopping to buy some whiskey at a drive-thru liquor store.

"Chris Kee," he whispered to the barely conscious man,

"I hope you don't remember anything you saw tonight. I'm sorry your life has been so miserable—but it's almost over."

He left.

13

The Four Corners Fiasco

"Sounds like the FBI and ATF guys know what they're doing." Ray only said that to reassure himself.

"I guess so," Tyee answered. "Still seem a little vague on how many people are in that camp. They say maybe thirty or sixty, or more, or less. Not a very precise estimate from the people who're supposed to be in charge."

Ray knew Tyee still fretted about the helicopter flight. He chose another subject. "Wouldn't surprise me at all if our sheriff was no longer there. He's the most likely suspect in the death of his wife. That could mean he left the camp site some time ago. Maybe he's in Mexico by now. If he's guilty, it wouldn't make sense for him to wait around for the feds to show up."

They were standing in the hall of the FBI offices in Albuquerque, outside a conference room where they had just attended a briefing about what would happen the next morning. As observers, they had been told by no fewer than three people that they were not to get involved. That was starting to be annoying.

Crawford, the lead FBI agent, walked up. "Ray, you and Tyee do understand you must stay way back from any sort of confrontation?"

Ray sighed. "My goodness. Yes, we understand. Look,

we're not fragile. We'll stay out of the way. Just stop acting like we're stupid or something."

Crawford waved his hands apologetically. "Okay. Sorry. I know it seems like we're being overly protective. But if we get some civilian hurt—or heaven forbid, killed—I'll spend the next six months on paperwork."

Ray had to laugh. "Well, *that* makes sense. I can understand your concern, now."

The next morning was all business. Everyone boarded the helicopters, all equipped with automatic weapons and geared for battle—except Ray and Tyee. It seemed very possible that within the next few hours someone could be killed.

Being a federal law enforcement operation using National Guard helicopters, they were given priority clearance to fly directly to their target. They maintained a fairly low altitude for the first part of the flight, but soon they approached impressive mountains and had to climb. The temperature began to drop.

Ray and Tyee sat next to one another but had not said anything. The noise made conversation almost impossible. Besides, there wasn't much to say.

They had learned in the pre-op meetings there would be no attempt to sneak up on the militia's camp. In fact, the plan was to fly around it and come up on its back side to land. They intended for the camp to be alerted by the noise. They hoped the show of force would be enough to persuade the militia members to surrender.

Near the back side of the camp they saw the landing zone marked by flares. Ray peered through a small window to see SUVs and crew-cab pickups waiting for them. The helicopters paused over the landing zone and abruptly made hard landings. The doors quickly slid open and everyone leaped out toward the vehicles. Ray and Tyee were pointed to one of the SUVs. Some agents stayed back to guard the helicopters.

The vehicles bounced down a primitive road and stopped about a half-mile from the landing zone. Crawford and several men got out to gather around the opened rear hatch of an SUV. Ray and Tyee walked up to observe.

An agent who had stayed near the camp for the past few days gave a report. "The only in-out traffic we've seen for the last several days was one old pickup entering their encampment. There was only one occupant. We could not identify the driver. Last night they sent out scouts who got fairly close to us, and we observed them on the video. They had mostly hunting rifles; one had a side arm. They stuck around a couple of hours and left. We've been able to recon the whole area and have not found any defense perimeters. We can approach the camp from any direction you want. We can even just drive in down the main road. We have not seen any guards or regular patrols."

Crawford frowned. "How can we communicate with them?"

"We've secured two speakers near the camp that work for about three hundred yards. Of course, the problem is, you can't hear them if they answer. Another approach would be to have at least one of us move nearer the camp with a radio. You could use the speakers to talk to them, and the lead guy could give you their response."

"Okay, let's go with that. And do it now."

Soon the speakers and the advance agent were in place.

"This is the FBI and ATF," Crawford announced. "We have your camp surrounded. If you'll surrender all weapons and come out, no one will be hurt. If you don't comply with our requests, we'll be forced to take action to close this camp. We are able to hear your response. Who is leading this encampment?"

Nothing happened. They waited.

"Well, looks like we'll have to go in and see if we can make contact." Agent Crawford didn't look happy about it.

The radio popped. "Sir," the advance agent spoke over it, "I can see someone standing in the middle of the entrance. He's saying the sheriff left yesterday with about twelve people and went up into the mountains. He says they don't want trouble. They'll put down their guns, walk out and surrender."

Over the speakers Crawford answered. "Very good. Walk out slowly with your hands in the air." Within an hour the feds had secured about forty people, identified each, and read them their rights.

Ray noticed how subdued the group looked. All hung their heads. "What about the sheriff and those other men?" he asked Crawford.

The agent grimaced. "Yeah, that's a problem. I'm not going to send anyone up into the mountains for them to ambush. We'll establish a base here and bring in more resources while we decide the next course of action. Unless, of course, you have a better suggestion."

Ray and Tyee had no alternative plan. They just wanted

to go home. "No," Ray confessed. "I'd thought they'd all give up once you guys showed up, so this is a surprise. As I told you, the sheriff is a suspect in his wife's death. He could be on some kind of suicide mission, and the guys who went with him likely are the most extreme members of his group." He thought a moment. "One thing I was wondering—could those speakers be repositioned and turned up enough to try and talk to them from here?"

Crawford nodded. "Sure. They can blast out pretty damned loud. Not sure what I'd say, other than threatening them."

Ray looked at him. "Let me talk to him. I have some info about his wife's murder he might at least want to talk to me about."

Crawford thought about it and shrugged. "Okay." He instructed his men to reposition the speakers to face the mountain and had the advance agent with the radio move closer to where they thought Jackson and his men were.

Ray took the mike. "Sheriff Jackson? My name is Ray Pacheco. I'm working with the governor of New Mexico to help with your department in Farmington. I've also been somewhat involved in the investigation of your wife's death. I thought you should be aware a man named Chris Kee has confessed. Maybe you don't care about that, but if you have information that would help, I'd like to hear it. I can meet you alone if you want to talk about it. The feds will not interfere."

Crawford exploded. "What the hell are you doing? I can't let you go meet with this guy. My god, Ray—what sort of grandstand play is this?"

Ray knew he had stretched his friendship with the agent, but still thought the best course of action was to get Jackson to come down for a parley, if he was alone. "Sorry. Seemed like the thing to say at the time." Ray shrugged. He hoped Crawford would let it play out.

Crawford glared at Ray with a look of admiration mixed with a hint of hate. He walked off.

"Looks like you've volunteered to be bait," Tyee muttered. "Maybe you should learn to keep your ideas to yourself. Indian will now have to find new sidekick."

"Let's hope not. I think if the sheriff will talk to me alone, there'll be little risk. At least that's what my gut tells me."

Tyee looked at him. "Your gut ever been wrong?"

"Yeah, a few times."

Crawford hurried back, still fuming. "Advance man says Jackson responded, and he's agreeable to meet with you. I just can't tell you how pissed-off I am. This is exactly why you should have never been along on this mission. There's no way we can fully protect you. If this guy wants to take you hostage, we won't be able to prevent it. I hope to hell you know what you're doing."

The fact was that Ray suddenly felt very unsure about the whole thing. Should he just call it off? Of course there was no way in hell he could back down. For better or worse, he had put his foot in it, and there was no way out of what his big mouth had gotten him into. "Agent Crawford," he confessed, "I'm sorry. I should have talked to you about it first. It just felt like something different had to be done, or people were going to die. Look, there are some things I know that you don't. The man I mentioned, Chris Kee, who confessed to the murder of the wife—he's Sheriff Jackson's father. He may want to meet with me to straighten out some things about that, and then go back to his men. But if I can talk to him, maybe I can make him see how foolish it is to get those guys killed just because of his personal problems. The sheriff has a troubling history, but I'm told he's not a bad person. If he's trapped, he and his men will fight. But there has to be another way."

Crawford stared like he was trying to make up his mind. "I shouldn't do this. It's my ass if something goes wrong. And if I ask my boss for clearance, he'll say, '*Hell no.*' But he always says that. I've got a stupid government form that says you're doing this on your own, and you understand the risks. You will have to sign it to release the FBI of responsibility. If you don't, I can't let you do it." Crawford paused, still not sure he was doing the right thing. "I sure as hell don't want you to take this risk. But maybe you're right. Maybe there is no other way. Just, please—don't get yourself killed."

"I know. The paperwork." They smiled at one another while Ray signed the form.

"We have an area that's fairly clear where you can meet the sheriff. It's about a quarter mile directly south of where we think they're holed up. It will take you about ten minutes to walk there; take him about the same to walk down." Crawford handed Ray a hand-drawn map.

Ray headed out. It was a cool day in the mountains, but

he was sweating. No one can walk into a situation of life-and-death possibilities and not be nervous. His thoughts turned to Sue, and how his life had taken on new meaning after his marriage to her. And he was risking everything. For what? He knew it probably wasn't a good time to have such thoughts, but he couldn't help it.

A small clearing seemed to jump up before him. And Jackson was there.

"Sheriff Pacheco?"

"Over here, Sheriff Jackson." Ray felt reassured by Jackson's voice. He sounded calm and, more importantly, sane.

They shook hands and traded manly nods to reassure each other that no one faced immediate risk of being killed.

Jackson spoke first and was remarkably composed, considering what he had to say. "I've fucked up a lot of things. Most of what's happened is my fault. I have no delusions about myself or my circumstances. I'm sorry I've caused so much trouble. But my father's innocent. If he's confessed to Barbara's death, I imagine it's because he's just confused about what he saw, and somehow he either believes he actually did it, or," he sighed, "he's trying to help me. He's hollowed out from years of grief and alcohol. He should be released."

"Trujillo is holding him because he has to—not because he thinks he did it. It would be helpful to your father for you to tell me what actually happened."

Sherriff Jackson paused for a moment, peering down at the ground. He then told Ray the story of how, in a fit of rage, he killed his wife with the frying pan. "I didn't know it," he said, "but my dad was standing in the doorway.

Even in his lifeless eyes, I could see he saw what happened. I didn't mean to kill Barbara. I'd gone to ask her to help my dad, and that was all. Then the argument started, and something snapped. I knew my life was over."

The calm with which Jackson told him the story chilled Ray's blood. But he had to make his appeal. "You still have lives in your hands, Jake. What you told me is enough to clear your dad. I'll do everything I can to get him into a place where he can get help and be safe. But you need to think of those men who followed you up here, and what's going to happen next."

Jackson only shook his head. "I will not surrender. Those guys with me now are ready to fight."

"You fight," Ray pressed, "and a lot of people will die. They can try to wait you out, but you know it will have to end. Your guys could die, and these federal officers could die, and all for what? Right now, no shots have been fired. This could all end with minor charges and no one hurt."

Jackson looked away. "You mentioned Deputy Trujillo. You should know he's not clean."

"What do you mean?"

"He comes off all friendly and everything, but he has his own agenda. He and the mayor have been buddies since grade school. You trust him, and you'll get burned." He took a step back. "I'll talk to the men. If the mood's right, I'll encourage them to surrender."

"And you?"

"I'm already a dead man."

He left, quickly. Ray headed back to report to Crawford. They waited.

14

Home Sweet Home or Hell

Big Jack was at the screen door of the cabin. "Where the hell is Ray?"

Sue fired back from the kitchen, "Don't yell at me, Big Jack!"

Big Jack deflated. "Sorry. Guess I was anxious to talk to him. And he's never here anymore."

"No shit." Sue flipped an egg with more emphasis than necessary. "I am sick and tired of him being gone all the time. He's supposed to be semi-retired." She stopped herself. "Oh, damn. Sorry, Big Jack. Guess I'm on edge. I sense something's wrong." She had not slept well for days.

"Shouldn't worry. Ray can take care of himself."

"Come inside, and I'll fix you a cup of coffee."

Their shared tension made for an uncomfortable few minutes while she made coffee.

"Damn." Big Jack wiped his face. "I don't know why I'm being such an ass. You've got real things to worry about, and I come around bellowing like it's all about me. Sorry."

"Oh, don't worry about it. I'm sure Ray's fine. I'm just a little edgy. Tell me what's on your mind this morning."

"Well," Big Jack began, "it has to do with the Hot Springs Inn. You know I've been analyzing whether there's a way to buy it and fix it up, a way that would fit into some kind of logical financial model. Bill's willing to sell it cheap, but it needs a ton of improvements. No matter how I squeeze or bully the numbers around, it just doesn't make economic sense. The cost to upgrade is too much. The Inn's been grandfathered into every new building requirement to meet code for over forty years, and it's a money pit just waiting for some damned fool to start pumping it in. I guess I wanted this to happen, but now it looks foolish."

"That's too bad. I think it would really help the town if the Inn was more of an attraction. But you sure can't just toss money at it. Have you thought of any options?"

"Yeah, a couple. You can get around some building codes by having the Inn declared an historical landmark. The problem with that is, once it becomes a landmark you're limited in what you can do to improve. You can restore, which is the most expensive option, but you can't alter the basic design. There's just no way around the cost."

"Does sound like you need to talk to Ray. He always has good ideas about how to solve problems."

"Well," Big Jack sighed, "that isn't all. I wanted to talk to Ray about what I'm doing. At one time, all I wanted to do was drink beer and run the bait shop. But since I became mayor and turned the store over to Chester, I've felt like I'm kind of lost. Before all the changes with Ray and my new identity, my whole purpose in life was just to hide and keep up my Big Jack act. But now it seems to me I should do more. So I've been thinking about moving up to Albuquerque and opening a law office."

"You could do that?"

"Seems I can. The FBI gave me a new identity along

with a valid attorney license. I haven't tested that, but I'd guess there's no reason I shouldn't be able to practice law again, if I want."

"What about Beverly? And being mayor?"

"Not sure about her. But being mayor is just a pain in the butt. It was a great honor to be elected, and beating that asshole Martinez was great. But being the actual mayor is just a tedious job with more headaches than it's worth."

"How about all the people who worked for you and helped you win the election? Wouldn't you be letting them down?"

"Yeah. Geez. You know, you're about as irritating as your husband. I never said I was honorable or some kind of dependable person. My goodness. I think I'll go to the bait shop and drink beer. If you hear from Ray, tell him I need to talk."

Big Jack left Sue feeling troubled by what he had said. Since they had all come together and bonded, their group had begun to feel like family. Now the family seemed to be coming apart. She didn't like that. And she was angry with Ray because he wasn't here to help make everything okay.

"We have movement," an agent radioed to Crawford after darkness had fallen. "Looks like some men are headed down."

"Okay. Tell everyone to be careful. No shooting unless I say." He found Ray and Tyee. "Looks like something is happening. Our best view will be from up above."

He led them on a climb of about fifty feet to a spot where they could see into a meadow illuminated by powerful lamps. It was the same one where Ray met Jackson. They could see Jackson's men with their hands on their heads and unarmed.

Agents moved in to surround and secure them with handcuffs. They had them sit on the ground.

Ray walked up to one and bent down to ask, "Where's Sheriff Jackson?"

"Far as I know, he's still up there," the man answered in a half-whisper. "He told us it was over, and we should come down and surrender. Told us we were outnumbered, and it would be suicide to fight. Then," he looked up at Ray, "he said things that didn't seem to make much sense, like stuff about his destiny and how he was going to return as a warrior and make everything right for his family. Kinda sounded nuts. Anyway, we all hesitated a bit. Then he pulled out his gun and said he would personally shoot anyone who tried to stay. We dropped our guns and headed down here. What will happen to us now?"

"Can't say. But you made the right decision."

Ray went to find Crawford. "Seems Jackson instructed everyone to surrender, even threatened to shoot them if they didn't. He's still on the mountain. But I can't see where he's any threat to anyone except maybe himself."

"Probably true. But, hell. I can't just leave him up there."

"Look—maybe I can get him to talk again. If you go after him, someone's—"

A shot rang out, high on the mountain. Then silence.

107

Ray and Tyee headed back to Albuquerque on the first helicopter available. Crawford's men found the body of Sheriff Jake Jackson slumped against a tree. Busses had taken the militia members to Durango, where they would be arraigned and held. Colorado's attorney general was also considering charges. His state police had officially taken possession of the camp site and all weapons, military gear, and supplies.

Ray knew Governor Johnson was probably blasting someone out about the theft of New Mexico assets by the asshole Governor of Colorado at that very moment.

Ray lay in his own bed. It felt great. He could hear Sue making happy sounds in the kitchen. Breakfast smelled like heaven. He thought nothing could be better than this. And he wasn't going anywhere from now on. How that would work out with Pacheco and Chino he didn't know. But for damn sure he was going to enjoy his life. He would not deal anymore with crazy people who seemed to be everywhere. He did enjoy the work, especially when it felt like the outcome was the right one. But he was too old to be gone from this wonderful life right here, always waiting on him. He would discuss his decision with Sue and see how he could make it work.

"Well, good morning, or maybe good afternoon. I take it someone is glad to be home." Sue knew her husband was happy to be home, and she was beyond pleased he was there.

Happy came running up, jumping and barking in a

complete display of true love. "Guess I'd better take him outside and let him burn off some energy before he wrecks the house." Ray felt comfortable. Home sweet home. "I can't tell you how glad I am to be home and to be with you," he told Sue. "Pretty sure I can't be gone the way I've been anymore. Not sure what that means for the business. But I'm not going to spend my remaining years trying to solve other people's problems. Can I just stay home?" He smiled at her.

"It's okay with me. However," she raised a finger, "before you retire, you need to talk to Big Jack. He seems about ready to explode. He's thinking about moving to Albuquerque and opening a law office. But mostly, I think he wants not to be mayor anymore. The fine folks of T or C are driving him nuts."

"That didn't take long."

"I know. You want to stay home, Big Jack wants to go back to being an attorney, Tyee wants never to fly again. Maybe it is time to talk about Pacheco and Chino and what makes sense going forward."

"What do you want, Sue?"

"You know that's a stupid question. I want you to be happy. But I don't want people being shot, I don't want you gone all the time, I don't want to be alone, I don't want to sleep by myself, I don't—" She started to cry. "Shit, I don't want to cry!"

They hugged. Ray stroked her hair. "I think we want the same thing. And, yes—it's time to talk about what we're doing. Maybe Pacheco and Chino needs a break."

❖

"Maybe it was Farmington," Ray opened the subject. "Or maybe it was Ruidoso. We had some pretty rough things to deal with at both of those assignments. After Ruidoso, I said we needed a break. Now here we are in the middle of the Farmington mess, and I need *another* break. Plus, Big Jack—you're thinking about moving to Albuquerque." Ray looked around the room. "Maybe it's just us. I thought it would be great fun to stay active, make a little money and catch some bad guys. It hasn't been. So, I want to hear what you're thinking. But I'm pretty sure I want to stop Pacheco and Chino for a while. What do you think?"

Tyee and Big Jack looked a little stunned. Sue just felt sad. She wanted Ray to stay home more, but now she worried that he was quitting in reaction to her needs and giving up on something he really wanted to do.

Tyee recovered to answer philosophically. "That's not a complete surprise. But I guess it's something of one. I don't know what to say other than without you, there is no Pacheco and Chino. So, what I think is not really important."

Ray shook his head. "Bullshit. Don't do that. You know this isn't easy for me. But you could continue doing most of the things we have going on with the FBI, and even the state. The computer stuff you do has nothing to do with me. I'm sure they'd want you to keep at it."

Tyee nodded. "Okay, maybe that was a little whiney of me. But if you quit, you know this deal will be over in a matter of months. So, let's be honest. Is it time for this to be over? Maybe so. I never wanted to be a cop. That's all you wanted to be. This was for you. I just tagged along."

Big Jack spoke up. "This, I'm sure, has something to do with my big mouth. I shouldn't have come up here and complained to Sue because you weren't here, and I was just in a bad mood. But, damn it, I *am* in a bad mood. I don't want to be mayor. Okay? So, that makes me a bad person, all of those people who helped me I'm just tossing aside like it meant nothing. And that's the problem. I can't do that. But I still don't want to be mayor, period. No ifs, ands, or buts—something has to change."

Ray looked sad. "I don't know the answer. But maybe that's something we can agree on: something has to change."

Sue had heard enough. "Listen to you. You're all unhappy about something, and you just know there has to be a change, but what you don't want is to lose your friendships. Just because we change the business doesn't mean you have to stop being friends." Sue was able to say things that three macho numbskulls could not.

A long pause followed while each pondered what this would mean. They wanted some things to change. They sure didn't want everything to change.

Ray broke the silence. "First, we have to finish Farmington. I'd like to just walk away, but that wouldn't be right. The governor is an asshole, but he's our asshole, and we shouldn't let him down. But, starting today, we won't take on any new assignments. Tyee can continue with computer projects for the FBI. Big Jack, you need to make up your mind on what you think is right for you. You can't stay here and be miserable just because you became mayor and now you don't want the job. Appoint someone else as the mayor until an election can be held, and go back to sleeping on the dock or go to Albuquerque and open a law office. But stop bellyaching all the time."

"You could've said that in a nicer way, but I agree." Big Jack began to smile, especially once he gave thought to who he could name as acting mayor.

15

Power Interruptions

"Hells bells, Ray, you can't quit, I won't let you."

"Governor, you have a lot of power, but you can't stop me from quitting."

"Shit."

"I just wanted to let you know that we'll finish our latest project in Farmington and then we're going to take a break. Not sure how long, but who knows, we may be back asking you for work before you have a chance to miss us."

"What the fuck am I supposed to do in the meantime? All those idiot sheriffs are still out there screwing up as we speak."

"One consolation; your term will be over in about a year. Then it'll all be someone else's problem."

The governor laughed. "There is that. Maybe I'll move down to T or C and live the life of leisure like Ray Pacheco. What do you think, Ray?"

"You'd be most welcome. Be happy to go fishing with you anytime."

Ray hung up. He could not help liking the governor. For all his bombastic ways, he got things done and never shirked his responsibilities to the people. Ray thought he might have a hard time adjusting to civilian life, though. He would definitely give him a call after his term and invite him to go fishing. First, Ray needed to finish *his* responsibilities.

Crawford was his first call. "Ray, good to hear from you. I hear the governor of Colorado is going to keep all your guy's army vehicles, apparently out of some old grudges."

"Yeah. I think their feud goes way back to their days in D.C. I've told the governor several times that junk wasn't worth anything, and he should be glad Graham's taking it off his hands. He seems to disagree. Still, he isn't willing to start the first war between two states over something like that. So I guess that part of that misadventure is over. I called you to let you know Pacheco and Chino is going to take a little time off. Tyee will still be available to do computer work, but we're not going to take any more field assignments that require travel after we're done in Farmington."

Ray felt a pause on the line. Agent Crawford had been a significant ally. Maybe he was taking this pull-back personally. "That's not good news. I don't have anything on the horizon. But you and your group have become a dependable resource for us. We'll have trouble filling that hole. Would more money help?"

"Ben, it's nothing to do with money. It's mostly to do with me. At this stage of life, my priorities are drifting all over the place. One week it was the business, the next week it was my wife, then it's fishing, or something. I just decided I needed time to think about what I wanted to do with my remaining years."

"I get it. Plus, I bet your new wife is not too pleased to have you involved in these life-or-death situations."

"I'm not too excited about that, either. While I was sheriff, I could count on one hand the number of times I'd been shot at. As a PI, everybody's trying to kill me. Never would have thought that."

"That's mostly just bad luck. But still, it's dangerous work."

"Maybe too dangerous for an old man. Especially one with a younger wife. Take care of yourself. I wish you the best, Ben."

"You too, Ray."

The phone rang, always an irritating sound to Ray, and—as he glanced at the clock—especially at four o'clock in the morning.

"Hello." Ray glanced at Sue, who was still asleep. He admired her ability to ignore interruptions from the outside world.

"Ray, it's me," the governor barked. "Going to see Grimes. Need to talk to the sonofabitch and see what the hell is going on. Driving down to Albuquerque and flying to Farmington from there. Can you meet me in Albuquerque this morning and go with me?"

No! No! he wanted to scream. "When and where?"

"We'll be at the Double Eagle II Airport FBO by ten. We'll wait for you. By the way, bring Tyee with you." The governor hung up before Ray could respond.

"Shit."

"What's wrong?" Sue raised up.

"The damn governor of New Mexico is what's wrong.

Got to get off of this treadmill before he drives me nuts."

Sue took his hand. "Just do the right thing and get it over with. You know you can't just walk away until some things are resolved. But do it quickly."

"Yeah, I know. Gotta call Tyee and make his life miserable." Ray smiled but did not feel happy.

Ray and Tyee were quiet, neither of them pleased with the idea of riding on a plane with the governor. While the trip from T or C to Albuquerque was only a few hours, it already felt like they had been driving all day. And it wasn't even dawn yet.

"Why do you think the governor wants to see Grimes? Sure seems like it has some risks associated with it, doesn't it?" Tyee would go along with the plan, but he thought it was stupid.

"There are. Plus, it's just plain stupid," Ray grumbled. "The governor has people who should talk to Grimes— and he definitely should *not*. But there's something he's not telling us, and that has me worried. He and Grimes go back a long way. There may be some things Grimes knows that the governor doesn't want anyone else to know. At this point, I'm not sure I care. We need to find out about Trujillo—is he a killer or what? If he is, we replace him as sheriff. If he isn't, we turn this stuff over to him and head home. Jackson seemed to say he was guilty of something. But the way he said it may mean he just wasn't loyal enough."

"Since we started, there have been three people killed.

Barbara Jackson, killed by her violent and crazy husband; the councilman Martin; and of course, Jackson killing himself. We know who killed Barbara, because Jackson confessed. So the only question is, who killed Martin? Or was that also a suicide? Let's say, based on what the dead sheriff told you, our best suspect is Trujillo. Why would he kill the councilman?" Tyee was using logic to get them pointed in the right direction.

Ray jumped in. "Most murders are based on greed or lust. I think we can rule out lust regarding Martin. So it has to be greed. Money. And so, if Trujillo did it, it's because he's going to get lots of money or wants to keep it hidden. The only place where lots of money might be floating around would be with Grimes."

Tyee smiled. "Everything comes back to the old bastard Grimes. And now we're going with the crazy governor to visit the crazy millionaire with the crazy wife. Do you see a theme here?"

"Yep, I do. Try not to call the governor crazy while we're on the plane, okay?"

"White Man has good words of wisdom."

As they approached the small airport, Ray spotted the governor's plane. He pulled into the parking lot next to the terminal. As they walked toward the plane, its side door opened, and someone lowered the stairs. The governor leaned out to wave Ray and Tyee aboard. Almost before they could get strapped in, the plane taxied, made its rapid trip down the small runway, and they were airborne.

"Glad you could make it, Ray. You too, Tyee. I know you guys must think I'm nuts to go visit with Grimes, and maybe I am. I've got big problems with him, and I need this to end without it becoming a major news story. That's not because of my reputation. It's because he's dangerous to the state's economy. He's the biggest employer in New Mexico. His string of convenience stores are all over the state, and he's got his dirty fingers in more corrupt business deals than you could imagine. How all this happened without some kind of investigation is beyond me. I met yesterday with the AG, and he has sufficient evidence to charge him with enough to rock this state to the core. I asked for one day to talk to him. Maybe, if he'll plead guilty, we can keep some of this quiet and not ruin so many lives. If he decides to fight, he's going to bring down a lot of politicians and turn the state into a laughingstock. I know you're a moralist, Ray, and you think, 'What the hell? Let him rot.' But it'll cause a lot of harm to innocent people. I'd like to avoid that if we can."

"I guess you know, governor, he could be a suspect in the murder of Councilman Martin." Ray watched for a reaction.

The governor only looked sad. "I won't shield anyone from any crime they've done, especially murder. But if there's some way I can work a deal to keep all the businesses open while this is worked out, it will save a lot of jobs."

The flight was supposed to be short, but already it felt long. Ray looked at the governor and remembered why he had thought, even with his faults, he was good guy. The man cared. "We'll help you any way we can."

The governor nodded. Still appearing emotional, he turned away.

The pilot announced they would be landing shortly and requested that everyone buckle up.

16

It's Going to Be a Bumpy Ride

Ray and Tyee stood back while the governor was surrounded by officials and law enforcement, hurried into a limousine, and whisked away from the airport.

"Think he forgot we were with him?" Tyee inquired, watching the governor's fleet leave.

"Probably. He'd make a lousy pal." In truth, Ray was glad the governor's circus had left.

"Do we call Trujillo to see if we can get a ride? And by the way, how do we get back to Albuquerque when we're done?" Tyee always wanted to identify an exit.

"Maybe before the governor leaves, he'll remember he brought us here. If not, we can get a flight or rent a car."

Tyee perked up. "I vote for a car."

"Excuse me, would you be Sheriff Pacheco?" The person asking was a Navajo policeman close to Tyee's size.

"Yes," Ray responded. "I'm Ray Pacheco, and this is Tyee Chino." Ray extended his hand.

The man smiled, quite warmly. "Nice to meet you both. I'm Captain Joshua Watchman, Navajo Nation Police. Do you have time to visit with me a bit?"

Rescued, Ray thought. Watchman had a car and offered to give them a ride to the Holiday Inn. They checked in and met him in its coffee shop.

"You guys need a car while you're here? If so, I can probably arrange something." Watchman's size and faintly scowling expression seemed to contrast with his gracious manner.

"Our trip was arranged at the last minute," Ray admitted, "but I believe we'll be able to secure a car from Acting Sheriff Trujillo. If we can't, though, we might take you up on that. By the way—how did you know we'd be on the flight with the governor?"

Watchman smirked. "The governor himself told me. There's a long story behind that. I contacted him almost a year ago about our nation's president and Grimes, and what I suspected to be a major crime involving gasoline taxes. I also communicated that to the Bureau of Indian Affairs and the FBI. Governor Johnson, being a very direct person, called me a stool pigeon. Thought that was a little crude. But maybe he was right." His eyes hardened. "Still, I don't give a fuck who it is—if you're stealing from the Navajo people, you're going to have to deal with me. Hard-charging the president could end up being my last act, though. I figured I ought to find some help."

Tyee jumped in. "You said you found this out a year ago?"

"Not exactly, my friend. I meant to say I *contacted the governor* about a year ago. I'd been working on this for almost two years before I had enough to talk about with anyone other than my wife. See," he continued, leaning only a little closer, "I believe our tribal leader is a crook. He and Grimes have been working a deal for years. Grimes steals gasoline taxes from the state and the feds—how much I don't know; it has to be millions. And he pays kickbacks to President Begay, who in return signs the falsified reports of how much gas gets sold on the reservation. The amounts are so stupid that anyone, involved or not, would wonder right away how that much gas could be sold on the rez. I don't really know if they're both that stupid or just that greedy. But the shit is just about ready to hit the fan."

After having been given all that interesting information, Ray felt uncomfortable that Watchman seemed to be spilling his guts like this after they had only just met. It struck him as odd. "Is any of this connected with Sheriff Jackson or his wife's death? Or the death of Martin, the councilman?"

Watchman shrugged. "I don't think so. Still, it could be. I don't know who killed Martin, if that's what you're after. I can say that Jackson and Trujillo were never in the loop with the state people or the feds about Begay and Grimes. Reason for that is there was concern that one or the other could tip Grimes off. Now," he raised an eyebrow, "the governor asked me to tell you all this because he seemed reluctant to tell you himself. I've known for a while that he delayed action that could have been taken because he's trying to manage the outcome." After that, Watchman appeared tired. He took a sip of his coffee. He seemed to be done.

But Tyee pushed a little further. "Do you think Johnson's trying to protect Grimes?"

Watchman leaned back, shaking his head. "Just the opposite, if he could have done it legally, he would have strung the bastard up, right in the town square. I think he's trying to protect the Navajos and the people who work in all of Grimes's businesses. Pretty sure the governor hates ol' Lewis Grimes."

Ray felt fatigued himself. There had been days while he was a sheriff when it felt like everybody was some kind of bad guy. That feeling was back. "What do you think will happen with Begay?"

Watchman sighed deeply. "The FBI will charge him with who knows how many crimes. Once again, Johnson has his hand in this, even if he can't stop them once they decide. For now, I think they've given the governor a couple of days to try to get something out of Grimes. Then they'll move in." He looked away. "This is going to be a major story once it breaks. The Navajos are going to look like shit, having a president stealing money just like American politicians."

Tyee shook his head. "What the hell is the crazy governor trying to do with Grimes?"

Watchman shrugged. "My guess is he wants some kind of ownership change so the businesses can still operate after Grimes gets tossed into prison. I advised him strongly not to talk to Grimes and let the FBI handle this. He said something along the lines of, I should mind my own fucking Indian business." He curled his lip. "He's a rude old devil."

"Yes, he is. He made it clear to me once that his family had a long history of killing Indians." Tyee grinned. Perhaps partly for that reason he'd grown to like the crazy governor.

Ray stood. "I need to find the governor and talk to him. I think talking to Grimes about some kind of deal is one of his dumber ideas. Could you take us to where he is?"

"Might be too late. You know, he didn't leave you at the airport by mistake. He doesn't want you to interfere." Watchman waited to see whether Ray would react. He didn't. The captain went on, "Something else you should know." He straightened up a little. "Acting Sheriff Trujillo was having an affair with Grimes's wife, the one he calls Vickie. I believe Grimes knows. She's much younger than he is, gorgeous and greedy. If Grimes was ever killed, the first suspect would be her. The second would be Trujillo. Sheriff Jackson knew too. He had pictures."

"Interesting. We know how attractive she is. We saw her—all of her—the day we visited Grimes. But how did you know that Jackson knew?"

"He told me one day. I always made it a habit to stop by to see him, usually just to chat a bit about the town and any trouble he might be having with our tribal members. He just told me that day that his deputy was having an affair with Grimes's wife, and he'd decided to fire him."

"When was that?"

"About a month ago."

Ray pondered that while the waitress refilled their cups. "I'm almost afraid to ask, but is there anything else we should know?"

"I've reason to suspect Vickie and Trujillo once searched the residence for a cache of money that Grimes is believed to have buried somewhere on the grounds."

Tyee leaned forward. "Buried? How much?"

Watchman didn't know. "You've met Grimes. So you know he's a little strange. Rumor was, he stole money from himself to avoid paying taxes on it and buried it somewhere on his estate grounds. It's just been a bar rumor for years, and I always thought it sounded bizarre. I mean, he's eccentric, not stupid. If he wanted to hide money, he'd move it to another country, or something. But the truth might be that he did both. Maybe he actually did hide some getaway money at his house. Apparently, his lovely wife thought so. Otherwise, why would she and Trujillo be digging up the yard?"

Tyee added his thought. "Maybe to bury a body?"

In another time and place that might have been funny.

Ray was on the phone with the governor, and hot about it. "I just don't understand. You asked us to help you, and yet you have a whole operation going on behind our backs. I think all we can do is go home and let your team take care of everything."

"Don't get pissed about any of that shit, Ray. I didn't tell you what they were doing because I didn't want you mixed up in it. I still want a functioning sheriff's department. Give me your recommendation on Trujillo, yes or no. Then, go home. All the rest is just one big mess, and you don't want anything to do with it. Do you?"

Ray paused. Johnson had him there. He wanted nothing to do with financial fraud or romantic affairs, or anything like that. "Okay. I'll have a report, one way or another, tomorrow. Can we get a ride back to Albuquerque with you?"

"Sorry, Ray. I'm at the airport right now—leaving in just a minute. Got another fuck-up to deal with back in Santa Fe."

Shit. No reason to get mad. It wouldn't do any good. "What happened with Grimes?"

"I gave him a week to transfer all his operating businesses into some kind of trust, or to his wife, or something, so they could continue to operate if he goes to jail. That bastard just laughed. Told me I was an old fool. My god, *he's* the old fool. Stealing millions from the state and the feds—what did he expect? Anyway, I gave him a week, then he'll be arrested. In the meantime, we'll keep an eye on him. If he tries to leave, the deal's off, he'll be arrested no matter what." Johnson scoffed. "God, I hate that bastard. He just kept laughing at me, like it was all a big joke to him. I think all of his years of drinking have rotted his brain. Gotta go. Get that report to me and bill me for the flight home. See ya." Click.

Ray walked over to Tyee, who stood staring out a window. "What's he done to us now?" He sounded beat. The governor had defeated the Indians, once again.

"He's leaving. We're stuck. Told him I'd have a report on Trujillo tomorrow, and then we're done. I swear I will never work for that old war horse again."

"What's your report going to say?"

"I don't know. Easiest answer: he should be fired. If Watchman's right, he's done enough wrong to be fired or arrested. Anyway, it would mean he's not qualified to be sheriff. But," he wondered, sullenly, "do we believe Watchman?"

"I guess I do. And that's not just Indian bias. I just think the guy wouldn't lie to us. He could be wrong about some of what he says and thinks about Trujillo. But I don't think he's wrong about who the guy is. Trujillo lied to us, big time. And maybe he's been plotting all along to steal his lover's husband's money." Tyee formed opinions quickly.

Ray sighed. "Do you think he's connected to Martin's death?"

Tyee shook his head. "We don't have anything to connect him. More than likely, the councilman killed himself. The coroner's report isn't completed for some reason—once we get the report, it will most likely be a suicide. And no, we don't know why he'd kill himself. But we have nothing linking Trujillo to him. I think we should go ask Trujillo about Vickie and the hidden treasure. See how he reacts."

Ray inquired. "You want to walk?"

Tyee scoffed. "I'd prefer to ride a horse, but I guess we can if we have to. If he's not in, maybe they'll loan us a patrol car. You know," he went on while they started on their way, "we should get more respect than this. After all, we're almost famous."

Ray pondered how, as big as Tyee was, he could still act like such a baby.

17

Sometimes Things Don't Go As Planned

"Fuck you!" Trujillo was in no mood to take questions about his married girlfriend.

Ray was beyond being patient with him. He had bounced between not being sure about him, then thinking he was a good guy, and at present dealing with facts that indicated he might be a bad guy. It was giving him a headache. "You'll either answer my questions," he said, flatly, "or I'll have you relieved of your duties today, by authority of Governor Johnson."

"Maybe I'll just quit. Then you can be sheriff. Or maybe you could appoint your Indian buddy." Trujillo cast a smirk at Tyee, as if he thought what he'd said sounded clever.

Ray burst upright, grabbed the acting sheriff's shirt and pulled him out of his seat until they were nose-to-nose. "I've had all the shit I'm going to take off you. You are relieved of duty. I will have your badge and gun."

Tyee already had Trujillo from behind, in a clench that kept him from moving at all. Ray slipped Trujillo's sidearm from its holster. Tyee shoved Trujillo back into the chair. The anger in the room was so thick it made breathing difficult.

Ray barked a question, "Were you having an affair with Vickie Grimes?"

"Yes. So fuckin' what? That's between me and Vickie and Grimes. That's not a crime." Trujillo's face turned red. But he kept still.

"Did you kill Thomas Martin?"

"Hell, no!"

"Do you know who did?"

Trujillo didn't answer right away, appearing to calm himself down. "Look. My affair with her's been over for months. It was all wrong. Caused all kinds of problems." He sighed. "I just couldn't resist her. I was stupid. My wife left me and took the kids to Phoenix to live with her parents. Now she won't talk to me, and she's filed for divorce. It's ruined my life. But," he almost pleaded, "I didn't kill anyone. And I don't know who killed Martin. I do know he didn't kill himself. He was having the time of his life. He'd always been this straitlaced guy; and then the next thing I knew; he was out running around with old man Grimes. Every time I saw him in the last six months, that was all he talked about—the sex, the booze. Like suddenly he was one of the cool guys. He wouldn't have killed himself."

"Was he involved in any business deals with Grimes?"

"Not that I know about. His family had money, and both his parents died over the last two years. He inherited a lot. But I don't think he would have gotten involved with Grimes when it came to business. He went wild, but he was basically an honest guy. He even told me a couple of times how he thought Grimes was doing illegal shit. I tried to get him to tell me what the hell that meant. But he'd say he couldn't prove anything, then he'd clam up."

"Would Grimes have any reason to kill Martin?"

Trujillo's eyes narrowed. "Grimes is a bad, dangerous man. He could do almost anything. If Martin confronted him, he might have worried about him being a risk. There's little doubt in my mind that Grimes wouldn't hesitate for a second to eliminate a threat. But," he admitted, "I don't have any proof he was involved."

Ray and Tyee both sat back down. Nobody said anything for a minute until Ray spoke, "Thad, we've got a big mess, involving a lot of powerful people. Soon it's all going to blow up, and some people in this town are going to be hurt. I have no reason to suspect you of any *legal* wrongdoing. I mean, you're right, having an affair with the wife of the richest man in town isn't a crime. But it does call your judgment into question. And I speak from experience—being a sheriff in a small town is a very difficult job. You're dealing with your neighbors, friends, relatives, old classmates, and everybody's connected. You cannot be anonymous, and you can't hide. You have to lead by example." Ray looked hard at Trujillo, but couldn't tell what he was thinking. "On the other hand, a sheriff doesn't have to be a saint. As a matter of fact, a saint would probably make a lousy sheriff." He leaned toward Trujillo. "I need to make a recommendation to the governor about what he should do about you. I can say he should fire you, and he'll send in some state police guy to run the department until an election. But that guy won't have the stake here that you have. Maybe I should have asked this at the beginning: Do you even want this job?"

Trujillo turned his eyes to the floor. "Thought I did, months ago. Today, I'm not so sure. Not sure I can handle the politics. Kissin' up to people is not one of my skills."

"I had the same issue. But politics comes with the territory. You handle that by being honest and treating everyone with respect, whether it's the richest guy in town or the poorest." Ray realized he sounded to himself like he was preaching. He didn't like that.

Trujillo looked up at Tyee and seemed to relax. "Would you want to be sheriff?"

Tyee glanced at the other two in turn. "Hell, no. You've got to be kidding? The pay's lousy. One day, everybody loves you, and the next everybody hates you. I'd go back to being a fishing guide in a heartbeat."

Trujillo laughed, a bit solemnly. "You're right about all that. But this is the job I want. I screwed up. But I know how to do this, especially in my hometown."

Ray nodded. "Even though I can't say I don't think there's a risk in doing it, I'm going to recommend the governor appoint you sheriff. If something else jumps out of your past that I don't like, I will come back and personally fire you. Now, you need to solve the murder of that councilman. We agree he didn't commit suicide. Find out what happened, and fast."

"Thanks. I'll do my best not to embarrass you, or Tyee." Trujillo smiled, if apologetically. "I should tell you, there is someone who I need to talk to about Martin's murder. But I have to warn you, that might cause some new conflicts."

"Who's that?"

"He's on the Navajo police force. A Captain Watchman."

Ray and Tyee exchanged looks. "We've met him," Tyee said. "How's he involved?"

"He and Martin butted heads. Watchman's involved in a lot of stuff in this town, some of it might have been illegal. Jake was investigating him when he went off his rocker. I know he'd discussed it with Martin, but I don't know what was said. Jake hinted to me that Martin was the key to nailing Watchman."

Ray exhaled. "You'd better be careful. And you should put anything you have in writing and pass it along to the state attorney general, just in case you need some back-up. Document everything. Going after a captain of the Navajo Nation Police sounds like dangerous ground."

"Yeah. I knew Jackson was afraid of Watchman. Still, I never was certain about what was real with Jake."

Ray and Tyee headed out in a borrowed patrol car with little idea where to go. They only knew they needed to leave the sheriff's department to allow Trujillo time to regroup.

"An hour ago," Tyee observed flatly, "Trujillo was almost sure to be arrested. And now you've decided to make him sheriff."

Ray almost snapped. "You have a better idea?"

"Nah," Tyee admitted wearily. "I'm as confused as you. Not sure what's what. I thought Watchman was being truthful. I thought Trujillo was guilty of something. I'm even starting to question your motives."

Ray sighed and ignored the offhand remark about his motives. "I know. I just want to go home and forget about all this shit. I'm sure there are very nice people who live in

Farmington. But so far, we've only met liars, or worse. First, there's Grimes, who's a big-time crook and scumbag. He could be responsible for all sorts of things—who knows? The ex-sheriff had serious family and mental problems, killed his ex-wife in a fit of anger, and that was witnessed by his father who might not be his father, who's some guy named Kee. Trujillo was having an affair with Grimes's sexy young wife, Vickie. Barbara, the wife of the ex-sheriff, who was killed by her husband, was having an affair with Grimes *and* the city councilman Martin, who himself is, we strongly suspect, a murder victim whose killer we can't identify. We don't know whether Martin was involved with Grimes's theft of gasoline taxes. And now we learn that Watchman may have something to do with something, but only on Trujillo's word. Meanwhile, Watchman's told us that Trujillo and Vickie have been searching for money buried at Grimes's house. We have the mayor, who seems a little nuts, but has some connections with Trujillo and Martin. And the president of the Navajo Nation is somehow involved. Is that about it?"

Tyee had something to add. "There is the question of what the governor knows. Also, what do the FBI and the BIA know? Or the attorney general? It seems odd to me how the governor can grant a man, accused of stealing millions from the state and federal governments, a week to decide what to do. Wouldn't it make more sense to arrest Grimes, and *then* sort things out? And anyway, does the governor have the authority to do what he said he did?"

Ray peered over the steering wheel. "Our buddy the governor might not want to talk to us about all this horseshit. Why don't we just go ask Grimes? If he causes us any problems, I'd be in the mood to beat the truth out of the old bastard."

"Giddyup! And watch out, all you fuckers!" Tyee smiled. He thought Ray was joking. Or, maybe not.

They rang the bell on Grimes's huge door. No response.

Ray looked around. "Looks like all the armed warriors got the day off." In fact, they hadn't seen anyone.

"Could be a warrior holiday."

Grimes showed up behind them, abruptly. "What the hell do you two want?"

They jumped a little. Ray cleared his throat. "How about a chat?"

Grimes sneered. "Fuck you. I'm going to Albuquerque. Gonna meet with my lawyer. No time to chat with cowboy and Indian." Just to make his point, he shot Tyee a dirtier sneer.

Ray kept his cool. "Won't take long."

"Look, you want to talk to me? Ride to Albuquerque with me. Or don't. I don't give a fuck."

"Ride, in a car?" Ray wasn't sure about getting into a vehicle with someone as old as Grimes behind the wheel.

"*Hell,* no. Got my own plane. I'm the best goddamned pilot who ever flew. Come on. It's just a short flight to Double Eagle II in Albuquerque. I won't kill ya!"

Was it smart to get on a plane with a maniac? Of course, their truck was parked there, so accepting the offer would solve some logistical problems.

Grimes had turned and was headed to the side of the house where the garages were. They had little time to make up their minds.

Ray could see Tyee turning pale. "What do ya think?" He wasn't sure whether he wanted to go, and all but positive Tyee would refuse.

Instead, he put on a confident yet nervous front. "What the fuck? I'm ready to get the hell out of here. If he does anything stupid, I'll just strangle him and figure out how to land the damned thing myself."

Ray called Trujillo to tell him they were at the airport and they would leave the patrol car there. He hung up before Trujillo could ask any questions.

The plane was beautiful, new, and probably worth more than a million bucks. Ray clung to those facts for reassurance that everything would be okay. Grimes barked, "All aboard!" With ill-advised and probably illegal speed, he fired it up, turned it onto the runway, and was airborne before you could say "here we go, ready or not."

Ray knew pilots were supposed to inspect planes, run up the engines and notify the tower first. Grimes had done none of those things.

"Did I ever tell you guys," Grimes shouted over the noise of straining engines and scratchy protests crackling over the radio, "that I used to be a fighter pilot in the Navy? Landing on an aircraft carrier in high winds was *some* of the most fun I ever had."

Tyee lost all his natural color.

Grimes leveled off at cruising altitude, completely at home flying his airplane. He talked about the plane itself, a twin-engine Cessna 425 Conquest, telling his thunder-struck passengers it was one of the best on the market. From there, he went on to detail the many upgrades and improvements he had made to the plane and how all of them had cost him an arm and a leg. A matter he discussed in particular, concerned the lengths to which he had gone to reinforce its landing gear. Ray and Tyee exchanged looks of dread. They could only imagine one fearful reason why a plane would need its landing gear reinforced.

But they never got a chance to ask about it, because Grimes dominated air time. He kept talking about the plane and circled back to tell stories of his experiences as a Navy pilot. It became clear they weren't going to discuss anything to do with Farmington.

"Hang onto your seats, boys," he announced abruptly. "Let me show you what it feels like to land on a carrier." With that he put the plane into what felt to Ray and Tyee like a nose dive. Grimes, smiling broadly, called to the tower and seemed to get clearance for his crash land-ing. And although Tyee and Ray felt certain they were in a nose dive, they weren't. Still, their angle was absurdly steep for an approach to an airport. From Ray's point of view, sinking into his seat, it certainly looked like Grimes indeed would crash the plane straight into the runway. It was at this point he extended the landing gear. The plane reacted to the additional drag by seeming to go into a steeper dive, or so it felt. Grimes, meanwhile, grinned like he was at his own birthday party, having a great time. At the very last instant, he pulled up and leveled off. The Cessna slammed into the runway in what without question was the hardest landing Ray ever experienced. It was more like a controlled crash.

"Fuck!" Grimes crowed, "Another perfect landing. How the fuck did you like that?"

Ray and Tyee just stared at him, each silently thanking God they were still alive. Grimes whipped the plane this way and that until it parked, at last at rest.

Tyee jumped up, flung the door open, flipped the stairs down, bounded out of the plane and sprinted for the terminal.

Grimes watched him with a smirk. "Guess the Indian doesn't like flying."

Ray thought about a punch to the arrogant bastard's nose but didn't want to hang around that long. "Fuck you." He went to find Tyee.

Tyee came out of a bathroom and walked up to Ray to announce firmly, "I quit!"

Their trip to T or C was silent.

18

Home Not So Sweet Home

"My god, Ray," Sue sighed after he told her about their plane ride with Grimes, "that is terrible. Where's Tyee now?"

"As soon as I parked, he got out and just walked off. I don't know if he was just going for a walk or leaving."

"You just let him walk away? Jeez. Men!" She went outside, calling for Tyee.

Ray was never much of a drinker but knew he needed something. He poured some scotch, added a touch of water, and sank into a chair. It had been years since the last time he had been shit-faced. He was giving the idea some real thought when Sue came back in.

"He's in the annex, working on his computer," she reported. "Said he didn't want to talk about anything. Just wants to be alone." She poured herself a shot, no water, and took a slug. "Something's going to have to change, or you and Tyee are going to lose your friendship. And that would be terrible."

Ray sank deeper into his chair. "I know. I also know you're pissed at me, and Big Jack is pissed at me. Tyee said he quit. And given another minute, I might have said the same thing. I've already said I wanted a break, but maybe it's more than that. Maybe I'm just done. Seems like the crazy-people population is growing too fast for me to deal with. I just want to be here with you. I want to hide from the crazies."

Happy, Ray's dog, came up and put his head in Ray's lap, knowing something was wrong. It made Ray smile, and he relaxed a little.

Ray made his way to Big Jack's bait shop, now run by Tyee's cousin, Chester.

"Hey, Chester."

"Mr. Pacheco! Great to see you. Big Jack's out on the dock." Chester got closer to whisper, "Glad you're here. He's started drinking earlier and earlier. Now it's a beer before coffee. He needs someone to talk to, before this gets worse."

Ray looked toward the door to the dock, then changed the subject. "Store sure looks great Chester. You've done a wonderful job. Smells good, too."

"Well, I try. Big Jack complains about the smell. Says he liked it better with the mystery odor." Chester frowned dubiously. "Do you think he really means it?"

Ray shook his head, smiling. "Probably not. More than likely something else is bothering him and he doesn't want to talk about it. You just keep doin' what you're doin'."

Chester smiled. He didn't get many compliments from Big Jack. Hearing Ray say good things made his day better.

Ray and Happy headed out to the dock. As soon as Happy saw Big Jack, he burst into a mad dash towards his best friend, other than Ray, of course.

"Hey, ya old mutt. Where the hell have you been?" Big Jack gave Happy an aggressive rub-and-hug greeting. Happy wagged his tail as hard as he could. Jack squinted up at Ray. "What the fuck do you want? Come to scold me about something?"

"Beer for breakfast? Pretty soon you'll be a slobbering old drunk who nobody wants to be around." Ray replied, matter-of-factly.

Big Jack shrugged. "Fine with me."

"Well, if that's gonna be your attitude, guess I'll join you." Ray reached into the cooler and pulled out a beer. He could see a slight smile on Big Jack's face. They sat and sipped a bit, saying nothing until Big Jack decided to own up.

"Okay. I'm all fucked up. So what? I've always been that way. I just can't be a mayor anymore. I don't want people to talk to me or act like they know me." He frowned bitterly. "It's just creepy. They come up to me and talk about their *toilets* for god's sake, or some problem with the road in front of the house. I don't care. Why can't they understand that?"

"You know; I've heard this story before. So quit."

"I've been thinking for over a month that I would do just that," Big Jack confessed. "I just didn't know how, until now. I've made a decision. This has been hard for me, because in a strange way, even though I hate all that, I didn't want to leave. And it'll still be hard. But I've got to, or I'll go crazy. This is what I'll do: I'm going to name Beverly acting mayor. She'll love having all these people talking to her about their damned toilets. And maybe then she won't be mad at me for leaving. And I'm going to sell the store to Chester—well not *sell*, right away. We'll enter into a partnership that won't cost him anything. He runs the store for five years and sends me a small percentage of revenue. After that, the store's his, free and fuckin' clear. As for me, I'm going to Albuquerque to open a small office; get back into law. Once I'm back up to speed, I'll move to the biggest town I can find, open a law office and be completely invisible. What do ya think?"

Ray laughed. a genuine belly laugh. They clicked beers. "Good for you. Do it!"

Next stop for Ray and Happy was to see Tyee. He knew the last thing Tyee had said to him came out of frustration, fright, and anger at Lewis Grimes, but only because he was part of a whole situation that had forced its way between them. Nancy had left, and Tyee wanted her back, but he hesitated to make an ultimate commitment to marriage. Pile too much uncertainty on, and a man gets surly. And boy, had Tyee been surly.

He found Tyee at his computer.

"I think you *should* quit," Ray said without preamble. "Big Jack's going out to Albuquerque because he hates being mayor. I'm yelling at people I care about because I'm tired of dealing with all these crazy assholes. We've got to make changes. I know you don't want me to tell you what to do, but I don't care. I think you should go see Nancy, tell her you love her, but also tell her you're not sure about getting married right now. And ask her what she thinks. She might surprise you. Might say she never wanted to marry you. What I mean is, don't just ignore the issue. Deal with it the best you can, and see what happens."

He paused for a deep breath. Tyee had not turned away from his computer screen. "But first—yes, but first—we've got to honor our commitment to our asshole governor. I wanted to just recommend Trujillo and walk away, let the rest of it be a problem for someone else. But I can't. I don't think you can either. How can we recommend Trujillo to be sheriff when we're not sure he wasn't involved in at least one murder, or in financial fraud, or in whatever else might be going on? I don't *want* to do it. But I've got to go back to Farmington and clean this mess up, once and for all. I'd like you to come with me. If you say no, I understand. We'll still be friends. And we'll go fishing every time we get a chance."

Tyee turned to look at him. "Well, none of that surprises me. When are you going?"

"Day after tomorrow. Leave early. Gonna drive. About five hours. So, leave about seven and get there around noon."

"I'll be ready." Tyee stood up and offered his hand. Ray instead gave Tyee an unexpected hug.

He let go and left quickly. He didn't want Tyee to see his tears.

Ray sat in the breakfast nook sipping tea and watching Sue make lunch. He felt more content then he had in a long time. He told Sue about his decisions and his talks with Big Jack and Tyee. She was pleased.

"Saw Beverly this morning," she said. "I dropped by the Lone Post and she was having coffee. She told me about

Jack and how she was going to be appointed mayor. She seemed happy and sad all at once. But she was already in politician mode, greeting everyone and telling them he asked her to handle things for a while. People were telling her all their problems and she was actually offering solutions. Who knows? She could be good at it."

"What did she say about Big Jack leaving?"

"Not much. I could tell she's sad. I guess they had more or less ended their relationship a while ago; they just didn't talk about it with anyone. So it might even be a relief for her to have him leave."

"What do you think's going on with Nancy?" Ray was genuinely curious.

"She and Tyee are in love, but they're both afraid of a commitment. And I believe she left because she realized how much she wanted to stay and be with Tyee, and it scared her. She didn't want to take the emotional risk. Tyee really feels the same—he wants to be with her, but doesn't want to go all in because he's afraid she'll say no. So everybody withdraws to their respective corners and waits. You know it's possible for people to be so damaged they can't form another relationship."

"You were hurt," he observed, "but you got over it." He wasn't comfortable discussing these matters. He didn't want to just shrug and move on, either.

"It wasn't easy," she said. "When I met you, I'd been running away from anything that looked like a serious connection. And that was the case for years. Then, all of a sudden, it seemed okay. I think—and don't get all sensitive on me here—it had to do with you being so vulnerable.

You were obviously a catch for some woman, and you didn't even know it. Because of your long-term successful marriage, you were completely innocent. What woman wouldn't be attracted to that?"

Ray blushed. "Innocent, huh? Guess I didn't see myself that way."

"Of course you didn't. You were a perfect match for me, and I found you right here in T or C, New Mexico, at the counter of the Lone Post Café. How romantic." Sue pretended to swoon. She could see Ray was still embarrassed. "Don't worry. I won't tell this to anyone else. Your secret is safe with me." She giggled. Ray grabbed her hand. They went into the bedroom. Happy stayed in front of the fire.

"Good morning." Ray greeted Tyee while he climbed into the truck.

Tyee grinned. "Good morning. Sure feel a lot better about going to Farmington in this old truck. Beats flying."

"Yeah," Ray cleared his throat. "No carrier landings for this old rig."

Tyee switched the subject. "Had some beers with Big Jack yesterday. His whole mood's different, talking about his new office in Albuquerque and how he is going to pick up some criminal cases. He seemed better than I've seen him in months. Soon as he gets settled, I'm going up to see him." He nodded. "Called Nancy. Asked if she'd see me. She sounded glad I called." A grin tried to work its way back onto his face. "Said, of course she wanted to see me. I guess maybe I imagined she was hating me or something.

Guess not." He glanced at Ray. The next part was tough to say. "Thanks for helping me with that little nudge to call her." He paused. Ray blushed. "So," he continued, "what's the agenda in Farmington?" Investigative stuff felt like much safer conversation ground than personal matters.

Ray relaxed. "First, go see Trujillo. Called last night; didn't get him. Left a message saying we'd be there about noon. That will be our first item, to see what's been going on while we've been gone. Then want to talk to Grimes's wife. Next is Watchman. Got to find out the truth about what Trujillo said. We know someone's lying and we have to find out who. And last but not least, we still need to talk to Grimes. Might even bring him in to the station to question him. That'd really piss him off. And I've got this idea that might lead to him saying things we need to know. If we're still alive after all that, we could circle back around and go see the mayor again, and then try to see the Navajo president. That ought to shake something loose."

"Sounds like White Man's plans involve attacking anyone standing and hope someone confesses to all of their sins—or points fingers at other sinners."

"Indian is wise beyond his years. If we had horses, we could ride in with guns blazing."

"Not so sure about the blazing guns part."

19

They're Back

With their long list of interviews, all with people who didn't want to talk to them, they entered Farmington sharing a sense of dread. They knew it was the right thing to do, but it still felt like something bad could happen. Without delay, or lunch, they headed to the sheriff's department.

Ray was smiling at the young woman at the front desk. "Would you let Sheriff Trujillo know that Ray Pacheco and Tyee Chino would like to visit with him?"

"Oh, I'm sorry, Mr. Pacheco. But the sheriff's not here. We haven't seen him since yesterday." She sounded concerned. Ray wondered whether or not that meant Trujillo had disappeared.

"Who's in charge?"

"I guess it would be Sergeant Hoover."

"Is he here?"

"Yes."

Ray struggled with dwindling patience. "Could you see if he'd meet with us?" She seemed only to react, not taking even ordinary initiative.

"Oh, sure." That seemed like a good idea to her. She picked up the phone, tried a number, and waited. For practically a minute. Then she hung up. "Guess he's not in his office. Let me call dispatch and see if they can find him."

Ray nodded and smiled, pressing his lips together. He listened while she spoke to dispatch. She hung up the phone.

"He's on his lunch break," she reported brightly. "They'll call and see when he'll be back. You can wait if you'd like."

Ray bit his lip. "We'll come back later."

They left the building.

"Something doesn't smell right." Tyee made his bad-odor face.

"Wasn't expecting this. One day Trujillo's a bad guy, the next day a good guy, and now he's a gone guy. I can't imagine why he'd disappear unless he's guilty of something." Ray sighed.

"I guess we should consider the possibility of foul play. We've already had two murders in this town."

Ray looked at Tyee. "You're right. I should've thought of that, but I guess I'm worried that Trujillo's dirty, so my first assumption was that he took off. It could be something else. We'll give him a little time." Ray paused. "Let's go get lunch. After that we can drop in to see Vickie Grimes."

Tyee grinned. "Maybe she'll be out by the pool again."

"Maybe I should leave you in the truck."

Mrs. Grimes pouted at them. "You do know my name's not Vickie, right?"

Ray exchanged glances with Tyee. "Not sure what you mean, Mrs. Grimes. You told us your name was Vickie."

"Yeah," she sneered. "That's the old bastard's way of irritating everyone, *all the fuckin' time.* See, his first wife's name was Vickie. So, along came wife number two, and the old fart decided he'd call her Vickie, too. He *said* that made it easier to remember her name. Now it's my turn as wife number three, and I get the same goddamned name. Vickie. I hate it. My name is Joyce Sanders. Or I guess, technically, Joyce Grimes." She huffed. "One of these days, someone's going to kill that old fool."

So much for matrimonial bliss. "Well, o-okay," Ray stammered. "Is this a good time for us to talk?"

"Sure, I don't know where he is, but if he comes back while you're here, all hell will break lose."

Ray had decided that there were no easy conversations to be had in Farmington. "I want to ask about your relationship with Sheriff Trujillo."

In a flash her demeanor changed from offhand to a look that could kill. "What kind of goddamned question is that? What the hell do you mean?" Her voiced grew louder. She leaned forward, as if ready to pounce.

Ray retreated into official reserve. "I'm sorry, ma'am, if that question feels inappropriate to you. But we're investigating a murder. That's a serious matter. We've been told you had an affair with Trujillo. Is that true or not?"

"Did he tell you that?"

"Please answer my question."

"Yeah, well," she straightened up, as if to project nonchalance, "it wasn't an affair, it was just a fling, some fun. My dear husband was having affairs with half the damn female population in town. What? I'm supposed to be pure or something?" She went back to a pout.

Tyee leaned in to get her attention. "We've been told you and Trujillo looked for buried money here. Is that true?"

"Jeez, what nonsense. Okay, one night we got shit-faced drunk. Grimes was off in Santa Fe or some place. Thad and I got to partying a little—it's just so damn boring here. So, after we got too drunk to do anything else, if you know what I mean, we decided we'd go look for the millions the old fart supposedly buried here. Thad dug a pretty big hole out back, and I *guess* one of those asshole guards saw us." She stopped and seemed to be thinking. "I don't know why I'm telling you this. Why don't you just fuck off? I want you out of here, right now." She stood, shot hot glares at Ray and Tyee, and left.

"Well, I guess *that* interview's over." Tyee watched her walk away—a very male thing to do. "Good guys zero. Bad guys—and gals—a perfect score."

They walked toward the car. "Let's head back and see if Sergeant Hoover's available."

"At this rate," Tyee observed, "we might as well just hide out and wait for whatever explosion is going to happen. We aren't making much progress." He was tired of being in the truck.

"I'm not so sure. We have Trujillo missing, and that's going to tell us something once we find out what happened to him. We have Vickie—and of course, by that I mean Joyce—telling us that she was having an affair, and that they did look for money buried at the house, and that it was witnessed by guards. Which reminds me, we need to talk to those guards. The treasure hunt sounded like a drunken lark, not a serious search. That's good information."

"But we're still basically in the dark about what happened to Martin."

Ray nodded. "Yep. You're right, there."

At the station the young receptionist handed Ray a note, while explaining, "He just now called and said it was very important that you contact him."

The message was from the city attorney, Mark White. It said he had important information regarding Martin. "Okay, thanks. Has the Sergeant returned?"

She smiled apologetically. "He did come back, but then there was a disturbance at one of the downtown restaurants. One customer hit another. He went out to handle that. Said to tell you he'd be back in an hour or so."

Ray handed Tyee the note and they headed back out to the truck. "Get the feeling the sergeant is avoiding us?"

"We are no longer popular."

They had been to the city offices before when they met with the mayor. It was a short trip and a much shorter wait this time. Mark White came out almost immediately.

"Welcome, please come in." White was tall and slender, young looking with clear blue eyes and prematurely graying hair. He looked like an attorney—or at least, the public's image of one.

Ray began to summarize an introduction regarding their authority in state matters as arranged by the governor.

White waved him off. "No intro needed. I've heard all about you two. I wanted to talk to you the first day you were here, but it seemed a lot was going on. I thought it best to wait until you had some time to look into our little nightmare."

Ray raised an eyebrow. "The 'nightmare' being?"

"Lewis Grimes." White paused to peer at his guests for emphasis. "If we were in Chicago, I'd likely say he was one of our biggest gangsters. Here in Farmington, he's our *only* gangster."

"That's a pretty bold statement for a city attorney. Do you have evidence to support it?"

White softened with a chuckle. "Well, no. Not really. At one time, I was working with Sheriff Jackson, and I think we'd uncovered a trove of evidence that Grimes was stealing gasoline tax money. But then," he inhaled, "the sheriff kind of went off the deep end. And before I knew it, he was gone and so was the evidence. I don't know if he took it with him or hid it somewhere. Trujillo wouldn't let me search the sheriff's office without a warrant. I got one and then had two state troopers drop in to make the search. They found nothing. About all I accomplished was to piss off Trujillo."

Ray's eyes were still wide. "Sheriff Jackson had proof that Grimes stole tax money?"

White nodded significantly. "Yep. Saw the documents myself. It was only one month's worth of detail. Still, the amount of tax money he was lying about was in the hundreds of thousands of dollars, just for that one month. If he'd been doing that for years, like we suspected, it had to be millions."

Tyee popped in. "Why didn't you turn that over to the

state, or the feds?"

"The only person who knows that for sure would be Sheriff Jackson—who, of course, is dead. He contacted me about the documents and brought them here for me to see. He wanted to know what to do with them. Of course, I told him he should contact the state and federal taxing authorities, and arrest Grimes while he was at it." White took a breath. "He said he'd do that once he was sure his contact was safe. But then, within a few days, he was off on some kind of weird military operation. If I hadn't seen those docs, I would've assumed that Jackson was completely nuts and none of it was true. But I saw detailed records showing that Grimes was moving money all over the place and falsely reporting gallons sold on the reservation at a ridiculous volume."

Ray asked White the obvious question, "You said he wanted to make sure his contact was safe. Do you know who that contact was?"

White nodded sadly. "Councilman Martin. The *dead* councilman Martin. According to Jackson, it was Martin who contacted him and told him what was going on. He was the source for the documents."

Tyee frowned. "We've been told Martin was a friend of Grimes; that they'd go out drinking together. Do you think Martin was involved in the tax scheme?"

"I don't think so, although I'm beginning to question everything I think I know. Martin was a long-time resident and for years a real straight shooter. It was the drinking and woman-chasing that led to his downfall. It might sound odd, but he might drink and womanize with

Grimes, but I don't believe he would've stolen a dime."

Ray took his turn. "How did he get those records?"

"My guess would be that Barbara Jackson gave them to him."

Tyee sat back, looking surprised. "Barbara Jackson—the sheriff's ex-wife who he confessed to killing?"

"Yep. Shakespearean, isn't it?" White rubbed his head like he had a headache. "She had a rather public affair with Grimes. I think she did it to try to hurt Jake, and sort of went nuts herself. Then Grimes announced in a bar one night that he was tired of her. Now, here's where the documents come in. She had connections in Grimes's office because of her political work. I think she managed to get access and stole them. But here's the thing: she wanted to nail Grimes, but I'd bet that she was terrified of Jake. I don't believe she wanted anyone to see a straight connection between herself and the documents. So I think, she started an affair with Martin, mostly to get him to do her bidding, part of which was to give the evidence to Jackson so she could get revenge against Grimes."

"Shit." was Ray's comment.

White nodded wearily. "Yep, big piles."

Tyee tilted his head skeptically. "Do you think Trujillo knows about any of this?"

"At one time I would have said yes, but today I'm not sure. No question, he's been in the middle of a lot of things related to this, like his affair with Vickie. But did he commit a crime or know about it? I don't have any idea."

20

So Much For That Plan

Ray eyed Tyee. "If we go see Grimes, you won't cause any trouble, will you?" He didn't need his partner locked up in a Farmington jail for strangling the town's leading citizen.

"If by 'trouble' you mean killing him, no, I won't. But I'm not going to be friendly." Tyee grinned while daydreaming about throttling the old fart.

"I don't like that grin."

Tyee got down to business. "What do you think he might know?"

"Everything centers around him, his affairs, and his questionable business practices. He was asshole buddies with the dead councilman, and he had an affair with the deceased, Barbara Jackson. It just seems reasonable to ask him more questions."

Tyee grunted. "So that means you have no idea what he might know."

"Something like that. And I'm not sure how to find the evidence White saw. I guess our best approach with Grimes is to annoy him enough to see if he'll accidently tell us something important. My instincts tell me he's involved in everything."

They once again drove to the out-of-place mansion. The guards were back.

Tyee got out to approach the one who kept the gate.

"No reason to knock," the guard told him. "They're all out."

Tyee noticed how friendly he seemed. "Know when they might be back?"

"Nah," he scoffed, "they don't tell us shit. The wife left early this morning. And Mr. Grimes, I think, went to his office downtown, but not sure. He left about an hour ago."

"Thanks." Tyee got back into the truck to report, "They're both out. Nobody for us to annoy."

"Oh, I'm sure we can find someone to irritate. Let's try the sergeant again."

"Hey, I wasn't avoiding you. I've got my duties I have to take care of. It's not like crime takes a break just because you guys are in town." Hoover smiled, perhaps to lend the impression he was just a good cop doing his job.

"Yeah, sure. I understand. Do you know where Trujillo is?"

"No," he shook his head as if mystified. "He just up and left. Told me he'd be gone a day or two but would be back. Told me to handle shit the best I could, and away he went." The sergeant shrugged.

"The city attorney told us he secured a warrant and searched these offices some time back. Were you here for that?"

"Yep. I was right here when they served the warrant. Worked with the state troopers; helped them any way I could. Trujillo stayed away. He told me he thought White overstepped his authority, and he wasn't about to cooperate."

"What did they find?"

"Couple of old *Playboy* magazines and a bottle of gin."
The sergeant went back to grinning.

"Anything else?"

"If you mean, 'Did they find the evidence they were
looking for?'—they didn't. Kind of pissed them off that
they spent so much time digging around these dirty old
offices and came up with nothing."

"So you knew what they were looking for?" Ray was
beginning to feel a little tired of the sergeant's silly grin.

"Oh, yeah. They told me."

"Do you know where those files might be?"

"No idea. If I was going to guess, I'd say Sheriff Jackson
took them with him when he left. Maybe he buried them
up yonder in the Colorado part of those mountains." The
sergeant seemed to think that was funny. He chuckled.

Ray and Tyee took a table at a nearly vacant IHOP. They
ordered coffee, sat back and went over what they had
learned.

The first lesson was, "The sergeant may be decent at his
job, but he's really damn annoying." Ray frowned.

"So I noticed," Tyee agreed. "I thought it was *our* job to
be annoying."

"You really are a wiseass Indian, do you know that?"

"White Man Leader has permanently lost his sense of
humor," Tyee observed. "Should have brought Happy with
us."

That made Ray smile. "Sorry. Yes. I really do miss my dog." He began to laugh.

Tyee laughed along with him, he also missed Happy. Then he steered their attention back to the subject. "Hoover may be annoying, but I think he might be right. Based on timing alone, I'd bet Jackson did take those files with him to Colorado. Did you see all the stuff up there? I'd bet you money the feds have done nothing with it and it's all still out there."

Ray nodded. "Yeah. I was thinking the same thing. If you know what we know then it's obvious, and that means that Trujillo might have come to the same conclusion. That may be where he went. I think we need to call the FBI, see if they have gone through all that stuff, and, if they have, find out if the documents are still there."

"We need to get some of those mobile phones," Tyee suggested, "so we don't have to go looking for pay phones anymore. I hear they're getting pretty cheap now."

Ray knew how much Tyee loved new technology, but resisted. "A mobile phone means people can call you all the time. I can't imagine a worse set of circumstances." He got up to look for a pay phone.

Tyee folded his arms and sighed.

Ray came back after some minutes, took his seat, and said, "Might want to rethink that mobile phone idea. Called Agent Crawford and what did he do but answer on his mobile. No receptionist, no switchboard or message machine. Pretty neat, I guess." He still wasn't sure he wanted one, however. "He said they had made a superficial search of the stuff and put together an inventory but had not examined anything in detail. They're still not sure who it all belongs to. The material could be evidence in a crime, but Crawford was not sure—which indicated it was a pretty low priority for them right now. They hired some private security guards after the Colorado State Police left, but other than that they're basically just waiting until they know how all of that crap might be involved in any potential crime. I told him we thought the sheriff might have taken a large crime file with him and that it's most likely still there. He didn't offer to do anything about it himself, but he said he was okay with us searching through the mess if we want; but we shouldn't take anything away without contacting him first. I told him I'd call him back."

Tyee started whining. "There were boxes all over the place up there. That could take forever. Besides, the drive's a killer. An hour or more to get there, and another hour to bounce our butts through the mountains."

Ray sat back to think. "Still, I do think it's logical that Jackson would have taken the evidence with him. And, no, given all that we need to do here, I don't want to spend days rummaging through who knows how many old boxes up in the middle of nowhere, where we might find nothing." He paused. "Maybe at this point, we give Trujillo a bit more time. If he did go there, and he isn't crooked, maybe he'll find those files and bring them back."

Tyee shot Ray his "You don't really believe that, do you?" look.

Ray sipped his coffee. He wondered what a mobile phone would cost.

Tyee spoke up, "If this was Las Cruces and you were

still sheriff, what would you do?"

"Good question." Ray gave it some thought. "I believe I'd go to a judge and get a search warrant for Grimes's house and office. Might even try for an arrest warrant."

"Based on what?" Tyee knew it was dirty pool. But he knew he needed to get Ray on point and fired up.

Ray sighed, perhaps finishing his own thought. "Well, I guess all I'd have for that would be White's testimony that he saw documents that proved Grimes was stealing gasoline taxes."

"Is that enough to get you a warrant?"

He shook his head. "Nope. It would get me a lecture from a pissed-off judge because that would be asking for a warrant against a powerful citizen based on gossip. I see your point. We need evidence. Let's go see the coroner. Bound to be better forensics by now for Martin."

"Giddyup."

"Just got off the phone with the State Police," the coroner informed Ray and Tyee in a tone that hardly concealed his annoyance with them. "They said you're authorized to receive whatever information I have on the Martin death. Still seems strange to me that some guy and his pal can walk in here and demand confidential information. But I don't run this damned state, thank god." Walter Strange was a medical doctor who spent a few hours each month as the county's acting coroner. Generally, his duty was mostly filing the right paperwork. But the Jackson and Martin deaths had more than tripled his time on the job.

He didn't like that and had resolved that he would quit as soon as he could. "After looking at the angle of the bullet," he continued wearily, "it is clear that Councilman Thomas Martin was murdered. His killer staged the incident in an attempt to make it look like suicide. But from the beginning, it was obvious to me that it wasn't."

"When did you know this?" Ray asked. "And who have you shared this information with?"

"I knew it the moment I viewed the deceased," Strange replied icily. "I saw at once he had been shot from an angle that he could not achieve himself. Some people think to fake a suicide, one only needs to have the gun touching or close to the head. There's more to it than that. The angle at which you can hold the gun is obvious, and any deviation from it raises suspicion. In this case, the angle was far too steep. The killer stood behind him and fired the gun into the upper part of his cranium, so the angle was a little behind and pointing slightly down. I *suppose* a person could get a gun in that position for self-inflicted gunshot, but it would be difficult and very awkward at best. The only reason someone intent on committing suicide would do that would be an attempt to make it look like it *wasn't* suicide. A strange thing to do, I should think.

"Even for all that, the most telling clue was the gunshot residue. There was none on his hand. Therefore, someone made a feeble attempt to make it look like a suicide. And the attempt failed. It was homicide. I told Sheriff Trujillo all this pretty much right away—Mark White, too. Both of them were bugging me, calling to find out what I'd found. By the next day I had a written a report that I sent to the District Attorney, Rick Travis."

"Did you hear back from the DA?" Tyee was mostly just curious, particularly because it seemed odd to him that they had not heard Travis mentioned before.

Strange rolled his eyes. "Travis is a known slacker. I have no respect for the man. And no, I have not heard a word. Now, I believe that is all I have to say, and I have other things to do." Strange lived up to his name. He turned and left without another word.

"Maybe it's something in the water?" Tyee watched while Strange slammed the door with clear intent.

Ray nodded. "We did learn a few things, though. It *is* murder, which we suspected, and it was not Trujillo. If he wanted to fake a suicide, I'm sure he could have done a better job. Also, it would appear that this information has been available for some time but not provided to us. Why would Trujillo not tell us for sure this was murder?" He thought again. "Let's go see Travis and see what he thinks. And don't say, 'Giddyup'. Okay?"

"Okay. Giddyup, partner."

"Was wondering when you two would show up," Travis greeted them. "In case you're curious, the city attorney and I hate each other. On several occasions he has threatened to have me disbarred. So, whatever he said about me is probably lies." The DA smiled but seemed on edge.

Travis was slim and stood tall, likely six foot six. He had wavy, prematurely white hair and bore an air of nobility. Ray figured that most likely *every* man hated this guy, not only White.

Tyee jumped in. "Actually, it was the coroner Strange who called you a slacker. The city guy didn't say much at all." He gave Travis an innocent smile.

Travis chuckled and seemed to relax at that. "That's not too surprising. He's my wife's uncle. He's always thought she should never have married me. Small-town connections, small-town attitudes."

Ray spoke up. "Have any theories on who killed Martin?"

"Well, you know, sheriff, it is our job to prosecute—not investigate. We've been waiting to hear something from the sheriff's department." With that, his tone turned a bit more serious. "I requested a meeting with Trujillo to see what the *hell* he thinks he's doing and have been told by the totally *incompetent* staff that he is out of town, whatever in the *hell* that means." He cleared his throat and composed himself a bit. "I was hoping your presence here meant you had something to tell me. Besides, you represent our wacko governor, I suppose I should be asking *you* for answers."

There was a long pause. Ray studied the DA, evaluating what to think about the man. Still, he had been right. It was not his job to track down suspects; only to prosecute them. "I will give Trujillo one day to come back from wherever he is," he informed Travis, tensely. "If he doesn't come back, I will request the governor appoint me sheriff. And I will raise holy hell in this town like you have never seen, until I find the killer or killers. And I will drop them in your fuckin' lap." He rose and left.

Tyee kept his seat while they watched him stride away.

He turned to Travis. "It's difficult to piss off Sheriff Pacheco, but I think this town's finally done it. We will find out who did this. And we will arrest that person, no matter who it is. See ya, Mr. DA." Tyee stood, intending to demonstrate that even if he was about the same height as the DA, he dwarfed him in mass. Tyee smiled and left.

"What now, chief?" Tyee found Ray outside, staring at a tree.

"You know that is not funny," Ray mumbled.

"I thought it was." Tyee grinned. "What's with the tree?"

"Thinking about fishing. Besides, I like trees." Ray gave Tyee a weak smile. "Let's call it a day. Trujillo will either show up tomorrow, or he won't. If he doesn't, I'm calling the governor, and he can either appoint me sheriff or send someone else."

"Sounds good. What'll we do if he does appoint you?" Tyee could guess, but might as well ask the horse since he was standing right next to him.

"Arrest Lewis Grimes."

"What's the charge, other than being an asshole?"

"Murder."

21

All Hell Breaks Loose

The phone rang and kept ringing. Ray wasn't sure he cared. Then he realized it might be Sue. Maybe something was wrong in T or C. He bolted up and glanced at the clock—twenty past one in the morning. This was not good.

"Hello." He listened. "Okay. Be there in a few." He called to wake Tyee.

Not until they were in the truck headed toward the Grimes's mansion did Tyee ask, "What did the sergeant say?" He looked tired and grumpy.

Ray still had trouble putting sentences together. "Said Grimes was killed. Shot by his wife. In their pool. They were drunk. Some kind of game, or something."

Tyee squinted at him. "Does that mean case closed? And we go home?"

Ray yawned. "Don't think so. I still think Grimes killed Martin. It's all that makes sense to me. But I needed proof, so my plan had been to arrest him and see if we could get him to confess. Then we'd go home. Now that he's dead, we have to think of some other way."

"We were going to beat a confession out of the old man and hightail it out of town?" Tyee glanced at Ray.

"Not sure about the 'hightail it' part. Besides, I thought we'd just dazzle him with our brilliance and he'd be so awed, he would confess to everything."

At the Grimes mansion it looked to them like every emergency vehicle available in the county was there. The blinking lights almost blinded them.

Tyee squinted and frowned. "Looks like a lotta folks are up early."

They hunted down Sergeant Hoover. "Tell us what happened," Ray snapped.

Hoover looked exhausted. He pulled a notepad out of his pocket, flipped it open and referred to his notes. "At about 12:45 this morning dispatch received a 911 call from Vickie Grimes of this address, saying her husband, Lewis Grimes, had been shot and he was dead. She also advised that she had been firing a weapon at the victim, but that none of the shots she fired struck the victim." He looked up. "Dispatch said she sounded hysterical." He went back to his notes. "Emergency was dispatched, and arrived in about, uh, seven minutes. They indicated they found Mrs. Grimes in the rear of the residence at the swimming pool, seated next to the body of the victim. Victim's body was half in the pool and half out. Emergency advised they observed an entry wound in the back of the victim's head, and that he was deceased." He closed the notepad and wilted a bit. "They were both naked as jaybirds. She's like, catatonic, now—in some kind of trance or something. Medical's taken her inside and drawn blood. I mean, you can tell she's been drinking, but we wanted to check for drugs. We got here about 1:08 and roped off the area. I have people searching the back yard and beyond the fence. Unless ballistics and forensics say otherwise, it looks like Grimes was in the pool, and Vickie was shooting at him, and got him, whether she meant to or not." He seemed done, until he blinked and said, "Oh, yeah—one other thing. Neighbors heard the shooting and told my guys they estimated eight shots fired. So," he shrugged, "I guess she fired those eight shots, and hit him in the head, deliberately or not. The first people here said she told them she jumped into the pool and tried to pull him out but could only get him partially out." He took a breath and let it out. "That's all I've got."

"You said she claims she didn't hit him," Tyee said. "What do you think that means?"

Hoover shrugged. "She could be saying she didn't shoot him. But at this point, it sure looks like she did. Maybe she really didn't mean to hit him. Until she's a little bit more lucid, it's all just a guess."

Ray looked around. "Since Trujillo is not present and his whereabouts are unknown, I'm taking charge of this investigation on authority of the governor. If Trujillo has not returned by tomorrow—or I guess, later today—the governor will appoint me as acting sheriff until some other arrangements can be made."

The sergeant nodded, looking relieved and exhausted. "What do you want me to do?"

"For now, what you're already doing. We'll want to talk to Mrs. Grimes before we leave. You finish up here, and we can meet later to decide what to do next."

The sergeant turned to leave, looking far more relaxed now that someone else was taking charge of the mess.

Ray approached Grimes's widow gingerly. "Hello, Mrs. Grimes. Or do you want to be called Joyce?"

"I don't give a fuck what you call me." She started to cry. "I didn't kill him." She seemed to have sobered up. She at least made some sense.

"Can you tell us what happened?"

She took a deep breath. "We were skinny-dipping." She swallowed, and her eyes hardened. "Then the old bastard told me he was tired of me, and that he was on the lookout for the next Vickie. I just completely lost it. I couldn't believe what he was saying. The only reason I stayed with the old goat was I thought he'd die soon, and I'd get his money. I know, that makes me a bad person. Well, so fuckin' what?" She looked up at Ray, eyes narrowed. "He was *evil.* Anyway, I went and got my pistol. When I came back with the gun, I could see the terror in his eyes. And I loved it. I didn't plan on killing him, but I sure wanted to scare the hell out of him. He started swimming to one side, and I shot into the water ahead of him. He turned and swam the other way; another shot. And I kept him going back and forth like that, like some penny-arcade game. And then," she said, staring away from anyone, "his head jerked in this weird kind of way, and—and blood went flying everywhere." She started to break down but kept talking. "But I didn't shoot him. I swear. I jumped in and got him and tried to pull him out, and then I called 911. Fuck! I didn't kill him." She surrendered to tears and convulsions. A nurse came to help her into the house.

Tyee had watched her closely. He believed she was telling the truth. "Unless she's the greatest actress in the world, she either didn't kill him or it was an accident. Jumping into a pool full of blood just isn't a thing someone who deliberately killed a person would do. They would leave them there, and get away, fast."

"Could be right. Go find the sergeant and have him make sure they search every inch of the fence perimeter, and keep an eye out especially for shell casings." He took a deep breath. "Guess I'm going to call the governor."

Ray gave the governor a brief overview on what had happened in Farmington.

"Dead," Johnson replied without emotion. "Can't say I'm sad about that in any way other than it's gonna create one hell of a disaster regarding his business activities. A lot of people are gonna be hurt by that old bastard even after he's dead. Do you think he'd die without a will, and just leave it all to his wife?"

At least the governor was an honest man. He hated Grimes while he was alive and still hated him now that he was dead. "I would guess he'd have a will," Ray replied. "At his age, death was nearby every day. I just can't imagine him letting everything go to wife number three."

"Yeah, me neither. So you think the wife didn't kill him." The governor had been grumpy due to the abrupt interruption at such an early hour, but now sounded alert and interested.

"I think if she did, it was an accident. Another possibility is that someone else was there and saw what was happening. That person intended to murder Grimes and stumbled across the weird pool scene and used it as cover. The wife is goofy, and even she admits she's a gold-digger.

But I really don't see her as a killer." Ray knew the governor's habits. It was a sure bet for him that Johnson would prefer that the wife had done it, so it could all be closed up and forgotten.

"I'll have an authorization statement making you sheriff sent out there as soon as I get to the office. Do you think Trujillo could be involved?"

"At this point, his actions put him on the list of suspects." Ray hated to admit it. He had trusted him and felt angry that he had been fooled.

"Even if he shows up, I want you to relieve him of duty until we get to the bottom of this."

"I agree. Too many unanswered questions about him to let him continue. I'll keep you advised." Ray hung up. Considering the circumstances, it had not been a bad conversation with the governor. He couldn't say that every time. He hunted down Hoover. "Sergeant, do you know who would be the number two guy at Grimes Oil Company?"

"Oh, yeah. Guy's been there forever. Name's Mathew Bowles. He's their chief financial officer. My brother-in-law used to work for him in accounting out there."

"Thanks." Ray wanted to talk to Bowles as soon as the office opened.

The McDonald's drive-thru was busy but efficient. Ray and Tyee had their coffee and breakfast biscuits within minutes of ordering.

"You know," Tyee observed with his mouth full, "I really like this stuff. Do you think it's bad for you?"

"The coffee's way too hot," Ray replied, "and these egg sandwiches taste too good not to have things in them that we shouldn't be eating."

Tyee twisted his mouth. "That's kind of a cynical view of the world, Ray."

Ray nodded with admission. He had become cynical. He needed to fish more and spend time with his dog. Alone time and the companionship of dogs kept men from turning old and grouchy. "You're right. They do taste good." Ray tipped his coffee, as if to propose a toast.

Grimes Oil Company looked austere. It was obvious fancy offices were not required for the mundane and dirty job of delivering gasoline to hundreds of convenience stores and service stations. Its aroma spoke of its core product, stored in great tanks, right on the grounds. Ray and Tyee parked in front of a nondescript two-story steel building. They took time to finish their tasty breakfasts before going inside.

"Good morning." Ray gave the receptionist his best smile. "Is Mr. Bowles in?"

"May I tell him who's calling?"

"Ray Pacheco and Tyee Chino."

She smiled at Ray, but looked sidelong at Tyee, as if suspicious he might pose a threat to peace and safety. She stepped away toward the back offices and soon returned. "He will see you in just a minute." She was no longer smiling at either.

It took closer to ten minutes before Bowles appeared. "Please come on back." They followed him through an open-style office filled with people busy at their desks and into his glass-enclosed corner office. They glanced at the suitcases stacked against the wall inside. Bowles noticed that. "Leaving this morning on a business trip. How can I help you?"

"Mr. Bowles, I am acting sheriff of San Juan County, appointed by the governor as of this morning. We need to inform you that Lewis Grimes is dead."

Bowles turned a sickly white. He looked like he might faint. His head lowered to his desk.

Tyee spotted a pitcher of water, poured Bowles a glass, and offered it. Bowles gulped it down, shaking visibly.

"Are you all right? Do you want us to call for help?" Tyee asked.

"No. Please. I'll be okay. Just give me a minute." He drank more water. "I knew something like this would happen. It was the sheriff, wasn't it? Is that why you're the sheriff now?" He was still shaking.

"You think Trujillo had something to do with Mr. Grimes's death?" Ray asked.

"I don't know. I just don't know. How can this happen? Everything is all screwed up. I'm going to jail, aren't I? My god. Everything's all screwed up." Bowles began to rise, and quickly collapsed. Two women, walking toward the office, screamed. Tyee called 911.

22

Chickens Come Home to Roost

They followed the ambulance taking Bowles to the emergency room at the San Juan Regional Medical Center. Standing next to the emergency entrance was a familiar face—Agent Ben Crawford.

Tyee spotted him first. "Looks like the FBI has descended on Farmington."

They parked and walked up to meet Crawford. "You're a long way from Washington," Ray said.

Crawford chuckled. "Yeah. *Very* early morning flight." Still, he seemed edgy, Ray noticed. "Your governor," Crawford said, "talked us into backing off Grimes for a few days. He insisted if we moved to arrest Grimes when we wanted, it would interfere with the state's investigation. He hinted the state's charges would be more important than the tax matters. He said all that to the guy above me, who is more politician than cop. I was instructed to let it go for a few days. Never should've agreed to it. So now, here we are trying to catch up to events we should have been out ahead of. Right after we heard Grimes was dead, we were proceeding to serve search warrants for the business offices and his home."

Ray was impressed. The FBI had moved fast. Within less than four hours they had made it to Farmington in full force. "I'm shocked you even knew he'd been killed. You guys have the whole country bugged or something?"

"Not funny, Ray. We have connections with the Navajo Police. They tipped us off. The search warrant was issued last week, and we were just waiting on our deal with the governor. So, we had to move fast. We understand his wife shot him, right?"

Ray nodded and glanced at Tyee, they both knew: it had to be Watchman who had told Crawford. How did Watchman know? And why would he act so fast to get the FBI involved? There were a lot more questions to be answered. "The wife— Grimes called her Vickie, but her real name is Joyce—admitted she shot at Grimes several times. He was in the pool, and they had a disagreement. She said she got a gun and started taking potshots, but never intended to hurt him. She claims she only wanted to scare him. He was shot in the head and, again according to her, she jumped into the pool and tried to pull him out. Then she called 911. So, we don't yet have all the necessary details, but I think she's more or less telling the truth. I think someone else could have been there, took advantage of the situation, and shot Grimes." He looked up at the hospital. "She's in here, too, experiencing some kind of mental breakdown. I assume that's why you're here."

"We got word about her, but we were en route to Grimes's office when we heard about his CFO. So, in fact, we're here waiting on you, because of Bowles. I wanted to have a quick word with you before we execute our warrants. We've been told that Jackson might have had evidence of Grimes's manipulation of reservation gasoline sales to embezzle the tax revenue. Are you aware of that? And do you know where those documents might be?"

"The city attorney told us he'd seen them. And he said Jackson had the documents but didn't know what he did with them. So he got a warrant and searched the sheriff's department offices. They didn't find anything. I believe Jackson might have taken those files with him when he took that military equipment to Colorado. Matter of fact, we think the Acting Sheriff Trujillo could be looking for those files up there right now. But you should know, we also think Trujillo could be involved in some of this stuff. Reason for that is, he just took off without explaining why." Ray threw up his hands.

Crawford shook his head and began to laugh. Ray and Tyee couldn't help joining him. "How the hell do you get involved in this shit?" he asked.

"I think it's Tyee's fault." Ray couldn't stop laughing.

After they got themselves under control, Crawford thought a moment and told them, "We've got some private security around that camp. But I'd bet they'd be easy to get around. Or if you looked official, they might not even interfere with you coming in to look around. So, Trujillo might just pull that off. Why do you think those files might be there?"

"Timing, mostly. We know he had some he showed the city attorney. We also know they weren't at the sheriff's office. And if Jackson thought those files were the key to arresting Grimes, I don't think he would've left them at his house. I believe he would have kept them with him, and when he left, would've taken them along. Now, keep in mind—this is a guy who was on the verge of losing his mind."

Crawford shook his head. "With Grimes dead, it's mostly a moot point, anyway. Plus, we have enough evidence to charge Grimes *and* Bowles."

"Looks like another example of our governor getting involved where he shouldn't have," Tyee said, almost grumbling. "If he'd let the FBI do its job, Grimes would be in jail, alive."

Ray wasn't going to defend the governor but refused to believe his motives were evil. "His heart's in the right place. It's just that sometimes his head isn't."

They nodded. Crawford added, "I understand his concern. There are a bunch of federal agencies waiting to jump all over the Grimes empire. They can't put the companies in jail, but they can fine them to death. Thing is, that means some negative financial impact here—and in some ways, all over the state."

"What do you think will happen on the Navajo side?" Tyee asked.

Crawford shrugged. "You're aware of the complications. But we're not the lead agency to deal with the Navajos. This gets hyper-political in a hurry. Nobody wants to jump in right away. We have heard a group of Navajo leaders are trying to work something out that would allow the current president to resign. The whole thing could just disappear for them."

"Man, that doesn't seem right." Tyee sounded disappointed.

"No. It doesn't." Crawford shrugged as he turned to go

into the hospital.

"Now what?" Tyee asked Ray.

"Before we can go home, we have two murders to solve, and then get the sheriff's department up and running." Ray frowned. That was a lot, he knew.

"That could take forever," Tyee grumbled. "I thought you believed Grimes killed Martin."

"I just thought he was the most likely suspect. We were going to arrest him just to shake things up. It's a wide-open investigation, especially now."

"Maybe when we get ballistics, it'll prove Vickie shot Grimes. Case closed." Tyee smiled at the thought of how those problems might be solved.

Ray shook his head. "You know you don't believe that. What we need to do is circle back to the Martin killing and do a better job of investigating. Start with the ballistics and forensics. Send the entire file to the state police lab in Albuquerque. Have them re-examine everything. We need clues. And we need to look at Martin. Who would want to kill him, and why? Who were his friends? Who were his enemies? We need suspects. We need to do the hard work. Something will jump out."

Tyee sighed. "Yeah, I guess so."

They arranged for security around Mrs. Grimes and headed back to the sheriff's department.

The first call Ray made was to Sue. "I'm sorry I haven't called. Things are worse." He related all the events to Sue, and how long he thought he and Tyee would stay in

Farmington. "Worst case, if we don't have solutions in two weeks, I'm turning everything back to the governor. He can appoint someone else sheriff. But we won't stay past that; I even hate doing that much. It's just that I'd feel a lot better if we could solve the murders and have some order in the department before someone else takes over."

"I understand. It's fine, Ray. I'm fine, and Happy's fine. Do what you have to do, but—stick with the two weeks. There are lots of crimes that go unsolved. Give it a good try, and then come home, okay?"

"Okay. Thanks."

"Just don't go crazy. And if you get a break, send Tyee to Albuquerque so he can talk to Nancy. If he doesn't do something soon about her, it'll be the biggest mistake of his life."

"I'll see to it that he gets time to go see her. I'll tell him that Mom said he has to go."

That made her start to cry. Her voice broke a little. "Be careful, Ray. I love you."

"I love you, too." They hung up. Ray went to find Tyee.

"Tyee, new plan. I think you should take the case file on Martin to Albuquerque, wait a couple of days and see what they can come up with. I'll call the governor and have him light a fire under them. You okay with that?"

"Sure. You sure White Man Leader will be okay without Indian Sidekick?"

"Well, actually, I'm not." Ray smiled. "Now, don't yell at me or anything. But I just talked to Sue. She says 'hi'. And she said you should go see Nancy before you screw up both of your lives."

Tyee smirked, hardly offended. "So, taking the file to Albuquerque is just a ruse to get me to go see Nancy?"

"Not really. When Sue mentioned the idea, I realized we needed to lean on this whole investigation—and hard—to get some kind of results. The best way to do that is to push on the governor. Let him light a fire under those guys. If you hand-deliver those files, it will be an obvious way to make the point that this is important and urgent. It all just came together in a flash." Ray smiled.

Tyee had to laugh. "Okay. I guess I'll buy your story. When do I leave?"

"I'll go call the governor now. Get your stuff together and you can go right away."

"Feels like the bum's rush."

"No comment."

Once on the road to Albuquerque, Tyee realized how right this trip was, and not only for the sake of the investigation. He knew he had to talk to Nancy and it needed to be right now. The trip took on a new sense of urgency. He calculated his route and a plan. The lab was on the northwest side of town, right on his path into the city. He would stop at the lab, leave the materials, and call Nancy. The obvious hole in the plan was that she might not be available. She might have gone to T or C to see her parents. Or she could be somewhere else. Or she could be with a new boyfriend. His doubts, always just below the surface, grew.

The collapse of his marriage had sent him into a tailspin. It flung him from a life as one of the most promising, happily married computer tech guys at an up-and-coming firm in Denver to the drunken Indian-stereotype guide of Elephant Butte Lake. He lost everything, mostly his confidence and self-respect. Deep into his miserable life at the bottom of a bottle, he met Ray Pacheco. Gradually he learned to trust again and joined Ray and Big Jack to start a new private investigation business. He dug himself out of a horrible hole, with a little help from his new friends. Still, he felt terrified of making a commitment to another woman. He never wanted to live through that kind of pain again.

23

Albuquerque Love Fest

The reception Tyee got from the state police lab people was almost embarrassing. Everyone treated Tyee like royalty. He figured the governor must have laid it on pretty thick about his mission and its importance. The head man, a Frank Millsap, insisted that Tyee wait in his office while they transferred the files and evidence bags from the truck into the lab.

"It's so great to meet you," Millsap enthused. "We've heard so much about the work you and Mr. Pacheco have done for the governor. It's almost like you're celebrities." He appeared to be serious. Still, Tyee thought the whole exchange seemed weird. "Our orders are to treat this as the highest priority, and we might have answers for you maybe by later today—but for sure by tomorrow." Millsap beamed.

"Thank you, very much," Tyee tried to seem untroubled. "Why don't I come back, say, a little after noon tomorrow, and check in with you?" He tried not to seem anxious to leave. Still, he did have other matters to deal with. He had other things to do, and Millsap's gushing was making him uneasy.

"Great. We'll see you then. Is there anything else we can do today?" Still gushing.

He hesitated to ask, but, "If I could have a quiet place and a phone for a few minutes, I'd appreciate it."

"Oh, please—use my office." Millsap gestured for Tyee to take his chair.

It seemed to Tyee that the governor might have threatened everyone at the lab with a list of terrible consequences if they so much as inconvenienced him. The visit was bizarre. "Thanks. This won't take long." Tyee shut the door.

He called Nancy's number and got her answering machine. "Hi, um, Nancy, this is Tyee. I know I should've called earlier, but, uh, I didn't. Which, of course, you know." *Jeez, I sound like an idiot.* "I'm here in Albuquerque. I know I should've called earlier—yeah, already said that, didn't I? Look, uh, if you have a little time, I sure would like to see you, maybe lunch or dinner or just coffee or something. I guess you're busy with school, but just a few minutes would be great. Not sure how you'd call me back. Ray and I talked about getting mobile phones, but don't have one yet. My goodness. I'm sorry, Nancy. I'm just rambling—."

She picked up. "Tyee? It's me, Nancy. Yes, I can meet with you. Where are you?"

"Good thing you picked up. I was getting nonsensical. I'm out at the state police lab, northwest of downtown. Maybe twenty minutes away from the school."

"You know where the Frontier Restaurant is on Central, just across the street from the university?"

"Sure, know right where that is."

"How about I meet you there in thirty minutes?"

"Yeah. That's perfect. I'll be there." He felt reluctant to hang up. He didn't quite know why.

"See you in a bit." She hung up.

He sat, first elated then suddenly nervous about seeing her. But that was exactly what he wanted to do—to see her and talk to her. He felt silly. He took a deep breath and walked out.

The drive to Central took longer than he had anticipated, through traffic a lot worse than he remembered. He spotted the restaurant and pulled in to park. As soon as he entered, he saw her in a booth. Something in his brain clicked. He knew he loved her. He wanted to be with her. It was all clear now. Why had he let her leave without telling her? Why was he such a fool?

"Nancy." He smiled. He knew he looked goofy. He couldn't help it and didn't care.

She stood and wrapped him in a hug. "Tyee. What brought you here?" She kept her eyes on his while they sat.

Good he thought, *something to talk about besides his feelings.* "I had to bring some evidence files out to the state lab. We—me and Ray—have been in Farmington working on some pretty bad things going on out there." He paused, realizing how wrong he was. He didn't want to talk about anything but them. He wanted to marry her. What should he say?

"I heard about some of that on TV. And read stories in the paper. Sounds bad."

"Yeah, a couple of murders and lots of money missing," he agreed in a rush, and blurted, "Nancy, I've really missed you."

"I've missed you, too." Her lip trembled.

"How's school?" *Great,* he thought, *why not talk about*

the weather next?

She shrugged. "It's good. Kind of hard to go back to sucking up to professors, especially now that some of them are younger than I am." She smirked at that. "But I like the law courses. Once I can just concentrate on law, I think everything will be fine." Her eyes softened. "Tyee, I was afraid. So, I ran away. I don't want to be hurt. I don't want you to be hurt. And it seemed like the best thing was just to not be together."

He took a deep breath. "I know. We're both afraid of another bad relationship. But since you left, I've been thinking a lot more about not being with you. And that hurts worse. I'm not one of the guys you've been with. And you're not my ex-wife. I think we both care too much to hurt each other, and I think we should try—oh, I don't know, I guess I think we should just get married." He looked up at her from under his eyebrows, bracing for what she would say, which he was sure would be, "Hell, no." But she didn't say anything. She just sat, staring, maybe too shocked. "I didn't say that well. Did I?"

She chuckled. He hoped that was a good sign. "You said everything just fine." She tilted her head. "Why are we making this so hard? I want to marry you, and you want to marry me. What's the damn problem?" She giggled.

Tyee got up, which others nearby noticed, given his size. He took her hand and helped her out of the booth. They embraced and kissed. He knelt. "Nancy Clark, will you be my wife?" He pulled out a ring kept in a plastic bag—not very romantic, but it was what it was. He had carried it with him for weeks. He took the ring out and handed it to Nancy.

She took it and put it on her finger. "Yes. I will be your wife." The room erupted in applause. Tyee didn't look around but noticed how he didn't feel embarrassed at all.

They went to Nancy's tiny apartment and for the first time in months, they felt complete.

The next morning, they walked around the corner to a mom-and-pop coffee shop. Most of its patrons were students, all bent over notebooks and texts. It was a comfortable atmosphere of belonging and privacy, all at the same time.

"What's Ray going to say about you moving up here?" she asked.

"Good riddance."

She punched him in the shoulder. "Come on, Tyee. You know that's not true." Nancy was smiling. In fact, she was joyous.

He shook his head. "He's already been talking about taking more time off. I think Pacheco and Chino is about done, no matter what I do. We'll always be great friends. But Ray seems tired. I think being with Sue changed things for him. He wants to be with her, and I think he worries more about the risks. You see, when we started, he made it clear we would only be working as advisors, never in the middle of the action. Well," he cleared his throat, "things didn't turn out that way. Ray's nature is to take charge, and where he sees a need, he jumps in with both feet. So we're taking more risks, usually without the kind of support he had when he was a sheriff. I don't know if he plans just to take some time off and then get back into it in a few months, or if this is the end. But my moving here to be with you won't interfere with anything he decides. And I know he and Sue will be happy for us."

She squeezed his hand. "What do you want to do?"

"Besides just being with you?" He smiled. "I want to get back into the computer world. I've learned a lot working with the FBI and seeing what they're doing in security. I've also learned a lot working with Ray. I think there could be a good niche for me working with local law enforcement agencies and their computer systems. I've got lots of ideas."

"You know what I think?"

"What?"

"Ray will take a few months off. He'll get bored and call you and say something brilliant like, 'Giddyup', and you will be right back in the saddle, off chasing bad guys."

Tyee laughed. "That *could* happen. I just don't know if it would. The governor's been our primary source of work, and he's just about done. This latest mess with Grimes will be a disaster for him once the news gets out about what actually happened. It could be really bad; he might even resign before his term's up. The FBI, especially Agent Crawford, might want Ray to keep going, but most of what they have isn't in our back yard. And Ray sure doesn't act like he wants to be away from home for long stretches anymore. I mean, there's fishing, and Happy. How can a man stay away from fishing and hanging out with his best dog?"

Nancy chuckled a bit sadly. "I know you're right. But

it doesn't feel right. You two were so great together." She thought a moment. "What about Big Jack? What's he going to do?"

"I forgot to tell you. He's moving up here. Going to practice law. Says once he gets his sea legs back, he may even go back to LA."

"Wow. What happened with Beverly? I thought they were an item."

"I guess Beverly's kind of a big reason why he's leaving. Big Jack lived a useless, good-for-nothing existence, what with his bait shop and beer drinking. Then Ray came along, and it changed a little. Then Chester came along, and it changed a little bit more. But Big Jack was still Big Jack. His 'fuck-the-world' attitude was still intact, mostly. But Beverly was a whole different story. She pushed him to become responsible, even respectable. I think he felt threatened by that, like he was about to become normal without agreeing to it. And it scared the hell out of him. He's running away, fast as he can."

"Will you run away from me?"

"I'm not Big Jack. And the answer is no."

Tyee was once again greeted like a hero by the state lab boss. This time, Tyee just grinned.

"We've got lots for you to review. We found numerous mistakes, and we have lots of new conclusions. The Farmington lab really didn't do much—we're guessing maybe they were told not to put in too much effort—but for whatever reason they missed a bunch. Now, our report is still not complete. We're running some more tests, and we promise you'll have a complete report by tomorrow. If you or Mr. Pacheco need anything else, just give us a call."

"Thank you."

Tyee drove away with a big smile on his face. Thrilled to be back on track with Nancy and have news for Ray about the investigation. Then curiosity overcame him, so he pulled into the parking lot of a burger joint to scan the report. It told him, of course, that Martin was murdered, and it was good to see their conclusion confirmed. But there was more. All surprises. He ordered at the drive-thru and headed out. He had to get it to Ray.

24

Follow the Bouncing Ball

Ray finished scanning the preliminary report from the state lab and looked up at Tyee. "This feels almost too neat and tidy; like something we'd make up."

"Yeah. Case closed. No need for evidence, witnesses, a trial—nothing. We're done." Tyee shrugged.

"Martin's fingerprints were on the gun that killed him. All part of the suicide charade. But a partial print's also on the gun, and it's someone else's. Now, if someone faked a suicide, wouldn't they wear gloves while they pressed Martin's hand around the gun?" Ray looked up at Tyee, frowning with skepticism. "And lo and behold, the partial print is one the lab can identify because they have examined the body it came from, which was Lewis Grimes. Grimes killed Martin, his drinking and carousing buddy. Nice and neat. For sure." He shook his head.

"It's the glove part I can't get past," Tyee said. "Grimes wouldn't be that stupid, not to wear gloves. But then, how did his print get there?"

"Who knows? I'm sure Grimes had been to his house. Maybe for some reason he handled Martin's gun. We need to check to see if Martin carried the gun around with him. If he did, there could be other circumstances where Grimes handled the gun."

"Okay," Tyee continued, "now for the hard part. Do we care that Martin was HIV-positive?"

"That could sure open up a whole can of motives. I know you're going to laugh, but I just don't think about that sort of thing being in these small towns. I know that's stupid and says a lot about me. But it just seems weird."

It didn't faze Tyee. "There are other ways to get the virus. Still, if he was a homosexual, it sure changes the image we had of him and the stories people told about him. Was he bisexual? Was the whole woman-chasing thing an act? Another question: did Grimes know?" Tyee saw it as a complete reset of what they had been thinking. Were Grimes and Martin lovers? That seemed bizarre, but it might fit some facts of the case.

Ray exhaled. "We've been lied to by more than one of the fine citizens of Farmington. Let's see if we can chat with Joyce. I bet she knows everything about Grimes's love life, be it woman or man. Also want to double back to the city attorney. His involvement seems to stick out, especially on the legal side. We're missing something. And we can't just let Trujillo be out there running around. If he's bolted, we need to find some reason to put out an alert. Let's get with the DA and discuss it. No way am I sure about Travis, but we need him to help us with the court side of things."

"Should I say, 'Giddyup'?"

"Sure. Why not?"

"Joyce, we're sorry to bother you. We know you've had a

hard time. But we need help to understand some things. Are you okay with talking now?" Ray's strategy was to treat her with kid gloves. Part of him couldn't be sure she wasn't involved more than she had said. He still needed to know more about her affair with Trujillo.

"Thanks. Sure. I can talk." She blinked. "I have no idea who'd kill him—other than me, of course." She attempted a weak smile. "He had lots of enemies. Matter of fact, almost anyone he was around pretty much came to hate the bastard. He was just a mean, greedy man who only thought of himself. But still, I can't point a finger at anyone and say, 'go there.'"

"Councilman Martin was killed with his own gun. I know some people think it was a suicide. We know it wasn't. Did you know he had a gun?"

She shook her head. "I didn't know much about him. He and Lewis would go out drinkin' and, I'm sure, chasing women. But I thought he was kind of mousy. It surprised me that Lewis liked him. Lewis was a macho kind of guy. Martin seemed, well—different."

"What about a gun?"

"I'd have no idea. Didn't seem like the type that would own a gun."

"I know this might sound out of line to you, so let me apologize in advance. But we need to get some answers involving some confusing information we're getting." Ray cleared his throat—this was not comfortable territory for him. "Do you think there could be any chance that Grimes and Martin were sexually involved? With each other?"

At first, she looked dumbfounded. Then she started

laughing, which led to coughing, after which a moni-
tor hooked up to her started beeping strangely. A nurse
dashed in to examine her, even while she kept laughing.
The nurse helped her catch her breath, all the while giving
Ray and Tyee the evil eye.

"If you can't conduct this meeting without exciting my
patient, I'll have to ask you to leave," she growled. She
looked ready to do that, too.

"Oh, no," Joyce patted her. "It's me, not them. I'm fine,
now. Really." She still giggled.

The nurse mumbled darkly and left.

"Look," Joyce replied at last, "that old bastard would
put his thingy into about anything—anything female,
that is. He treated women like they were there just for
his physical pleasure. But, it's beyond belief that he'd be
involved like that with a man. It's just absurd."

"Do you know if Martin was, you know, attracted to
men?" Ray actually blushed. He wanted this to be over. He
saw Tyee grinning out of the corner of his eye.

"That's a different story. I don't know for sure about
Martin. I can say whenever I was around him, he did
seem different. I wondered if he really caught any of those
women he was supposedly chasing with my unfaithful
husband."

"It was our understanding Martin was having an affair
with Barbara Jackson, Sheriff Jackson's estranged wife,"
Tyee put in. "Do you know if that was true?"

She wagged her head. "I had heard that, but I didn't
believe it. Barbara had her little, out-in-the-open, sleazy
affair with my husband, and he dumped her—big shock.

I thought she might be trying to get back at Lewis by spreading a rumor about an affair with his wimpy drinking buddy. I think she was attracted more to brute types—the macho, slap-you-around guys. She just didn't fit with Martin. I think he would've been afraid of her." She snorted a quick, dark laugh.

"Do you know if your husband had a will?"

She shrugged. "He told me he did. I never saw it. But he said he left everything to me, at first, anyway. Of course, that was what started our last fight. He told me we were done, and I was out of his will. So I guess I can't say what his will says." She sagged, out of energy.

"Looks like you need to rest," Ray said. "We'll leave now."

Tyee had one more question. "Who would've prepared your husband's will?"

"Not sure," she replied, snuggling into her pillow. "He had lawyers everywhere. Before he got to be city attorney, Mark White handled all that for him. He might know." She yawned and closed her eyes, either to sleep or to signal their interview was over.

Ray and Tyee stood outside her room. "Mark White seems to pop up in odd places," Tyee remarked.

"Yes, he does." Ray said, thinking.

"A surprise visit might be in order." Tyee was ready to move the investigation along.

"Come in, come in," White waved them into his office again. "Good to see you guys. Man, that's just *awful* about

Lewis Grimes. He's the biggest name we have in this town. People are just shocked. I've heard his wife shot him. Is that true?"

The man acted way too friendly, and it was too annoying for Ray's taste. He nodded to Tyee to take the lead.

"I'm sure you understand our investigation is still ongoing, and we won't be commenting on any aspects of it at this time. I can tell you there are factors involved which may implicate other parties." Tyee smiled in the most unfriendly way he could. "It has come to our attention that you used to be Grimes's personal attorney. Is that correct?"

"Yeah. But he always had lots of attorneys working for him. I really don't think he liked lawyers." He uttered a short, nervous laugh. "But, before I ran for city attorney, I did do some work for Mr. Grimes. Some of it was personal and some was related to his businesses."

"Did you prepare a will for Grimes?"

"Oh, yes. Actually, I prepared several. Mr. Grimes was something of a volatile man. Every time his circumstances changed, like if he married a new wife, he'd have me draft a new will. And on at least a couple of occasions, he had me change aspects of his will based on some feud or business disagreement."

"Such as?"

White tilted his head disagreeably. "I really don't think I should say. It would be confidential information and privileged communication between a client and his attorney." Tyee could see he was getting nervous.

"Your client's dead." Tyee wasn't smiling, which seemed to unnerve White even more.

Still, he held his ground. "Doesn't matter," he shot back. "The Supreme Court has said legal obligation remains in place, even in that circumstance." He shrugged, letting the highest court in the land do the talking.

Tyee went on to something else. "You told us earlier that you believe Barbara Jackson gave Martin some stolen documents that proved Grimes was stealing tax money, and Martin then gave them to Sheriff Jackson. That's what you said, correct?"

White hesitated, thinking. "Actually, I believe I said something like that would be what I would *guess* happened. I didn't know anything for sure. What I knew was that Sheriff Jackson had evidence Grimes was stealing state and federal tax dollars, lots of them. I only guessed at how he got that evidence."

Tyee bored in. "So you don't think Barbara stole those documents and gave them to Martin, or you don't think Martin gave them to Jackson?"

White turned testy. "That's not what I said, and you know it. I don't know what's going on here, but if you have some suspicion that I'm involved in this, then I won't answer any more questions. I believe it's time for you to leave."

Ray spoke. "Mr. White, I would advise you not to play games with us. We have the unsolved murder of Mr. Grimes and the unsolved murder of Mr. Martin, and you have connections with both. I think it would make a lot of sense for you to just answer our questions."

White stood. "I'm not saying any more without an attorney."

"Do you know where Trujillo has gone?"

He looked confused. "Hell, no. How would I know where he went?"

"Were you aware that Martin was a homosexual?"

"Thomas Martin? That's just stupid. I've known him for years." He lifted his chin at them. "You're slandering a dead man, and I will not stand for that. I'm calling the governor. You have no right to come into this town and spread salacious gossip. What kind of goddamned investigation are you running? Get out—now."

Ray and Tyee left, as part of what was becoming a familiar pattern.

Ray stopped to lean on the truck. "If he's innocent, we've made an enemy. If he's guilty, he might do something stupid and maybe help us find out what the hell's going on. Which way would you bet?"

"My gut says he's involved somehow, especially with the money. I don't think he's a killer. But he knows a lot that he's not sharing with us. That makes him a bad guy. How are we going to watch him with just the two of us?"

"I think we're going to have to trust the sergeant. We can't cover all the bases without his help."

"You know what else my gut says, besides that it's time for dinner?"

"What?"

"That Navajo, Watchman—he's involved somehow, too. And he's dangerous. Another bit of psychic insight: that old Navajo, Kee, that the sheriff was protecting, knows something. We need to find him and talk."

"I agree. Keep stirring the damn pot." Ray smiled. He

really liked the chase. "By the way, were you able to see Nancy?"

Tyee smiled, looking goofy again, and not caring, again. "I'm getting married."

"'Bout time."

25

Nothing's Black and White

The sergeant clearly did not look pleased, yet he did as ordered and made arrangements for surveillance on Mark White. "You should know, sir," he told Ray, "we're running short on deputies. At this rate, we're going to have a shit-load of overtime this month. And a lot of griping."

Ray was used to managing the workload in a sheriff's department. Often the most time-consuming part was trying to keep everyone happy. "How many deputies are at the hospital?"

"Right now, four. At any one time we have two there, each working twelve-hour shifts, one for each patient. The FBI's keeping two men there, too, on the same shifts."

"Pull the two guarding Bowles. He's the FBI's concern. Keep two on Mrs. Grimes for now." Ray reminded himself to call Crawford and touch base about the FBI's plans.

"That will help." Hoover now seemed pleased. He had to listen to the complaints, so anything was a help. He left to see to his duties.

Tyee and Ray were using Trujillo's office although it felt like they were intruding. Ray called Travis to arrange a meeting. "Don't think the DA has warmed up to us yet," he told Tyee after hanging up. "That whole exchange felt pretty guarded. Let's go get something to eat before we see him."

Tyee cheered up immediately.

Ray gave Travis a recap of where they stood on their investigations of the Martin and Grimes murders. "We think Acting Sheriff Trujillo may have skipped town. *Or* he may be looking for those lost files the previous sheriff supposedly had. Anyway, we think we should issue some kind of alert to law enforcement in the area and see if we can locate him. But we wanted to go over that with you first."

The DA seemed attentive, if slightly bored. "Do you suspect Trujillo's done anything illegal?"

"At this point, I guess almost everyone is a little suspect," Ray grunted, feeling somewhat testy. "But we have no evidence that he has. As we've discussed, he did have an affair with Grimes's wife. And they each admit they'd spent time searching the Grimes property for buried money. None of that was technically illegal."

The DA rocked back in his chair to peer at the ceiling. "Of course, you can issue a BOLO or APB, or even an ATL," he said, referring to three different types of police alerts: be on the lookout, all-points bulletin, and attempt to locate. "But I wouldn't. Trujillo may have just left for his own reasons. He's a free man in a free country. Maybe he just got tired of the whole mess and went to Nebraska or something. He has a right to do that. So," he continued, as if thinking his way through the matter, "issuing alerts to law enforcement, unless we have reason to suspect he committed a crime or is some kind of danger, does not seem appropriate." He leaned forward. "Did he take a county vehicle when he left? If he did, that would be a different matter."

"No." Ray shook his head. "He drove his own truck."

"If he's looking for those tax files, it seems that would be a waste of time now, don't you agree?"

"Yeah, probably is. I don't think the FBI ever needed those files, actually, and with Grimes being dead they're not really relevant to anything. But of course, Trujillo may not know that, so he might still think they're critical to making a case against Grimes."

"Well, still. It's odd behavior for him just to take off and not let anyone know what he is doing. At any rate, I'd be careful about doing anything that could come back and bite us."

Ray and Tyee noticed how Travis seemed to have become more engaged in the matter. It was the first time either had heard him say anything like "us," perhaps indicating he might be on their side. "I understand your concern," Ray replied, "but I think if we don't hear from him in another twenty-four hours, I will put out an alert. We'll do it as an attempt to locate. It seems to me that if the acting sheriff disappears, we shouldn't just ignore it. He could have enemies because of his duties, and his absence might not be related to the Grimes case at all."

Travis nodded. "I agree. Put the bulletin out tomorrow." He cleared his throat and changed the subject. "You should know that I have talked to the governor." He chuckled. "Or, more correctly, I have *listened* to the governor. He expressed deep concern about the continuity of the Grimes business enterprise. Now, I don't believe that should be any concern of his, but he ignored my advice, of course. In a move that I'm sure exceeds his legal authority, he has authorized the New Mexico National Guard to send fifty troops here to guard the headquarters of the business." He leveled his gaze at Ray and Tyee. "I know you work for this man. But I must tell you, I fear he may have lost his mind. During our conversation, he mentioned something about Colorado's governor. And I may have misunderstood him. However, he *sounded* like he was declaring war against our neighboring state."

Tyee perked up. "He can't do that. Can he?"

"He's got troops, and Graham has, too. Fuck, who knows what crazy people might do?" Ray's greatest concern was for his friend—the wildly eccentric Governor Johnson.

As soon as they stepped into the sheriff's department, Sergeant Hoover came running. "Just got off the phone with Deputy Avery," he announced, gasping for breath. "He was the one we had watching White. Said White went to the hospital and tried to strangle Bowles. The FBI broke it up. The deputy arrested White. He's transporting him back here."

"Was Bowles hurt?" Tyee inquired.

"Don't think so. Avery said he was scared for sure. The nurses gave him something to calm him down. We think he's okay, though."

"What the hell is that about? Has this whole town

gone nuts?"

Ray didn't expect an answer, but the sergeant offered his opinion. "White was Grimes's attorney before he became city attorney. And Bowles, he has to know everything. Maybe White didn't want him talking to the FBI."

Ray shook his head. "That's logical, in a sick kind of way. But to go to the hospital where the FBI are guarding the man and try to kill him—that's just plain ol' stupid."

Hoover nodded. "I used to arrest White and some of his pals when they were just kids, out smokin' and drinkin' and carryin' on. That Mark White has one hell of a temper. Jake let him go more than once after fights all over town. If he and his family weren't so well connected, he'd probably be in prison by now."

The receptionist came up. "They're in the back with Mr. White. Where do you want him?"

"Put him in interrogation room two." He glanced at Ray hopefully. "You want to talk to him?"

"Yeah."

"What the hell was that about?" Ray was in no mood for small talk. He and Tyee sat across from White.

White slumped. "Gross stupidity. We got to talking, and it got heated, and I lost my temper. I wasn't going to strangle him, no matter what the FBI guy says. I was just—just wringing his neck a little. Stupid. That's what I should be arrested for—just being a dumbass."

Ray wasn't buying. "Well, counselor, as I'm sure you know, being a dumbass is not a crime—at least not in this state. But assaulting someone with what appeared to be the intent of killing that person—that is. Still, my understanding is that Bowles says it was all just a misunderstanding, and he doesn't want to bring charges. But the FBI can testify to your actions. That could still lead to a charge of assault. But," he leaned forward, "for the time being, let's just pretend this matter gets dropped. You walk out of here with no charges from what just happened with Bowles. How does that sound?"

"Sounds like you're offering a deal. What do you want me to do?"

"Just tell us the truth." Ray was pretty sure that this offer would not be agreed to by the DA or the FBI. But at this point he didn't give a shit. He needed facts.

White didn't bite. "No reason I should trust you."

"No reason at all. Just say no, and we will proceed with the charges."

"Fuck." White wilted. "I knew about the money—the tax money Grimes was stealing. Jeez, you've got to understand, I was not the only one. He'd get drunk and brag about it. He was a rich old fool who thought he was a goddamn genius. But he wasn't."

"Who else knew?"

"Well, of course, Bowles knew. Martin, his drinking buddy, knew. Although, I don't think he understood the amounts involved. He wasn't the brightest guy. The sheriff knew."

"You mean Jake Jackson?"

"No—fuck, no. Jackson didn't know shit. He was half nuts. I mean Thad Trujillo knew. Vickie knew, of course.

She told Trujillo. Barbara Jackson knew. And his honor the mayor knew."

Tyee spoke up. "My god, who didn't know? How could this have gone on so long without someone doing something?"

"Everybody was afraid of Grimes. He was a crazy man. He always carried a gun. He talked about all the times he'd killed people—and I, for one, believed him. He had money, power—it was just too risky."

"Did anyone else get any of that money?" Ray asked, peering at White.

"I sure didn't. I think Bowles did, but I don't know. If he gave anyone money, it was probably like a gift. You know—an envelope with a few thousand in it; that sort of thing."

"What did you mean the mayor knew? How was he involved?"

"I don't know. He called me once and asked if I knew anything about Grimes stealing money from the Navajos. At that time, I had no idea what he was talking about. That's what I told him."

"Do you know who killed Martin?"

"Martin came to me and said he was done with Grimes. Said he hated him and that he should be in jail or an insane asylum. I had never seen him that angry and vocal; he was always so subdued. He told me Barbara had brought him files that showed how Grimes was collecting the tax revenues and using bogus reservation sales numbers to cover it all. He took the files to Jackson, and he said Jackson told him he was going to arrest Grimes. Of course, Jake hated

Grimes because of the affair with his wife, so it was easy to believe he might do that. Martin said he was letting me know because we had been friends for so long, and he was worried I might be involved. We'd known each other since grade school, like a lot of people in this town. There is a lot of history." He looked depressed.

"I'd think Jackson also hated Martin because of an affair with his wife, wouldn't you?"

White shook his head quickly. "I never believed that. Just a silly rumor. That wasn't Tom."

"What did you do after Martin told you that?" Ray asked.

"I made a big mistake. I went to Grimes and told him. He went ballistic. He said he'd get those files from the dumbass sheriff, and nobody was going to talk to anyone or they'd all end up dead. He was obviously mad—a complete lunatic. I didn't tell anybody. I just laid low. Pretty soon, in just in a few days, Barbara, Tom, and Jake were all dead."

"But Grimes didn't kill all of them." Ray was a little confused about what White was saying.

"All I know is he said they'd die, and they did. I'm sure he killed Tom. The way it happened; it was Grimes. I'm sure of it."

Ray leaned back. "Let's be clear. Sheriff Jackson confessed to me that he killed his wife in a fit of anger. And I was on that mountain when he killed himself. Grimes wasn't. But you're probably right that he killed Martin."

He stopped to wonder what to do with this horrible man who was too much of a coward to save a lifelong friend's life. Just let him go? No. "You know something, Mr. White? I believe you need a good attorney. You're under arrest for aiding and abetting the theft of millions of dollars from the state and the federal government, and for obstruction of justice." Ray opened the door. "Sergeant."

Hoover leaned in. "Yes, sir."

"Arrest this man and throw him in a cell—literally, if you wish."

White sat, shocked. "I thought we had a deal."

"We did. No charges for strangling Bowles. Everything else I can think of though; you will be charged. Lock him up!"

26

Bad Pennies

Thad Trujillo stood in the lobby of the sheriff's department—*his* sheriff's department. The receptionist kept her eyes on him, noticing how he looked like he was waiting on something. He hadn't said anything.

She notified Sergeant Hoover, who bustled in and confronted him. "What the fuck, man? Where in the hell have you been? Do you know what's been going on around here?" No reaction. "My god, say something."

Ray walked up. "Let's take this to the conference room." It was not a request. Tyee, Ray, and the sergeant all squeezed in to face the subdued Trujillo. "Okay," Ray began, "let's do this with some order. First, do you know who killed Martin?"

"Don't you want to know where I've been?"

"I want answers," Ray shot back, struggling to control his temper. "Do you know who killed Martin?"

"No. I suspected Grimes. I don't know why anyone else would kill him. He was a threat only to Grimes."

"You have no evidence against Grimes?"

"No."

"Do you know who shot Grimes?"

Trujillo's jaw dropped. "Grimes has been shot? Is he dead? Did Vickie shoot him?"

No one answered, all frowning. "You didn't know?" Tyee asked.

"How could I know? I've been gone."

Hoover repeated his earlier question. "Where the hell did you go?"

Trujillo waved his hands. "Look—I know I should have told someone about this. But it was such a long shot, I thought it was best for me just to go and see. I knew Jackson had files from Grimes's CFO that proved he was stealing the gas tax money. But he also had photos and tapes of meetings between Grimes and Begay. I don't know how long he'd been working on it, but he told me he had all the evidence he needed to put both of them away. After he went nuts and left with his little army, I thought I might find it all here, but I didn't. So, I decided he must have taken it with him. That's why I went to Colorado, to look for it. And I found it, all of it—everything. Files, pictures, videos, audio recordings—it was all in some old, rusted-out tank."

Ray looked confused. "Video? Tapes? I thought it was all paper stuff that Barbara gave to Martin. Never heard about videos or tapes. How would she get those?"

"No idea. But I found them, all labeled as surveillance of Grimes, with dates. And there are lots of them."

"Do you have these things with you?"

"They're outside, in my truck."

"Your keys," Ray demanded. "Sergeant, go retrieve those items. Let's set things up in the media room and see what we have."

Hoover hustled away to Trujillo's truck. Ray and Tyee

stepped outside for coffee.

"What do you think?" Tyee asked.

"If this checks out, it'll lock down the case against Grimes and Begay. I'd be real surprised if there's anything related to Martin's murder, though. One thing it does for sure is to put Navajo Nation Police Captain Joshua Watchman on our list of people to talk to."

The sergeant set up the videos, which were so clear everyone could tell they were shot on high-quality equipment. Even ones taken in low light showed everything and everyone—mainly Grimes and Begay—with unmistakable clarity. Several captured Grimes handing packages to Begay. One showed Begay opening a package and fanning a bundle of cash. They also watched videos of Grimes talking with Martin and White. They switched to the audiotapes, each referenced to tie in with videos. Again, the evidence was damning.

But the main suspect was dead, and the other was beyond the county's jurisdiction. Ray shrugged. "Looks like we'd be arresting Grimes today, if he wasn't dead. I'll get hold of the FBI and BIA and let them know. They'll have to deal with Begay. Sergeant, please lock all this up in the evidence room."

The receptionist leaned into the room to say, "Mr. Pacheco, you have a call from the governor."

Ray took a deep breath and went to Trujillo's office to take the call. "Governor."

Johnson sounded strained. "Ray," he said, "I'm old and tired. And now my fuckin' doctor says I've got cancer. What an asshole. But it looks pretty bad. I'm going to fight it. Who knows? I've won long shots before. But I didn't call to get any fuckin' sympathy. Just wanted to find out if you'll be able to wrap things up pretty soon. What do you say?"

Ray hesitated, dumbstruck. The governor, odd and troublesome as he was, had become a friend and, in a strange way, a man he admired. "Sorry to hear about your, uh, your health, governor. If anyone can beat it, it would be you." There were a few ticks of silence. Ray told the governor about the piles of evidence they had found that would nail down any doubt that Grimes was stealing money in collaboration with Begay. "What's still an open question is who shot Grimes. I think we've got a strong circumstantial case that Grimes killed Martin, most likely because Martin was working with Sheriff Jackson to prove he was stealing tax dollars. With both Grimes and Martin dead, it may be pointless to push that matter any further."

"How about Trujillo? Does he get a thumbs-up or down?"

"He's made some big mistakes. He's apparently in the gossip loop of the town, which means he's been aware of some of the whispered secrets, but I'm not sure that should disqualify him. His biggest mistake was his romantic involvement with Grimes's wife. That might be a dumb enough move that he shouldn't be sheriff, but the choices are slim for a replacement. When it comes down to it, I think he's a decent lawman. Let the voters decide if he's a decent man."

"Always the philosopher. I agree. What do you have left to do?"

"Need to find Grimes's killer, and I have some ideas. Probably a little housekeeping with the Navajos, FBI, and BIA, too—but I can do that from T or C, and it's not really our concern. I'll give it a couple more days of digging, and if we can't point to someone as the killer, we'll go home."

"One favor while you're still there. I don't want Grimes's business to collapse, if it can be avoided. That's a few thousand employees and a major supplier of gasoline, especially in small markets. Letting it die would be very disruptive. Any idea who will inherit it?"

Ray bit his lip, sorry to listen to Jeremiah Johnson not being his usual loud, in-your-face self. Even at that, he felt impressed by how concerned he was about the people who worked for Grimes. "It's possible, of course, that everything will end up with his wife. I wouldn't describe her as a businesswoman. But, hell—who knows? Maybe she's smarter than the dumb blonde girl character she plays. And even if there's a clear path to a new owner, the business is facing massive fines. It's possible that it can't be saved."

"Get involved a little," Johnson urged. "Let me know what you think can be done. Ray," he added, "I'm thinkin' about resigning. It's not fair to the state for me to be in a hospital, unable to do the job. The lieutenant governor's a complete idiot, but he's got a good heart. He'll try his best, and that might not be worth much. But it's better than me being half dead and hangin' on. Think that announcement's gonna come in about a week. Now, if you could come up with some way to salvage that business for those good folks before then, I'd greatly appreciate it. Keep me posted. Good luck, Ray." The governor hung up.

Ray just stood holding the phone. He felt old and tired, too, but he wasn't dying. Still, he felt sorry for the governor, and for himself, if for a somewhat different reason. *Shit.* What could he do about a complicated business matter in just a few days? With or without a will, the business was almost certainly doomed. Nobody would want to touch a business stuck in the middle of an epic legal battle with the state and the feds, let alone rescue it. That was a losing proposition. Hundreds of convenience stores and gas stations would have to be shuttered all over the state and on the reservation. And the whole mess traced to the egomania of Lewis Grimes. The moment was far too late for a white knight.

Or was it? He pondered, still holding the buzzing receiver. A deal could be struck with the state. And the feds were likely most interested in punishing Grimes and Begay, so shutting down the business might not be a priority for them, either. Ray was aware of the inkling of an idea taking shape in his mind.

Tyee and Trujillo were still talking when Ray returned to the main office area.

"Going to be around for a few more days," he announced, and turned to put his eyes on Trujillo's. "At this point I want to hand the reins of the department back to you. You should know I just now gave a lukewarm recommendation to the governor to appoint you sheriff until an election, whenever that might be. Lukewarm or not, it was a recommendation and I expect him to take it. Don't screw up anymore—at least, not while I'm still in town. Okay?"

Trujillo nodded, smiling faintly.

"What's the plan now?" Tyee sensed maybe they were nearly done, and thought that a loud "yippee" might be in order if they had been outside.

"We need to find Watchman. I believe he's the source for all this evidence. We need to hear his story. Thad, how would you find him?"

"I'd call him. He has one of those mobile phones." Trujillo pulled out a notebook and shuffled the pages while Tyee turned to Ray with a meaningful grin, which Ray ignored imperiously. "Here's his number."

They pulled into the McDonald's, which Ray had picked for a meeting spot with Watchman because it was Ray's favorite food and he was driving.

"We really need to have mobile phones," Tyee remarked on the way. "Navajos shouldn't have better shit than Apaches."

"We're not going to have some kind of Indian war in here, are we?"

"You mean like one where I take his stupid mobile phone from him while I wave my tomahawk?"

"Well no, that wasn't exactly what I meant. But now I'm really worried—be nice, okay?"

"Have any idea why Watchman would collect all that evidence and just turn it over to Jackson?"

Ray parked. "No clue. If he was protecting Begay, he wouldn't have made any of it, nor would he have given it to the sheriff. But we know the real threats were the feds, either FBI or BIA. So, did he give all that to the sheriff to keep it out of their hands? The part that really confuses me is Jackson. One minute he's nuts, and the next he's in the middle of a major crime investigation. I know he confessed to killing his wife. But is he a bad guy or a sort-of good guy?"

"Crazy people often act crazy."

"Is that an old Indian saying?"

"No. Just common sense."

Ray smirked at Tyee while they entered the restaurant. They were a few minutes late and expected Watchman to be there. He was not. Ray bought coffees, and they took a booth. After about twenty minutes it was clear Watchman had stood them up.

"Now what?"

"Go see the DA. Based on what we've uncovered, maybe there's enough to arrest Watchman for obstruction of justice. Likely that's complicated because he's a policeman for the Navajo Nation. But he can't stand us up. No more Mr. Nice Guy."

"I like it. Be nice to us, or we'll haul your ass to jail."

27

How Did That Happen

The *Albuquerque Journal's* headline read, "Governor Threatens War Between the States." Many readers had to be curious about what the hell that meant. Within the article, they discovered Governor Johnson was quoted as saying he would use the National Guard, if necessary, to secure and return the military equipment that the State of Colorado held illegally. It went on to say the governor also had directed the state attorney general to file a lawsuit against Colorado to force them to return the hardware. The paper quoted Colorado Governor Tom Graham as saying he had "real concerns about my old friend and his mental health."

"Fuck that bastard Tommy Graham. He's always been a goddamn crook, and he's still a fuckin' crook." The governor was reading his morning paper and was not pleased. "Call the goddamn AG and tell him I want to see him."

His beleaguered chief of staff had aged noticeably since coming on board about a year ago—the previous one was rumored to be in hiding somewhere near Taos—took a deep gulp before he replied. "Governor, I *have* had conversations with Colorado's attorney general. He said we can have our equipment—just come and get it. He reassured me that *if* Governor Graham implied something else, he *has* changed his mind."

"What?" Johnson glowered. "Why should *we* come get it? They're the ones holding it. They should bring it to the border." The governor loved fighting more than anything. And this was likely his last fight.

The attorney general walked in, already briefed about that morning's tirade. "Sir, you might recall it was our San Juan County Sheriff who took all of it into Colorado. And at least according to the attorney general, their governor may have overreacted a bit during one of your conversations when he said they would hold it until hell freezes over, but in any case, all we have to do is send people to that camp, and they can drive everything back here." The AG smiled broadly to indicate what a good idea that was. He did not smile because he felt at all happy to be in the middle of a pissing contest between two bulls, even if they were just about all out of piss.

The governor made a sour face. "You know, in 1925 the U.S. Supreme Court settled our border dispute with Colorado. They said the border would be the thirty-seventh parallel, based on surveys conducted by two groups. The two crews started at opposite ends of the state and would join in the middle. Well, wouldn't you know it? They fucked it up. Yep, there were morons back then, too. They missed each other by maybe two miles. That's why we have a kink in our border with Colorado. A fuck-up. Now, wouldn't you think that could be fixed? Oh, no. They just joined the two ends with a line—and that's the state border. Now, there's a road that runs right down that line. It's just inside the line, in New Mexico. But it serves mostly the people who live on the other side, in Colorado." He narrowed his eyes at the chief of staff, who wilted with dread. "You tell that fat-ass governor he can keep that military junk. But *I* want Colorado to pay for the annual maintenance of that highway. You tell him if he says no, I will have DOT tear the damned road out—completely gone. Then he can build his own road on his side of the border and pay for the maintenance."

The attorney general stood speechless. He began to speak but seemed to change his mind. "Yes, sir. I will let them know." He left.

"All right," the governor nodded conclusively. "Now we're gettin' somewhere." And he began to cough. Then he couldn't stop. He rose from his chair and collapsed onto the floor with a loud thud.

Emergency medics already stationed at the capitol were steered into the governor's office. They quickly examined him and placed an urgent call to the hospital. All the signs looked bad. They lifted him onto a gurney and rushed him to an ambulance, but he did not live to reach the hospital. His term was over. He had a long run.

Ray walked woodenly into the conference room where he and Tyee had been drinking their morning coffee. "Just took a call from the governor's office. He had a heart attack this morning. He's gone."

He turned and left, and did not stop walking until he was outside, where he stayed for many minutes before he went back inside and found a quiet room to call Sue.

"Don't know if you've heard or not but . . ."

"I did. I'm sorry. Do you want me to come out there?"

Ray almost broke. He felt weak. He swallowed. "No. I'm sure the funeral will be quick. It'll be in Santa Fe. I'd like for you to be there."

"Sure. But just say the word, and I'll come to Farmington."

"I'll be fine." Ray paused. "We'll get this wrapped up in a day or so. We're going to hand this back to Trujillo pretty quick, and we'll head home." He wanted to change the subject. "Have you heard from Nancy?"

"She's so happy. Tyee's a lucky man. She really cares about him. I think they're going to be great."

"Sue, I love you. I'll be home soon."

"I love you, too. Be careful."

Tyee burst into the office. "Ray, just got a call from the DA. An attorney from Albuquerque called and said he had Grimes's latest will. He wants to meet with Travis to give him some information. And Travis wants us there." He suddenly realized Ray was not reacting. "You okay?"

He seemed to refocus. "Yeah. The governor dying just kind of hit me hard, I guess. I'm fine. Hey, uh, talked to Sue. She said she talked to Nancy and you're one lucky guy." Ray smiled, or gave it his best shot.

Tyee smiled back. "Yeah, I know. Time to wrap this up. We've got bigger fish to fry."

"So, when does the DA want us in his office?"

"The attorney was already in town, so in about forty-five minutes."

At the DA's office the receptionist took them straight back to the conference room to meet Travis and someone new.

The DA handled the introductions. "Ray Pacheco and Tyee Chino, this is Paul Unger. Paul's an attorney from Albuquerque, and he prepared Lewis Grimes's most recent last will and testament." They both shook hands with Paul, a slight man of slim build, about five-feet-six inches, with deep brown eyes, dark, thick hair worn long in the back, and a manner of notable intensity.

Tyee opened the questions. "Have you done a lot of legal work for Grimes?"

"Not at all. I'm just a one-man shop. One day about a year ago, he walks in and asks if I do wills. And that is a lot of what I do. Anyway, he hired me to do his, and I never heard from him after that. Then just lately I saw in the paper that he died—all so unusual, especially with him being killed. At first, I thought somebody would contact me, but no one did. So, I filed a copy of his will with probate court yesterday. And I drove here to see if I could find the beneficiaries and give them copies of it."

The DA asked him, "Could there be later versions?"

"Like I said, I haven't talked to anyone, especially not Mr. Grimes, since I prepared it. I guess he could have had later ones done. But I thought I should operate under the assumption that this is his valid last will and testament."

Tyee peered at him. "Did you find the beneficiaries?"

"Yes. Matter of fact, it was Mrs. Grimes who asked me to contact the DA and give him a copy."

"So she was named in the will?" Ray asked.

Unger handed Ray a copy. "As you will see, there are two beneficiaries: one Joyce Sanders aka Vickie Grimes, of Farmington, and one Chris Kee, address unknown. The estate is basically split down the middle—fifty percent to Mrs. Grimes and fifty percent to Chris Kee."

"Did Mr. Grimes identify to you who Chris Kee is?"

"No, he didn't. If I may say, I believe it was seeing Kee's name on the will that prompted Mrs. Grimes to suggest I should get the DA involved. So, who is Chris Kee?"

"Apparently we're not sure." Tyee remarked, almost under his breath.

Unger seemed to ignore that. "One of the odd things that happened, after I prepared the will, was I received a letter from Mr. Grimes in which he named me as executor. Sort of a weird thing to do, but the letter came with a very nice check. While I thought it was strange, since we had only met once and I hadn't seen him since, it was still legal. I decided that, for his own reasons, he wanted someone who was not involved in his day-to-day life to handle his estate. So, unusual? Yes. But legal."

Travis cut his eyes toward Unger. "Well, Mr. Unger, I believe you may find being the executor of this estate to be a very interesting job."

Unger thanked them for their time and left.

"What does that mean?" Ray asked anyone who might know.

The DA spoke. "I have some knowledge about Kee, as I think you do, too. And based on what I know, there's no accountable reason for Grimes to leave him anything, much less half of everything."

"We've been told Kee is Sheriff Jackson's father. Do you know if that's true?" Ray asked.

Travis shook his head slowly. "I have no verifiable information about him. Just rumors, like you have."

"Under normal circumstances, this would be Kee's lucky day. But with all the legal problems, his estate may not be worth much." Tyee seemed almost sad.

"Wonder what Vickie—or Joyce—is thinking about now?" The DA pondered.

"I think we should go ask her." Ray stood, ready to move.

"Before you leave," Travis said, "we should discuss your plans for Mark White."

"My plans went so far as locking him up. Maybe I should ask you what he should be charged with."

He chuckled. "I've talked to him. He called and raised a ruckus. Wants to charge you with false imprisonment." Travis grinned, clearly relishing the matter. "I told him that would be a waste of time and that he was in a lot of trouble. I reminded him about conspiracy charges that he could face besides ones for withholding evidence. And with a little thought, we could probably come up with other ones. He wants to talk a deal to avoid jail. I said I'd talk to you."

"My job is to find evidence and arrest people. I'm not a deal guy. Rubs me the wrong way. White contributed to an attitude in this town that led to all this. Maybe he didn't do anything himself, but he sure didn't do anything to stop it. I'm not sure I could make it stick, but if we really push, we might even be able to charge him in connection with Martin's murder."

"I hear you, Ray. The biggest problem there is that we can't prove Grimes did it. So, we may not like it, but there are a lot of holes in your case against White. Sometimes it's best to take what you can get, rather than shoot for the moon and miss everything."

Ray looked at Tyee and frowned. This was the part of the law he didn't like. "What can we get?"

"He'll plead to a misdemeanor, interfering with an investigation. And he'll surrender his law license and take two years' probation. That means he'd have to resign as city attorney."

"What would you do?"

Travis looked wistful. "If I could, I'd throw the book at him. He's that kind of privileged lawyer who thinks the law doesn't apply to him. And that rubs me the wrong way. But what I *would* do is offer the deal and consider it a job well done. Otherwise, I think there's a good chance he just walks. And probably sues us."

"Tyee, what's your opinion?"

"Never take big bites. You might get choked."

The DA looked at Ray. "Does that mean anything?"

"Yes. Offer him the deal."

28

It's All In The Past

Tyee took a gulp and grimaced. "Another day, another great cup of coffee."

Ray looked at Tyee. "You're being a wiseass, right?"

"I was only complimenting this wonderful cop coffee."

"I know. It's awful. Hey. Let's go to McDonald's and get some real coffee." Ray was smiling.

"Seriously? McDonald's?"

"Sure. I like their coffee."

"It's too hot."

"It'll cool."

"Okay."

About halfway there, Ray suggested they stop and see the mayor.

"The mayor doesn't drink coffee," Tyee grumbled. "Only booze." He didn't hide his disappointment that they weren't going to McDonald's.

"His honor will be with you in a few minutes." Ray noticed the mayor's receptionist was not the same person as the one they had seen in the office before.

After waiting a good ten minutes, Ray approached her again. "We need to see the mayor *now*," he said firmly. "Please inform him that this is a law enforcement issue."

She rose from her desk, looking annoyed and disconcerted, and went to the office door. She lightly tapped on it. No answer. She did it again. Still nothing. Ray pushed past her and opened the door. The untidy office was empty.

He turned to her. "I am the acting sheriff of this county, and I am working in association with the FBI. You should know that if you have lied in order to allow the mayor to leave by the back door, you *will* soon find yourself in jail." The woman's eyes widened with alarm, but she didn't say anything. "Was he here when we first came in?"

"Yes."

"What did he say to you after you told him we were here?"

"He said to stall. He said he didn't want to see you. He said he was leaving through the back door." She pointed.

"Damn. Do you know where he went?"

"No." She started to cry.

It almost made Ray feel bad, but only almost. "You were not here when we saw the mayor before. Are you new?"

"Yes," she sniffled. "I started just a few days ago. I'm sorry if I did anything wrong." Now she was really crying.

And Ray did feel bad. "It's okay. The lady who was here before—what happened to her?"

"That was June Walters. I think she quit. That's what the mayor said."

"Is she still in town?"

"I think so. Most people live here till they die."

More tears and some sobbing. Ray said he was sorry and they left.

"Let's call the office and see if we can get an address for the mayor and June Walters."

"No coffee?" Tyee whined.

"Later."

They called dispatch and talked to the officer on duty. That person gave them the addresses and directions for both houses. The dispatcher also mentioned that the mayor had inherited the place from his parents. Not much privacy in a small town, especially if you're the mayor. They headed to the mayor's house to see if maybe he had gone home to avoid them.

The mayor's house was a large, plantation-style structure that needed paint. They knocked and got no response. Walking around the house, they saw more up-keeping problems, including some cracked windows.

"Nice old house. Needs some work." Tyee remarked as they came around one side.

"Yeah. Looks like money might be a problem for his honor."

June Walters's house was much smaller, and very well kept. The house, the yard, the trees—everything was neat and tidy. June Walters was someone who liked order. They rang the bell and waited only a moment.

She recognized them at once. "Mr. Pacheco, Mr. Chino. Please, come in." June Walters appeared to be dressed for work. Or maybe that was how she looked every day. The inside of the house exceeded the outside in neatness. It was immaculately clean and orderly. Ray surmised that she lived alone. "Please have a seat," she offered. "May I get you some coffee or tea?"

Tyee was just about to say yes to coffee, but Ray butted in. "No, we're fine. We were just at the mayor's office for a visit. For whatever reason, the mayor left before we could speak with him. The new secretary said she thought you'd quit. We were wondering if you could share with us why you left your job?"

June paused to take a deep breath. "I'm a Christian woman. My nephews say I'm a straitlaced old fuddy-duddy." She smiled. "My nephews are right. I'm not a modern woman. I guess I live in the past. And I like it that way. Being polite in my world is as important as almost anything. Now," she went on, "I've known the mayor since he was a baby. I was great friends with his beloved mother, may she rest in peace. Mr. and Mrs. Chavez were some of the nicest people in this town—we went to the same church. And when Frankie became mayor, I couldn't have been prouder if he had been my own son. So when he asked me if I would be his assistant—that's what he called the job—I was honored." Her expression resolved from a beaming pride to a furrowed brow. "But after a while, he started to change. He was drinking in the office during the day. It was shameful. And he just got worse. That awful man Grimes started to visit with Frankie a lot." Her eyes narrowed. "I can smell a slimeball a mile away, and Lewis Grimes was the worst I'd ever met. I'll tell you one thing— he scared me. He was dangerous. And poor ol' Frankie thought he was something special. He'd go out drinking with Grimes and that Martin fellow. The next morning, Frankie couldn't do anything. He'd just sit at his desk and moan. It was disgraceful." She paused to wipe her eyes with a delicate pink handkerchief.

"Is that why you quit?"

"No. Should have quit right then, but I was worried about Frankie. I thought if I stayed, maybe I could keep him out of trouble. I *should* have quit and read him the riot act as I was leaving. But, no—I stayed."

"What happened to make you leave?"

"When you guys came to talk to him and he drank himself silly and left, I decided I had to do something. I knew he must know something about the Martin killing, yet he didn't say anything to you. The next time I saw him, I told him I was going to talk to you and tell you everything I knew about the way he and his friends had been acting." Her eyes flung open wide. "He threatened me. I couldn't believe it—little Frankie Chavez was threatening *me*. I'll tell you, even though I might have been able to take the little fat weasel, he kind of scared me. Suddenly, I'm wondering what he's got himself mixed up with. I went home, locked my door and have hardly stepped outside since. My neighbor's been getting my groceries. I think I had a panic attack or something. Anyway, I've not been myself. Strange—just yesterday, I decided I was going to call the sheriff's office and talk to someone about all of this, but I got sidetracked with cleaning and forgot. And now, here you are."

"What had he been doing?" Tyee asked, minding that he kept his voice calm. His sense was that June Walters was hanging on by a thin thread.

"Well, I have to tell you, the most shocking thing happened, and it was some months ago. Like I told you, I'm a prude. I don't have to defend that because that's who I am, and I'm comfortable with my morals. He was having a meeting with Martin, that's the Councilman Thomas Martin—I knew his parents, too, lovely people, always so generous, especially to the poor. Plus, my goodness, I worked for a while with the councilman's wife, and I knew his children; it's just all so awful. I can't believe people can *behave* that way."

Tyee and Ray traded glances, each out of the corner of his eye. "What way do you mean, ma'am?" Tyee asked gingerly.

"Oh, yes." She blinked, as if coming to. "Well, I walked into the office—sometimes I would forget to knock—and it was shocking. They were kissing. I almost screamed. I turned around and left, immediately. I went home and had a good cry. I was *so* embarrassed to see something like that." She wiped tears away. "Frankie called and left a message saying I had misunderstood, that he was just helping Thomas because he had something in his eye. Well, I knew that wasn't true. But anyway, I went back. But when I heard Thomas was killed, that's when I really started to worry. I knew Frankie had to talk to you and tell you *all* his sordid secrets."

"Do you think," Ray asked, "the mayor might have killed him?"

She seemed shocked by the idea. "Of course not. Don't be ridiculous. Oh, he's a sinner, all right. I know that. But his parents were church people, I know they taught him the Ten Commandments. He wouldn't kill anybody. That's just crazy. Why would you even think that?"

"Thank you, Ms. Walters."

Ray and Tyee were back in the truck. "Now what?"

Tyee wondered.

Ray was thinking. "I don't see how we could justify putting out an alert on the mayor. So we're back to waiting until we can find him and get his side of the story."

"Still," Tyee looked out the window, "this is news. It tells us there was a lot more going on than we suspected between some of our victims and suspects. I would say the mayor is now the number one suspect in Grimes's murder." Tyee, like many people, often wanted black-or-white answers in a world full of grays.

"I agree. Let's give it a day to see if he shows up and we can talk to him. If not, we go full blast to find him tomorrow. For now, let's go see if Mrs. Grimes will talk to us."

Ballistics results had by then persuaded everyone that someone else shot Grimes, so she no longer had guards at her room. However, she still had a frowning nurse to admonish them that they should not disturb her for long.

"How do you feel?" Ray's bedside manner wasn't the best. At least he smiled.

"I'm fine. There's no reason for me to be in here, except maybe mental. I understand I'm no longer a suspect. So, who do you think might have shot Lewis?"

"Well, technically, discharging a gun in the city limits is a crime, but we're not pursuing that, so you're free and clear. The evidence suggests your husband was shot with a 30-30 rifle from somewhere along the back fence. At that distance, it was either a lucky—or I guess unlucky—shot, or the shooter used a scope. We found two spent shell casings. But your husband was only struck once. We should make you aware that the other shot could have been for you, and just missed. As for the identity of the shooter, your husband had enemies in business and, of course, his personal life was littered with people who could be pretty angry with him. But we have not identified a specific suspect."

"You really think someone was shooting at me?"

"We don't know. But I think you have to consider that a possibility."

"Why would someone want to kill *me?*" She sat up, becoming alarmed.

Tyee spoke up. "Money would be the most likely answer. Your husband was a rich man. And if he was dead, you would inherit his estate. Maybe someone didn't want that to happen."

Joyce thought about that, then asked, "Have you seen the will?"

Ray answered, "Yes, we have."

"Do you know who Chris Kee is?"

"He's an old Navajo. Some call him the town drunk. It was rumored that he was the old sheriff's father." Ray responded.

"The sheriff who killed himself in Colorado?"

"Yeah. We're not sure it's true about him being Jackson's father, though. At any rate, he's disappeared, and we're looking for him."

That didn't calm her down. "Could he have been the shooter?"

"I suppose, but he's not in the best of health, mostly because of his age and his heavy drinking over the years. I'd be a little surprised if he could get his hands on a rifle or have the strength to fire it. But he's still someone we want to talk to."

She sank back into her pillow. "I knew Lewis was doing something wrong with the business. He was always hiding things or shutting me out of meetings at the house. I didn't know it involved so much money, and damned sure didn't know it was all so illegal. Maybe I *am* just a bubble-headed blonde, but mostly it was that I just didn't *want* to know what he was doing. He scared me. I wasn't going to challenge him. My dream plan was just to leave and hide somewhere where he could never find me. I always believed if he ever thought I was a threat to him, he'd kill me, just like that."

Ray sighed. It was time to steer the subject toward his obligation to the governor. It wouldn't be easy. "I don't know all of what's going on with the FBI and the BIA, but I doubt they suspect you of being involved. You also should know that this will be a real mess to clean up. Millions of dollars are involved. And at this point, no one knows for sure where to find that money. Even if it was all returned to the state and the feds, the fines would likely almost equal the amount stolen. And that would bankrupt the Grimes Oil Company."

Joyce perked up. "Do you think there's any way I could keep that from happening?"

Ray felt a mixture of relief at her interest and dread for the task ahead. "It'll be very difficult. There are too many people and agencies involved. The governor might have been able to accomplish something. He wanted the business to continue to operate because of all of the people it employed. But, as you might have heard, he just passed away." He shook his head. "I don't know of anyone else who could pull it off."

Tyee looked at him. "How about you, Ray? You know the people involved—or at least, some of them. It would be what the governor wanted."

Ray gave Tyee a dirty look. "Yeah, I know it was what he wanted. But nobody's going to want to listen to me. Plus, I think this matter with Kee is going to confuse the issue. Why did Grimes leave half his business to the town drunk? Unless we can answer that question, I don't think anyone's going to stick their neck out and try to keep the business alive."

"The reason has to be because he's a Navajo."

"Maybe so. But there are thousands of Navajos. Why leave a fortune to this particular one?"

"I wonder if Begay would know the answer?"

Ray nodded. "Let's go ask."

They said their good-byes to Joyce, saying if they learned anything regarding the business or Kee, they would contact her. It seemed polite, but no one expected much of anything to happen.

29

Strangers in a Strange Land

Before they could leave the hospital, a security guard waved them down. "Mr. Pacheco?"

"Yes."

"The sheriff's office is calling you."

Ray followed the guard into a tiny office. "Ray Pacheco."

"Trujillo. Just got a call from Captain Watchman. Said he was supposed to meet with you but didn't because of an emergency. He wants to meet now, at the same place. Then he hung up. Do you know where he's talking about?"

"Yeah, I do. Thanks. I'll—"

Trujillo interjected, "Be careful around Watchman. Some say he's crooked and dangerous."

"We'll be careful." Ray hung up. "Watchman called the office," he told Tyee. "Still wants to meet at McDonald's, right now."

Tyee smirked. "Sounds good. If he stands us up again, at least we can get something to eat." Tyee didn't appreciate McDonald's the way Ray did, but food was food.

Watchman was easy to spot—big and scowling. No one sat close to him.

"Captain Watchman." Ray nodded.

"Sit." It sounded like a command.

"We would like to interview Begay," Ray said, up front.

"Do you think he will agree?"

"Hah," he snorted, "Not too damn likely. Whatever you think he has done, you're all wrong. You have no idea what all this is about." Watchman was in a fighting mood.

But Ray wasn't in the mood to back down. Okay. It was time for an explosion. "I've got two unsolved murders—that's what it's about. I want to solve them so I can go home and forget about Farmington. I've got a new boss, the lieutenant governor, who doesn't know shit about anything, and he'll do whatever I tell him. If I don't get some answers soon, I will request a full team of state troopers to join the fifty National Guardsmen already here, and I will arrest Begay if I think I should, with or without permission. Fuck the reservation."

Tyee tensed. He knew he could handle Watchman, but he had to be prepared and not allow him to get an advantage.

Instead, Watchman leaned back. "Calm down. Begay didn't kill anyone. He's been a fool, just like a lot of other people mixed up in this. And he probably would have been just fine with the idea of shooting Grimes, but he didn't do it. And Martin has no connection with Begay at all."

"Do you know who killed Martin?"

"I can only guess, and my guess would be Grimes. They were pals. You know most people are killed by friends, and not enemies."

"How about Grimes?"

"A long list of suspects there. Begay hasn't been off the rez in weeks, so he couldn't have done it."

"Do you know where Chris Kee is?"

"He's in the hospital, on the reservation. That was my emergency—the reason I missed our meeting. Got a call saying he collapsed outside one of his favorite bars." He shook his head. "It was bad. He was bleeding from his mouth and his nose. I took him to the hospital. He was in a coma by the time we got there and hasn't come out of it. The doctors say his kidneys and liver are shutting down. Probably hours, or maybe days, and he'll be gone."

"Could he have shot Grimes?"

"I doubt it. Physically, I don't think he could have done that, and mentally he was completely lost. I don't think he would have even remembered who Grimes was. When you get to the point he's at, any anger he had toward Grimes was buried a long time ago in his own decay and misery."

Tyee leaned forward. "I don't get it. How does Kee fit in all of this? Is he Sheriff Jackson's father? And why would Grimes's will name him as a beneficiary?"

Watchman sighed. "Chris Kee used to be one of the leaders of the tribe. After the last president died, the two people who were going to run for the position were Begay and Chris Kee. Now, everybody knew Kee had a drinking problem. But he was still the favorite. He was full of life, had a big personality, and was one of the smartest people I'd ever met. It was just the drinking that kept him from being a shoo-in. It was about that time that Lewis Grimes came into the picture. While the presidency was vacant, Kee sort of assumed command. That was Begay's weakness, you see? He was not a fighter, he just wanted to get along with everybody. Anyway, Kee and Grimes seemed to hit it off and they started drinking together. Grimes took him to Vegas, I don't know how many times, and spent a lot of money on him. He wined and dined him—mostly wined. And even in Farmington they were drinking and raising hell almost every night. Well, Kee got arrested several times, and the word got back to the reservation. People were saying he was turning into a town drunk. So, the election came, and Begay won. That really pushed Kee in the wrong direction. That was about the time he started staying with Sheriff Jackson's mother."

"Does that mean he was the sheriff's father?" Ray asked.

"Nah. The timing is way off. Jake Jackson was probably seven or eight about then. I'm sure his mother probably didn't know who the father was. Could have been she just said whoever was around at that time. There's no way it could have been Chris Kee."

Tyee wondered, "Why would Grimes become buddies with him, though?"

"Well, you're probably thinking about the Kee you know now. He used to not be like that. He was big, handsome, and he loved the ladies. So he and Grimes liked to drink and chase women together. They were kindred spirits. Why he got to know him in the first place was because Kee was, in essence, the acting president of the Navajo Nation at the time Grimes came to town. Grimes was just small-time then and he wanted to open convenience stores on the reservation and sell gasoline. He just bought a couple of run-down stations. So he approached Kee about a contract with the Navajos. Of course, technically he wasn't president, so he didn't have the authority to sign a contract. I think Grimes just played around with him until he saw how the election came out. Then Kee lost, and he turned his back on him."

"But he did get the contract," Ray said. "How did he do that? Through Begay?"

"Some of this I know because Kee told me, but only when he was falling-down drunk. So take it all with a grain of salt. One night, I got a call from the sheriff's department saying they had picked him up. Sometimes they'd throw him in jail, and sometimes they'd call me to come pick him up because that was easier than doing the paperwork. Besides, he was a sloppy drunk and hard to handle. I got him that night, and I was taking him back to the reservation to sleep it off. He got to talking about how he was going to be rich. He said he had a written agreement with Grimes for half his whole damn business. He and Grimes were 'partners,' is what he said. I made some wiseass remark I thought he wouldn't even respond to, something like, 'Why would Grimes make him a partner in anything?' He said, 'Because I killed the SOB.' Well I had no idea what he meant by that, and he passed out about then. Anyway, you know it's a pretty long trip to Shiprock, and he woke up again. So, I was curious, and I asked him, 'Who was the SOB he killed?' And just like there'd never been a break in our conversation, he says, 'Bill McCullum.'"

"Bill McCullum?" Tyee asked, glancing at Ray. "Who was that?"

"He owned the Phillips 66 distributorship for this part of the state. Very successful. Hated by everyone. No great loss when he died. Died in an accident when his car ran off the road. After he died, Grimes bought the business from his widow."

"Did you tell anyone what Kee told you?" Ray was not sure he believed anything Watchman said.

"Nah. The sheriff before Jackson was an idiot. Hell, all of these damn sheriffs are idiots. He investigated the accident and closed the case—accidental death. I could have pressed the issue, but that particular sheriff hated me, and I hated him, and it wasn't my problem."

Watchman looked defensive. Ray looked at Tyee, then back to Watchman.

"Do you think Kee being named in Grimes's will was because they did actually have an agreement?"

"Grimes was a strange man with a strange sense of humor. I guess somehow in his mind he could have thought he owed half the business to his old partner, if Kee's story was true. I can't think of any other reason he'd leave it to him. As far as I know, they hadn't talked in years. I really never heard Kee even mention Grimes after that night I took him to Shiprock."

"But that doesn't answer why Begay signed the contract for the stores on the reservation," Tyee brought up. "Why did he do that?"

Watchman rubbed his face. "I'm not completely sure. I challenged him on it one day. He told me that Kee had told Grimes something that Grimes turned around and used to blackmail him. He said that on top of that, Grimes gave him fifty thousand dollars to sign the contract. He told me he needed the money to help his wife, and I knew something about that. She died about that time, of breast cancer. I know she spent her last months in a Houston hospital, and that had to be expensive. Also, Begay told me that Grimes used the same things to threaten him into signing those fake gas sales reports. He told me he didn't get any more money from Grimes for doing that."

Ray's skepticism kicked in. "We've seen videos and audio recordings that would indicate otherwise. Didn't you make those?"

"I did. That's how I got Begay to tell me what was going on. That bag of money is a little deceptive. Grimes knew I was tracking him. He gave it to Begay and he told him to use it to buy me off, or he'd have me killed. I took that money from Begay. But I put it in a box, along with a note, and left it on Grimes's front porch."

"Any proof of that?"

"No."

Ray nodded, but had something else. "Grimes was shot with a 30-30 rifle from long range. Whoever killed him either had a scope or was one hell of a marksman. Why do I think you're someone who prides himself on being good with a rifle?"

Watchman grinned. "Probably because you'd like to go home, and arresting me wouldn't ruffle any feathers in Farmington or Santa Fe." The look on his face suggested he might have found pleasure in doing just what Ray asked about. Before he could go on, his mobile burbled and rattled on the table. "Yes." He listened, and quickly disconnected. "Kee just died. He never came out of the coma." Another pause. "If you decide you have to talk to Begay, I think I could talk him into meeting with you. Like

I told you, he has done some things that are wrong, and maybe he should be punished for them. But I guarantee you, he did not kill anyone. Talking to him isn't going to get you home any sooner." Watchman stood, eyeing Tyee. "That was going to be one hell of a fight, if I'd lunged at you. I could see you were ready." A quick smile crossed his face and he winked.

They kept their seats while he left. Tyee observed, "If everybody keeps dying, we won't need to arrest anyone."

Ray chuckled. "All's well that ends well." He sobered. "It's hard not to feel for Kee. But I think I believe Watchman about him being involved in a murder. It just seems like something Grimes would have done—talk someone into doing his dirty work. And that Bill McCullum's death was no coincidence. I'd bet Grimes had something to do with it. The strangest thing about all of this is him leaving Kee half his estate. He didn't know Kee was going to die, so what did he think he'd do with it?"

"Maybe it was a way to punish Vickie?"

"That sounds like Grimes." Ray took a slug of milkshake.

"What happens now to Kee's half of the will?"

"Don't know. We should find out."

"Sounds like giddyup time."

30

Better Alive than Dead

"Just talked to Unger. He said the will has a survivorship period requirement written into it. Sort of scolded me, saying it's very clearly set out in the will. Guess we should have read it before calling him. Anyway, if a beneficiary doesn't live forty-five days past the death of the person who made the will, that portion of the estate goes to the other stated beneficiary, which in this case is Joyce Sanders." Ray sat back and put his feet up on Trujillo's desk—Trujillo not being in the room.

Tyee was frowning about something. "I guess that's good. No feuds with Kee's relatives, if he had any. Of course, now she's the only one left to fight with the feds and the state to try to keep everything together."

"I know you think I should get involved. But I don't know if that's the right thing to do."

Tyee leaned forward. "Well you said the biggest problem was having the mystery of why half of the estate went to Kee, now that part's solved. He died."

"That's kind of cold-hearted."

"Yeah, maybe. But I don't think Kee cared much anymore. And it does simplify things regarding who the new owner is."

Ray was tired of almost everything and everyone to do

with this case. "Is Joyce still in the hospital?"

"Trujillo told me she checked out and went back to her house. Must be kind of strange to be there."

"Yeah. Let's drive out there and talk to her." Ray took his feet off the desk. He felt fidgety.

"Should we call first?"

"Nah. I need to get out of here, anyway. If she's not there, or doesn't want to see us, let's just take it as a sign that we should move on to something else."

"Divine intervention. I like it!" Tyee shook his fist at the ceiling.

There were no guards, and the house seemed smaller. It was obviously an illusion, but it was odd—somehow it had genuinely lost some of its grandeur.

"Considering we just told her someone could have been shooting at her when her husband was killed, you'd think she might have some security."

"Maybe she didn't believe us."

"Tyee, everybody believes us, we're the good guys."

"Oh yeah, I forgot."

They rang the bell and soon Joyce answered the door, wearing sweatpants and an oversize hoodie—quite a contrast from her ensemble when they first met. "Come in." She stepped aside as Ray and Tyee entered the house. They noticed how empty it looked and felt.

"No servants?"

"Nah." She shrugged. "They always made me nervous. I'm only going to be here a few more hours, myself. Until things get settled, I'm moving into one of the hotels downtown. Just getting some things packed." She rubbed her arms like she felt a chill. "It just feels wrong to be here. Like I'm trespassing."

Tyee nodded. "I understand that. The hotel will be better."

Joyce smiled at him. Ray noticed how she seemed younger, and smaller. She was barefoot. Before, she always wore heels. "So. What brings you by?"

"Wanted to tell you about Chris Kee. You know he was elderly and in poor health. We just got word that he died." Ray never enjoyed the notification part of being a sheriff. Even though Joyce had no connection to Kee, it still felt sad.

"Oh, my. And he just inherited all that money. He could have had a different life. That is so sad." She walked into the living room to flop down on a sofa. "What happens to his part?"

"It now goes to you."

"Not his next of kin?"

Ray explained how the conditions of the will made her the sole beneficiary.

"That still doesn't seem right." She looked up at them. "But why would Lewis leave half of everything to him in the first place? Was it something from way back?"

Ray hesitated, unsure of how much to share with her. What they really knew was next to nothing, all secondhand information mostly based on hearsay and the word of a drunk. But he decided she was entitled to at least some idea of why Grimes did what he did. "Maybe the only person who really knows why he did that is Grimes. What we've learned won't hold up in court. It's all based on bits and pieces of information we got from people who may or may not actually know, or even want to tell us everything."

"It's okay, counselor. I won't hold you responsible." She smiled. "Dish out the gossip."

"When Grimes first moved to Farmington, he and Kee became drinking buddies. Apparently, during this time, Grimes thought that Kee could help him get business on the reservation. The tricky part is that Kee indicated to one of our sources that he may have murdered a man who owned a business Grimes wanted to buy. And as a result of that man's death, he was able to buy it, and it became Grimes Oil. Kee told at least one person, while he *was* drunk, that he killed that man. He also told that person that Grimes was going to give him half of everything as a sort of payment. But his life started to tumble down into a bottle, and soon he had nothing to do with Grimes. I guess it's possible Grimes left him half the business because that was their deal. Or maybe he thought it was a joke, or it would make you miserable. We can't know."

Joyce laughed. "What a strange man Lewis was. But that fits. Even when he was causing someone pain he always kept his word. Isn't that odd? Have you found out who shot him?"

"No. Kee was in no condition to do that, we don't think. We're investigating a lead as we speak, but I'm not able to give you any details." Ray started pacing. "We should discuss what you want to do with the business, and whether you want to try to keep it running."

She sat up. "I've thought about it. I don't know anything about running a business, especially one with thousands of employees. If there was some way to deal with the fines and everything, I think I'd sell it to someone who knows what they're doing."

Ray nodded in approval. "I think that's very smart. And it's an approach that might work to your advantage. If there was a change of ownership, it might go a long way toward dealing with those problems. I'm sure neither the state nor the feds want to shut down Grimes Oil. But they probably feel obligated to take some action if anyone associated with Grimes was planning to keep it." He stroked his chin. "Matter of fact, I think that is a great plan. Now we just need to find someone who might be interested in buying it."

Joyce looked up. "Another thing I would like to do," she said, "is to set up some way, legally, so half of everything would go into some kind of trust or something to benefit the Navajos in Chris Kee's name. Maybe a program to fight alcohol abuse, or something."

Ray and Tyee regarded her like they were seeing her for the first time. "That's great," Tyee responded at last. "Just great. That attorney Paul Unger, I bet could help you do that. He said that's the kind of law he practices. That really is very thoughtful of you."

"Hey, just because I'm a blonde bimbo doesn't mean I'm not nice." She smiled and giggled. She seemed pleased about her decisions.

✵

The discussions seemed to go on for days. The state wanted some assurances, the feds others. Paul Unger proved to be a very competent attorney and negotiator. And there proved to be an unexpected attraction between Joyce and Paul—love is a strange thing.

In the course of the discussions, the feds revealed that much of the money had been recovered. It had been traced to numerous banks, some overseas, but given the clout of the Treasury Department almost everyone had cooperated and returned the cash. There were still millions missing, but the majority of the stolen tax dollars had been found. Just to be sure, the FBI spent a considerable sum having the entire grounds of the Grimes estate dug up looking for the remaining millions, but to no avail. The rumor persisted in Farmington gossip, at hair salons and in bars, that the money was still buried there, but in such a way that the feds couldn't locate it. This led to many schemes, concocted over whisky and beer, on ways to uncover the mysterious loot. The next owner of the Grimes mansion was going to need a very secure fence.

No purchaser of Grimes Oil had surfaced yet, but there was interest from several individuals and a couple of large corporations, all of whom were doing due diligence, so a sale seemed imminent. With the assistance of the now ever-present Paul Unger, Joyce hired a national CPA firm to provide a temporary CFO to run the business during the transition. Almost immediately, the business took on a new professionalism throughout its operation. With much of the craziness that had been interjected into operations by Grimes purged, policies and procedures were implemented that improved efficiency and profitability, all of which had a positive impact on the prospective buyers.

Ray had contacted Watchman and told him what Joyce wanted to do. He was pretty sure that Watchman had teared up a little—for sure he had trouble talking for a moment or two. After a pause, Watchman said he would talk to Begay and let Ray know what program they thought would benefit the most people.

Tyee climbed into the truck.

"Well, superman, looks like our work here is about done."

"You really are annoying."

"No, I'm not. Well, maybe a little." Tyee was feeling good. They hadn't arrested anyone for Grimes's murder, but it was past time to head home—they would let Trujillo solve the murder and be the hero. "'Bout time to head home and finally get a good night's sleep."

"Yeah. I hate leaving without resolving everything, but maybe that's our only choice."

"Can't fix every problem. I think we've done a good job. I know this latest little coup, keeping Grimes's business operating, would please the governor."

"Okay, one last thing, though. Let's go to the office. I want an alert out on the mayor. He's the loose end I can't walk away from."

Trujillo met Ray and Tyee at the door. "We've found him.

He's at the old schoolhouse on the north side of town. It's been abandoned for years. The deputies say he's drunk and he's armed. He told them he's got a 30-30, and he's threatening to shoot them or himself. I told them to back off and wait."

Ray told Trujillo to direct his men not to do anything. The last thing they wanted was a dead mayor. He and Tyee headed out.

"The mayor's holed up with a 30-30 rifle," Tyee noted. "You think we've found our shooter?"

"I know some things pointed his way." He shook his head, eyes on the road. "But I'm having trouble with him being the shooter. It just doesn't fit." Ray frowned. The matter could end in another death, and still no complete answers.

"It sure fits a pattern," Tyee countered. "Sex and money. Greed and lust. Human weakness strikes again."

"Yeah. But I'm still uncomfortable with the whole thing. He just doesn't fit as a killer. Especially one that would take a shot at Joyce. Can you see him doing that?"

"Crazy people do crazy things."

"I know, that could be the answer. But it just feels so hollow."

They pulled in near the small schoolhouse and saw the emergency lights of six patrol cars and two ambulances. "Sure hope he doesn't try to run for it," Tyee said. "He'll be dead before he gets ten feet out the door."

"Yeah. We need to defuse this before someone gets hurt." Ray spotted Hoover. "Look, we need to calm every-thing down. I know he's armed, but I think this is more a mental crisis. The more threatening we look, the more likely he'll shoot. Take half the cars and deputies and move them back down the road. And have those ambulances move out of sight."

The sergeant looked confused. "You know he threatened to shoot us, don't you?"

"I do. And I don't want that to happen. Do we have any way of communicating with him?"

"All we've been doing is yelling. We've had trouble hearing him."

Tyee wondered, "Do you have a bullhorn?"

The sergeant held up a finger, dashed to his patrol car and back, and handed a shiny white bullhorn to Tyee.

Tyee quickly handed it to Ray.

Ray shrugged and turned the thing on. "Frank? This is Ray Pacheco. I want to talk to you. Will you please put down your firearm and come out so we can talk?"

No answer. Ray moved a little closer, careful to stay behind a broad-trunked tree. "Frank? Come on out, and nobody will be hurt. Frank? Can you hear me?"

Silence, then some movement. Ray spotted Frank standing behind the open front door. "I hear you. I'm drunk. I don't want to die. I thought those deputies were going to shoot me. I told them I'd shoot them because I was scared."

Ray heard a tremble in his voice. "Frank, if you'll put your gun down so I can see it, I'll come in and walk out with you. You will not be hurt. Okay?"

A minute passed before Chavez slid the rifle onto the porch. Ray eased toward the door and went inside.

"You okay?"

"I think I'm going to throw up." Which he did, all over the dirty tiled floor. Ray waited, then took him by the arm and walked out.

31

Well, Well, How 'Bout That

The drive back to the sheriff's department passed mostly in silence. Two deputies had transported Frank Chavez. He was to be placed in the interrogation room. Ray and Tyee were already tired and they knew the day wasn't over.

"You know it almost has to be him," Tyee said after a long silence on the way back.

"I know. The rifle, his involvement with Martin, the likelihood Grimes killed Martin. Sure, all points to Chavez. But it still doesn't seem right. Do you think he's a killer?"

"I sure haven't been doing this as long as you. But, you know what? I don't see a pattern. Nice people kill, bad people turn out to be nice—it's all confusing. I think all you can do is go where the evidence points. And it points to Mayor Chavez."

Ray sighed deeply. "I know. We'll get the ballistics on that rifle and if we have a match, we have our shooter. I know the motive is most likely revenge because of Martin, but it still doesn't seem to fit. That was a very long shot. Maybe Chavez was the Boy Scout marksman of the year, or something like that, and he had the skills to make it—but if not, you don't hit Grimes at that distance with a lucky shot. And the second shot? Why would Chavez want to hurt Joyce? Just because she was there?"

"Maybe the second shot wasn't at Joyce. Maybe he took the first shot and didn't know right away that he hit Grimes, so he let off another round, which missed because Grimes moved slightly when he was hit."

"So, you're saying Mayor Chavez is such an excellent marksman that he fired two unbelievable shots—remember, there was no scope on his rifle—in rapid succession, and hit one and barely missed the other."

"Yeah, that's what I'm saying. It could happen." Tyee was getting annoyed with Ray's stubbornness.

When Ray and Tyee entered the interrogation room, Chavez had his head down on the table.

"Frank?" Ray asked him, "Do you need a doctor?"

He looked up. "I don't think so. I just feel pretty bad. What's going to happen to me?"

Ray spoke calmly. "I don't know. Right now, we need you to answer some questions. Okay?"

"Okay."

"I'm going to read you your rights. If you don't understand what's going on, or if you think this should wait until you have an attorney, that's fine." Ray pulled out his card and read Frank his rights. "Do you understand?"

"Sure. Look, I'm hung over— not stupid. I want to tell what I know. I didn't kill anyone. Period. I didn't shoot at anyone. That old gun was my dad's, and I'm not even sure it would fire. I've had some kind of mental breakdown, so lock me up. But not because I killed anyone, okay?" Frank's voice raised while he spoke.

"You had nothing to do with Lewis Grimes's death?"

"Nothing! Nothing! I told you, I didn't kill anyone. I hated Grimes, and I'm glad the bastard is dead. But I didn't do it."

"Did you have anything to do with Martin's death?"

"Jesus Christ. Listen to what I'm saying. I did not kill anyone. No one! Kill Martin? My god, are you crazy? He was my life. I loved Tom. I know that's not allowed in Farmington, but I was in love. It was that monster Grimes who killed him. If I was anything other than a sniveling coward, I would have killed Grimes. But I didn't."

"How do you know Grimes killed Martin?"

He looked up. "He told me. I confronted him about it. He said, 'Yeah, so damn what? I killed him.' Just like that, he confessed. Said if I didn't keep my mouth shut he'd kill me, too. He killed Tom because Tom decided he was going to tell you everything he knew about him, which was a lot. Tom told Grimes that. Told him he was finished, that he was going to see him go to jail. That's why Grimes killed him."

"Was Martin having an affair with Barbara Jackson?"

"Of course not. They were great friends, though. It was mostly because of her that Tom decided he had to do something about Grimes. He told me he thought Grimes had gone mad and had to be stopped. I begged him to leave it alone. I wanted us to go away somewhere together and forget everything else. But he said he couldn't just leave. He had to deal with the monster." Chavez laid his head on the table, breaking down.

Ray instructed the sergeant to take him to the hospital and have him admitted for a mental evaluation.

"Don't you have to have a court order for that?" Hoover sounded sure about it.

Ray looked at him. "Just have someone take him there, please. I'll call the DA and have him take care of it." The sergeant left.

"We're getting to the end of our rope. In lots of ways." Tyee sounded nearly done.

"Give me just a minute to call the DA. Then we can head out."

Tyee gave Ray a quizzical, slightly hopeful look. "Head out where?"

"Navajo reservation."

"President Begay will see you now."

"Thank you." Ray and Tyee entered the rather grand office of the president of the Navajo Nation.

"I wasn't sure if you would come or not. Watchman said you would because he would do the same." Begay gestured for Ray and Tyee to be seated.

"Where is Watchman?"

"I'm not sure." Begay looked troubled.

Tyee spoke. "Being evasive with us only delays the inevitable."

"You're Apache, right?"

"Yes."

"Apaches are our brothers. You should understand better than anyone that our lives are different. We are hearing different music than the white man, and it causes us to think differently. Those different thoughts involve not just us, but everything in this world and the one beyond. The world is not divided. Only people are divided. Watchman," he added significantly, "is one of our spiritual leaders. And I have been honored to have known him."

Ray was losing patience. "Watchman killed Lewis Grimes. Didn't he?"

"The short answer is yes. The long answer is more complicated."

"We've got time. Tell us what that means."

"He was forced to kill Grimes because he's a Navajo warrior. He had no choice once Grimes became an enemy of the Holy People."

Tyee nodded, but Ray asked, "Holy People?"

"We don't believe what you believe. But we have many similarities. Our spirits live with us. Kee was a Holy Person. Why and how that came to be doesn't matter. For us, he was a special gift from our gods. The Navajo warrior protects the Holy People, and Watchman was a great warrior. And even if to your eyes, Kee was alive, Watchman had determined he was already dead. And his death had to be avenged. The person responsible for that was Lewis Grimes. Watchman had no choice."

"You can call it whatever you want," Ray said, keeping his impatience and anger in check, "but whether you're in Farmington or on the Navajo reservation, what you're describing is murder. Where is Watchman?"

Begay shook his head. "When Watchman killed Grimes, he also died. From the point of the death of

Grimes, he was doomed. He won't take any food. He'll survive for some time—who knows how long—but he will be dead, in time. You can try to find him, but it would be futile. He has gone into the wild part of the reservation, to places where no white man has ever been. He is gone, and will die in peace."

"I could probably have charges brought against you." Ray was not pleased with any of this.

"If that suits your needs, then by all means, do it. But I'm not guilty of any crimes, except maybe spiritual ones."

Ray thought about Begay's story. He wasn't sure he understood everything he had been told. Still, he was sure he was not going to arrest him. He also felt a tremendous sorrow in the pit of his stomach for Watchman. He knew he was a warrior, and he had not met many like him. He turned to Tyee. "Time for us to leave." Ray got up.

Tyee stood to address Begay. "Navajo warriors live forever. I'm deeply sorry for your loss."

The ride back to Farmington was long and quiet. Something good had died in order that something bad could be purged from the world.

"Well, Thad Trujillo," Ray smiled at the newly appointed San Juan County sheriff, "you must be pleased to see us leave."

Trujillo chuckled. "It's been interesting. Still, I hate to think of what would have happened if you and Tyee hadn't been here. I want to thank you for what you've done for me and my town." He softened. "I went by the hospital this morning and visited with Frank. Ms. Walters was there reading to him. He seems a lot better."

"I hope things turn out okay for him. Any news on someone buying the Grimes Oil Company?"

"Heard yesterday a big oil company made an offer, and it looks like Mrs. Grimes is going to take it. Sounds like she'll be set for life. Guess everything worked out for some." After a moment of awkward silence, Trujillo extended his hand to shake with Ray and Tyee. "Be careful driving home. Come back and see us anytime."

Tyee looked thoughtful on the way out of town. "Been thinking. I may never come back to Farmington. If someone offered me five hundred bucks, I wouldn't set foot in that lovely town again. I believe I'm going to hold a grudge."

Ray smirked and shook his head. "How about five hundred *thousand* dollars? Would you *live* in Farmington, then?"

"Half a million? Damn right. I'd live there and marry Ms. Walters. Life would be good."

"It's good to know you have a price."

"Oh, I do. It's really less than half a million; I'd rather not say how much."

Ray laughed. "Wonder how much Joyce is going to get for her half of the business?" Ray really didn't care, but it felt nice to talk about meaningless things.

"One of the deputies told me more than eight million. How he got that, I have no idea."

Ray felt mischievous. "Wouldn't it be interesting if she and Paul Unger plotted the whole thing to get the money?

Since Unger prepared the will he knew she would inherit half, and also he knew if Kee died before the forty-five days, she would get it all. You saw how their romance sure did seem to blossom real quick. Maybe they'd been lovers all along, and it was all one big evil plan by the small but smart Paul Unger. How do you like that for a plot?" He watched Tyee for a reaction.

"That's not nice, Ray. Now *that's* in my head. Nah. Can't be right. We know what happened." He pouted.

"Yeah, maybe." Ray was having fun.

"You really are a wiseass."

"It's the company I keep." After a few more miles, Ray asked, "Do you believe what Begay was saying?"

"He wouldn't lie about something that important. The problem is, we don't understand how he and Watchman see the world. It's different. We live in the same world, but it's not the same. Was it right for Watchman to kill Grimes? Not by our laws. By theirs, it might have been. I'm not Navajo, and I'm not a spiritual Apache. When I lived with my relatives, I was often confused about how they thought. They thought I was the odd one. And I thought *they* were. Maybe I should have tried harder to understand the way the old Apaches saw the world, and how we fit into that world. The Navajos believe in a different order. But," he nodded, "I completely believe Begay was telling you exactly what he thought. And in his world, Watchman had no choice but to deal with Grimes. And here's what we have to understand: even in the Navajo world, even if that world sees what he did as right, there will be consequences. Watchman has to pay the ultimate price for his act, even if not in the way we think he should, with a trial and a judge. He has set his own punishment."

"It's a different kind of justice," Ray admitted, "but maybe it *is* justice."

"I think so."

32

Hello and Farewell

Ray woke up in his own bed. He almost laughed, it was so wonderful. Sue was still asleep, so he didn't. Instead he headed to the kitchen to make coffee. Happy got up to come over and greet him with an aggressive, tail-wagging good morning. Happiness was being home with a lovely wife and faithful dog.

Sue walked in. "My, but you look happy."

"I am happy. Wow, am I ever." Of course, every time Ray said "happy," his dog jumped. "I think my dog wants to go outside and play."

"I'm sure he does. You know he misses you a lot. You go. I'll make breakfast."

Ray hugged his wife, and they kissed. "Did I tell you how happy I am?"

"Ray, you're just making the dog crazy."

Ray followed the bouncing and tail-wagging dog outdoors.

The breakfast of hash browns, fried eggs, and bacon was unusual for Sue, who usually insisted on a healthier option. But for Ray's return from Farmington, she went all-out.

"It's really great to be in good old T or C," Ray said with a smile. "I know this likely isn't so, but it seems to me it even smells different here."

Sue laughed out loud. Next, he saw she was crying.

"My goodness, what's wrong?"

"Oh, nothing. I just missed you so much."

"I'm never leaving home again."

"You do remember we're going to Santa Fe tomorrow for the governor's funeral?"

"Okay, then. I'm never leaving home again *after* we get back from Santa Fe."

"That's an okay with me."

He sighed. "I know I said yes because the governor put it down in his final instructions, but I dread giving a eulogy. You would think he'd pick a fellow politician for that. They love to talk. I don't."

She laid a hand on his arm. "Maybe you just answered you own question. He was a great friend of yours. He was odd, even strange, but he admired you and you admired him. Just tell people that. It doesn't have to be long-winded. Just tell them what you feel."

"I will do that. Thanks." Ray smiled. "Are Tyee and Nancy going to be there?"

"That's what Tyee said yesterday before he left for Albuquerque. I sure hope everything works out. I have a really good feeling about them."

"Me, too. I hope it works."

Ray spent the afternoon writing out a few thoughts for the eulogy. He was not comfortable speaking in front of a lot of people, even if it was an honor. And he wanted to make sure he didn't come off like a hick sheriff.

An early morning departure got them to Santa Fe in plenty of time. They had reserved a room at the La Fonda, the memories of the famous margaritas were a major factor. They agreed they would give those another shot.

Their room wasn't ready when they checked in, so they left their luggage at the desk. Ray was thinking a cup of coffee would be just the thing he needed before leaving for the service. After some time alone, they were ready. It was a beautiful day and they decided to walk. They had time. As they approached the capitol it was clear there was going to be a huge crowd.

The service was in the rotunda. Ray was relieved it was not at a church, which would have made him even more nervous. As they entered, several people came up to Ray to offer condolences. That seemed odd to Ray, but he only smiled and moved on. They spotted Tyee and Nancy, who had saved seats for them. The service began with songs and speeches by several people Ray didn't know. Quicker than Ray preferred, the lieutenant governor made a statement that sounded like a political speech, then it was his turn.

"When I first met the governor, I thought, 'I'm going to hate this man.'" Ray smiled and looked across the crowd. Everyone was paying attention. "As I got to know him, I became one of his biggest admirers. I regret now, that I didn't tell him how much I admired who he was. But that would not have mattered to him. He never seemed to notice whether people admired him or hated him. He just did the job the best he could, regardless. The governor didn't care what important people thought of him. He knew he rubbed many elites the wrong way. He cared most about whether the people of this state thought he was doing his job to make their lives better—especially the ones who didn't have wealth or power. He worked every day to make their world, their state better for *them*. The important people never did understand him. Many thought he was a buffoon. But what they did not understand is that he knew who he was—he was someone who cared about the people he represented. Every one of them, and the weakest were the ones he cared about most. Any powerful man could demand all he wanted from the governor, but if it was not good for the state, he would not budge. A weak man, someone in trouble, someone under the thumb of some bureaucrat or fighting the power structure didn't even have to ask for Jeremiah Johnson's help. He wanted to help. I had lots of dealings with the governor, and there was always one thing he'd ask me, 'Is it fair?' He wanted everyone treated the same, and it had to be fair. You might say, 'Well, what does that mean?' Being fair to everyone is not as easy as it may sound. In all my dealings with the governor, his sense of fairness was always exactly right. He never wanted to split it in the middle, because that's not fair. It's arbitrary. He would make the right choice every time, no matter who was involved.

"He taught me a lot. For sure, he taught me some words I will not use here today. While his language was colorful and not always suitable for everyone, he was a kind and forgiving man who wanted the best for everyone. He cared. I did not know his wife, Jane. I know her death was a great tragedy for him. He once told me she was why he cared so much, because *she* had cared, and he was the one left. He had to go on and do the best he could, for her.

He cleared his throat. "I have recently experienced something that has caused me to question a lot of things. A man who considered himself a Navajo warrior took actions that many will question and even condemn because he did not choose the easy path of just standing back and letting someone else deal with a difficult issue. His was a path in which you take responsibility for everything you touch. In that path, the world and you are the same, and you cannot hide from responsibility. Governor Johnson was not a Navajo warrior, but he could have been.

My friend Governor Jeremiah Johnson will be greatly missed."

Ray stepped toward his chair, suddenly aware that everyone was applauding, and they were rising to stand while he passed. He kept his head down and found his seat.

Sue leaned over to whisper, "Perfect."

The service ended. Many people came up to Ray to thank him for his words about the governor. He felt totally out of place, and he and Sue left as soon as it seemed appropriate.

"How 'bout a margarita? This walk is making me thirsty." Sue smiled at him.

"Sounds good to me. Are Tyee and Nancy joining us?"

"No, they went back to Albuquerque. She has some kind of important test and needed to study. They did say they're coming down to T or C to stay with us this weekend." Sue was anxious to talk to Nancy.

They settled into the colorful, crowded bar and ordered two giant margaritas. The drinks arrived quickly in glasses so large they looked too heavy for a person to lift. It was a good thing they came with straws. Soon, Sue and Ray were feeling much younger—maybe even smarter.

"I think we've been here before. It's about now we say adios and go to our room, correct?" Sue was giggling quietly.

"Yes. I want to be alone with you."

They were up early the next morning, checked out and headed home.

"Do you think we'll get tired of each other?"

Here we go again, Ray thought. "What does that mean?"

"I don't know. You just see people who've been married a long time and they seem kind of tired of each other."

He grabbed her hand. "I don't think that will happen with us. How could you ever get tired of me?"

"Yeah. Right."

They drove in silence and with a great sense of belonging and caring.

Ray got up and fixed coffee. The early morning with Happy asleep by his feet and sipping coffee in his wonderful cabin, surrounded him with comfort. Then the stupid phone rang.

"Ray Pacheco."

"Agent Sanchez, Ray. Sorry about this early call. Wanted to give you a little update. Got a minute?"

He wanted to say he didn't care anymore, but instead said, "Sure."

"The Bureau of Indian Affairs convinced Begay to resign. There won't be any charges brought against Begay. They sent a team onto the reservation to search for Watchman. Of course, they didn't find him—not even a hint of where he could be. The San Juan County DA filed an arrest warrant for Watchman in regard to Grimes's death. Of course, it would have no value at all on the reservation. We expect Watchman will die on the reservation and will never be charged. The tax people wrapped up their investigation into Grimes's scheme. They agreed to waive most of the fines so the business could keep going and get sold. They levied a few fines against the Grimes estate, specifically Joyce Sanders, which have been paid. Those were mainly wrist slaps so the tax guys could say the estate didn't get off scot free, even if that's what happened. The state of Colorado agreed to a bizarre arrangement where it will pay for road maintenance on a stretch of highway in New Mexico for five years in exchange for being allowed by New Mexico to keep the military equipment abandoned in Ignacio. If Governor Johnson wasn't dead, I'd swear this would be the kind of deal he'd have made. Anyway, that avoids any disputes over that old military equipment. In a bit of odd news, the mayor of Farmington has returned to his job, and by all accounts looks like he will be re-elected. Guess that's about it for the Farmington stuff."

"Good to know. That town could use a break. How about Trujillo? Think he's going to stick?"

"Looks like it. He's been working real close with us on cleaning up some lingering issues we had with some drug traffic. Seems capable." There was a pause. "How 'bout you,

Ray? You and Tyee still in business, or did all that Farmington shit break you guys?"

Ray chuckled. "We got close to breaking, that's for sure. Right now, I'm not sure what's going to happen. No question, we're taking some time off. Tyee's getting married, and I'm going fishing."

"Look, Ray, this is from me and Crawford. If you decide you want back in the game, we've got lots of stuff going on where we could use you. Some in New Mexico, but definitely in the region. I think we worked well together. And we would like to have you and Tyee as a resource."

"Agent Sanchez, I just really don't know. But when I decide, you'll be one of the first people I call." Ray hung up and wondered. Was he done? Or was this just a break?

EPILOGUE

Agent Ben Crawford. Agent Crawford worked for the FBI for what seemed like most of his life. After the Farmington case, he took time off to visit Ray Pacheco in Truth or Consequences. He spent five days in Ray's cabin, enjoying Sue's great cooking and fishing every day. He still cared a great deal about the world and how it seemed to come unraveled. Still, at some point he realized he could not fix it. He bought a rundown cabin on the shore of Elephant Butte Lake and resolved he would fish every day. He became a daily regular at the bait shop, where he often talked politics with Chester. It had no meaning at all, and he loved it. Chester said Crawford reminded him of Big Jack.

Chester Chino. Chester became something of a tourist attraction after he took his Uncle Tyee's advice and started talking and dressing like a stereotyped Apache Indian. The regulars knew Chester to be a thoughtful, intelligent man who salvaged a failing business and turned it into a success. They thought his latest gimmick to attract more tourist business was hysterical. Chester opened a whole new section in the store offering all sorts of Apache trinkets, some of which were not made in China. He opened a day-trading business in the back of the store, and the rumors were that he soon was worth a small fortune. He stuck with the Apache gimmick because he liked it.

Beverly Evans. As mayor, Beverly was in her element. Communication in a small town like T or C was driven in great part by gossip, which was Beverly's forte. She opened a small taco restaurant along Main Street, and soon felt like she had been born in T or C. She thought about what might have been with Big Jack, but knew he needed more than a life in a small town. She didn't. It was her life. Her kids started visiting each summer and soon they were almost a family again. Beverly never remarried and devoted herself to the success of her adopted hometown. She became an institution in T or C and was re-elected mayor six times. When she retired, the entire town gathered to give her a standing ovation. She cried.

Nancy Chino nee Smith. Nancy and Tyee married and almost lived happily ever after. Of course, as is the way, there were bumps. Nancy got her law degree and became an advocate for the downtrodden. She didn't make much money, but she developed a reputation in Albuquerque and Santa Fe courts for being tough as nails when it came to defending her down-on-their-luck clients. Nancy's passion for justice sometimes conflicted with the need for a softer side in her relationship with Tyee. She became increasingly harsh and cynical. That led to some bad days. But their marriage appeared to be solid and durable.

Big Jack/Jack Parker. Big Jack established his law practice in Albuquerque, at first taking on any and all clients. His manner and outspokenness made him a media darling in a rather tame market. Soon he was being hired by anyone looking for a foul-mouthed, tough-guy lawyer. After some time, he decided he had outgrown Albuquerque and needed richer lowlife clients than were available in New Mexico. He went home to LA. He worried—even with a new name and his new, slimmer, more athletic shape—that some of his old enemies might remember him. But he learned all of them were dead. Nevertheless, it was a tough life being a tough guy. In a reflective moment one night over a bottle of whisky, he realized he would likely be long dead if he hadn't spent those glorious, unproductive years in New Mexico. He thought about Ray and Tyee, but never called.

Sue Pacheco nee Lewis. Sue was content. She loved her life. After experiencing the great trauma of death and heartache, she had run away to nowhere, thinking all the good there was in life was over for her. But Ray changed everything, and she was comfortable just being Mrs. Pacheco, living in the small cabin by the lake. She did know Ray needed his space, and to accommodate a few hours of away time, she began volunteering at the local hospital. Using her medical skills and knowledge immediately brought her a sense of accomplishment and made her feel complete. She still worried about Ray, their age difference, and his risk-taking, but put it all out of her mind as best she could, and just enjoyed each moment.

Tyee Chino. Tyee was overjoyed to be married to Nancy. He acknowledged they had some differences but was satisfied they were committed to each other. He returned to the university to finish a master's degree in computer science. The school had already offered him a teaching position, and he was thinking about whether he should take the job. He often visited Ray to go fishing. They were living in different worlds, which meant sometimes they didn't have much to talk about. But that seemed fine. They enjoyed fishing and each other's company, even with little conversation. Tyee often suspected he would hear from Ray about teaming up again to track down some bad guy or solve some mystery. But, so far, he hadn't been able to say, "Giddyup." He was always ready.

Ray Pacheco. Ray woke up most mornings feeling a great sense of joy at just being home with Sue. There were moments when he missed the action, the risk, and the camaraderie with Tyee. But he would look at Sue and realize it just wasn't worth the risk. He had everything he wanted at home. Law enforcement had been his life, and it was the reason he was alive. It was hard to drop that and just be. But he was learning. He fished a lot more and became a budding professional. He hadn't mentioned it yet to Sue, but he was thinking about joining one of the pro fishing tours. It would not be the same thrill as capturing murderers, but it would be a lot safer. He knew he should call his son, but didn't. He knew he should tell Sue he loved her more, but didn't. He was still not a complete human being. But he was trying.

Happy. Happy couldn't remember ever being a show dog. He was an adventurous, on-the-prowl dog who frequented the woods and knew everything about all kinds of animals, even snakes. Show dog? Don't be ridiculous. He was getting older, but he still thought he would be there for a long time to take care of his owner. His owner was great, but a bit reckless. Happy needed to watch over him. It was his dog duty.

AUTHOR'S NOTE

Four Corners War continues the story of Ray Pacheco and his unusual team. When I lived in New Mexico, I visited Farmington on many business trips. This story includes several events that actually happened in that unique multi-ethnic community. My strong connection to New Mexico has had a great influence on my writing. The locations featured in this series are some of my favorite places.

You may not know this but Ray Pacheco was introduced in my first book *The Bootlegger's Legacy*. If you haven't yet, you might want to read *The Bootlegger's Legacy* for additional background related to *Four Corners War*.

If you have time, a quick Amazon reader review of *Four Corners War* would be most appreciated. Reader reviews are a great way to communicate directly with the author. It may come as a surprise to you that I read every review, and while some are more appreciated than others—each one has value.

To leave a review, just go to Amazon.com, make sure you're signed in, and click "Your Orders" to look at your past orders. Find *Four Corners War* in the list and click the button that says "Leave a Product Review". That's it!

I look forward to reading your review and hope you will read some of my other books. For a list of my books, please visit my website at **www.tedclifton.com**.

KEEP IN TOUCH

Once a month, I send my readers a newsletter with a little of everything in it: southwest US culture, be it art, recipes, or local sights; my thoughts on writing and reading; book recommendations; updates on my current writing project; and from time-to-time a short story.

To sign up, visit www.tedclifton.com and either wait for the pop-up window, or scroll to the bottom of the page. Everybody who signs up receives a mystery gift, with my compliments.

You can also learn more about me and my latest books by visiting www.tedclifton.com or emailing me at ask@tedclifton.com.

Thanks for being a reader!

ABOUT THE AUTHOR

Ted Clifton has been a CPA, investment banker, artist, financial writer, business entrepreneur and a sometimes philosopher. After many years in the New Mexico desert, he now lives in Denver, Colorado, with his wife and grandson.

BOOKS BY TED CLIFTON

All books are available from Amazon.com, or by request at your local bookstore.

The Bootlegger's Legacy

Meet Ray Pacheco, pre-retirement, in this prequel to the Pacheco & Chino Mysteries.

When an old-time bootlegger dies and leaves his son Mike a cryptic letter hinting at millions in hidden cash, Mike and his friend Joe embark on a journey that takes them through three states and 50 years of history. What they find goes beyond money and transforms them both.

An action-packed adventure story taking place in the early 1950s and late 1980s. It all starts with a key, embossed with the letters CB, and a cryptic reference to Deep Deuce, a neighborhood once filled with hot jazz and gangs of bootleggers. Out of those threads is woven a tapestry of history, romance, drama, and mystery; connecting two generations and two families in the adventure of a lifetime.

"Superb character development ... vivid backdrops, brisk pacing, and meticulously researched ..."
—*Kirkus Reviews*

"A rollicking good time." —*Self-Publishing Review*

"... interesting characters, true-to-life situations, and intriguing twists ..." —*Stanley Nelson, Senior Staff Writer, Chickasaw Press*

Pacheco & Chino Mysteries

#1: Dog Gone Lies

Sheriff Ray Pacheco returns from his introduction in The Bootegger's Legacy to start a new chapter as a private investigator, along with his partners: Tyee Chino, often-drunk apache fishing guide, and Big Jack, bait shop owner and philosopher.

#2: Sky High Stakes

Lincoln County, New Mexico was best known as the site of The Lincoln County Wars, featuring the likes of Billy the Kid. Martin Marino, the acting sheriff, is also short in stature, just like The Kid—and no doubt also like The Kid, Marino is crazy. Lincoln County survived Billy the Kid, but Martin Marino might be a different matter.

Ray Pacheco and Tyee Chino have been asked by the state Attorney General to find out what the hell is going on in the Lincoln County Sheriff's department. Ray is sure there's some big trouble waiting for them and his gut is right: murder, lust, madness and greed are visiting the high country.

#3: Four Corners War

Navajos, Apaches, militias, good sheriffs, and bad sheriffs

are all drawn to a small town by millions in stolen money and a small army's worth of stolen military equipment. Is this the start of a Four Corners War? Nothing is as it should be as Ray Pacheco and Tyee Chino try to untangle the mix of greedy businessmen, corrupt politicians and a slightly unhinged sheriff—along with the usual dead bodies.

Farmington, New Mexico's unique mix of cultures is the backdrop for Ray and Tyee's most dangerous assignment to date from the bombastic Governor of New Mexico.

Vincent Malone Mysteries

#1: Santa Fe Mojo
Vincent Malone, a classical private investigator at the end of his career, finds himself in the middle of a murder mystery in Santa Fe, New Mexico with a dead big time sports agent and his professional athlete clients as suspects.

#2: Blue Flower Red Thorns
One dead body; many suspects. Sex, money, hate, love, artistic egos explode in Santa Fe high-end art community; Vincent Malone, down-and-out legal investigator, wants to know whodunit!

#3: Fiction No More
A mystery author staying at the Blue Door Inn claims she is being followed. Vincent Malone volunteers to find out what is going on, and things quickly get complicated. The author's first book details a murder that took place forty

years in the past, but is suspiciously specific. The victim's adult son would like to know how the author came by this information. Soon, a bullying sheriff and a wayward priest are involved, along with a priceless—and stolen—collection of Pueblo Indian artifacts. When the situation turns deadly, Malone must find out who committed the murder, and why. Past misdeeds long buried will come to light, and fiction will be separated from fact, as Malone pursues the truth.

Muckraker Mysteries
#1: Murder So Wrong
Follow Tommy Jacks, a recent journalism grad, as he becomes involved in his first newspaper job in middle America during the tumultuous 1960s. Within days of Tommy being on the job, a reporter from the competing newspaper is found dead at the state capitol. Tommy's beat is politics but he cannot ignore the murder of a fellow reporter right under his nose. His quest begins. Tommy's dad had been a leader in politics until he was framed and went to prison. The connection with his dad had led him to the OK Journal, a fledgling newspaper competing with a well-established media giant. It was the owner of that powerful newspaper who had his dad framed and tossed into prison.

As the story develops we are introduced to an amazing cast of characters: Ray Jacks, Tommy's dad, Taylor Albright, mentor and tormentor; the Gilmores, father and son, who run the entire state, Joe Louongo, Attorney and oddball—and many more; including Judy Jackson, Tommy's soon to be girlfriend and a co-worker at the capitol. Mystery, adventure, and some romance come together in this story of personal growth and great tragedy. This is the first book in the Muckraker Trilogy which leads Tommy into the complicated world of state politics and the newspaper business.

#2: *Murder So Strange*

Tommy Jacks has taken on a new role as a political columnist and he is making enemies, very powerful enemies. Tommy's recent tragedy involving sudden and violent death has left him shaken and emotionally damaged. Spending most of his adult life on his own he is discovering a whole new family life with his new "mother" and recently out-of-prison father. Also entering his world is the most beautiful person he has ever seen. Tommy can't stop staring.

This story begins with the sudden and unexplained death of the state's U.S. Senator. Tommy Jacks and his fellow journalists don't believe the police chief's story blaming it on natural causes. It has the smell of a crime.

Many strange things are happening in the city. New crime bosses seem to be causing lots of mayhem. Tommy has a lot to write about in his "My View" political column, including some not so subtle references to the police chief. Lurking in the shadows is the powerful and corrupt chief, who seems to think it might be best if Mister Jacks, even if he is very young, was dead.

#3: Murder So Final

Tommy Jacks, reporter, encounters new love and old threats while covering one of the most brutal U.S. Senate races in history. With a massive oil fire threatening the city of Tulsa, three candidates face off: a ruthless oil baron, an idealist college professor, and a reverend running under the God Party. When the race suddenly turns deadly, the winner may be the last man standing.

The final book in the Muckraker trilogy, Murder So Final brings to a close the stories of Louongo, Albright, Robbie Gilmore, Tracy and Ray Jacks, and Tommy himself.